Also by Hugh Leonard

FICTION
A Wild People

AUTOBIOGRAPHY
Home Before Night
Out After Dark

PLAYS
Da
A Life

SCREENPLAY
Widow's Peak

TELEVISION ADAPTATIONS/DRAMA
Great Expectations
Nicholas Nickleby
The Moonstone
Wuthering Heights
Good Behaviour
Parnell and the Englishwoman

Fillums

HUGH LEONARD

Methuen

1 3 5 7 9 10 8 6 4 2

Published in 2005 by Methuen Publishing Ltd
215 Vauxhall Bridge Road, London SW1V 1EJ
www.methuen.co.uk

Methuen Publishing Limited Reg. No. 3543167

A CIP catalogue record for this book is available from
the British Library

ISBN 0 413 77167 9

Printed and bound in Great Britain by
Bookmarque Ltd, Croydon, Surrey

For Kathy, with love

Trailer

When the playwright Peregrine Perry set it down in his will that his private papers should not be published or even inspected during his wife's lifetime, it could hardly have crossed his mind that Babs would live to be 106. The promise I had made him still nagged to be kept, but there seemed little point in writing the biography of a man already forgotten.

The first time I met Perry Perry, as he enjoyed being called, was on an evening at the National Library back in 1964. It was his seventieth birthday, and he not only marked the occasion by donating his manuscripts, letters and scrapbooks to the library, but was there for the occasion, as if to prove what was uncharitably said: that he would have attended the opening of a kitchen window. My own first play was in rehearsal at the Abbey, and I was still young enough to have heroes, so when my director, Ria Mooney, asked if I cared to accompany her to the ceremony, I kept the excitement out of my voice and told her I didn't mind.

Demigods walked the streets in those days; one might in a lunchtime espy Flann O'Brien – or Myles na Gopaleen, as we knew him from his column in the *Irish Times* – half-seas over and hanging on to the railings of the Huguenot Cemetery in Merrion Row; or pass a sauntering Micheál Mac Liammóir, his face a death mask of Leichner No. 3½ in summer or a careful blend of 5 and 9 in winter, with a white line of No. 20 keeping his nose straight all the year round; or see Brendan Behan stalking Patrick Kavanagh around Parson's bookshop on Baggot Street Bridge.

To my delight, another near-titan, Sean O'Faolain did the honours for Perry and made the formal speech of acceptance in the Round Room of the library – there was not yet a Minister for the Arts to pocket for himself such stray crumbs of glory. He spoke briefly and made sly nose-tapping mention, as became a Corkman, of the private papers, wondering aloud what lurid skeletons they might contain. 'Could Darby,' he said, 'have secrets from Joan?' and at this there was fond laughter. Even as an outsider, I could tell that Perry was held in ungrudging affection, which in Dublin meant that a writer was too old or too chronically a failure to provoke envy.

The guest of honour replied modestly. He was tallish, whippet-thin and almost bald. His smile was infectious; his good nature shone. He paid tribute to Babs' part in whatever success he could lay claim to, beginning with the words 'I have a wife, a companion for life.' The rhyme, intentional or not, was somehow familiar and caused my mind to stumble as if I had walked on a broken pavement. I righted myself and listened again while the speechifying ran down like a Hong Kong clock.

'Do you want to meet him?' Miss Mooney said and led me over.

I still called her Miss because I was in awe of her; she had played Rosie Redmond in the first production of *The Plough and the Stars* back in '26 and so was part of history. As Perry shook my hand, compliments spilled out of him. He had heard that my play was only massive, and sure the whole town had the good word for it. It would run till the cows came home. (It did not run; it loped for two weeks and limped for a third.) What the Abbey needed, he was sick and tired of saying, was new blood. 'I've had my day,' he sighed cheerfully, at which Babs, petite and bottle-blonde, gave him a slap on the arm and said, 'You're bold. No such thing.' When I addressed him as Mr Perry, he insisted in his Ringsend accent that his first name was Paddy, or Perry for preference – in interviews, he regularly declared that when young and in a fit of foolishness he had adopted 'Peregrine' as a

2

first name because it sounded author-like. 'Wasn't I the right gobshite? Peregrine! Jay, do I look like an effin' falcon?' He was a great man for alliteration, even ornithological.

The next time I saw him was weeks later at my first night. He came up at the second interval – there were still plays in three acts in those days – and pumped my hand with 'Didn't I tell you? It's the berries.' When the final curtain fell, the reception was polite, and to my dismay I heard two size nines thumping the floor as if tamping down the clay on the play's grave and a solitary voice shouting 'Author, author!' Of course it was Perry Perry.

One of the comforts of writing a novel is that bad reviews come like robbers, often unnoticed, over a period of weeks, whereas with a play the comeuppance is instant and brutal, with the Sundays around the corner to deliver the *coup de grâce*. The *Irish Times* notice by Seamus Kelly was sour and dismissive, saying that the Abbey had laboured mightily and brought forth a mouse, and in the *Independent* Mary McGoris, who sported a cigarette holder and wanted to be mistaken for Marjorie Proops, roasted me and mine. I spent the day at home, rather than at my desk in Merrion Street hearing some wag ask if anyone had seen a mouse just now or if maybe a lady clerk was missing a cheese sandwich. I licked my wounds and watched a film on television. It was an oldie, even then: *The Pride of the Yankees,* with Gary Cooper as the baseball player, Lou Gehrig, struck down by motor neurone disease. At the film's end, he gave a moving farewell address at the Yankee Stadium. When I heard him say, 'I have a wife, a companion for life,' I blinked. Perhaps Perry's use of the words at the library had been an unwitting trick of memory on his part; or it may have been a coded 'our song' between him and Babs. For all I knew, *Pride of the Yankees* might have been what they would have called 'our fillum'.

That evening, I was leaving for the pub to find out if my sorrows could float when he, of all people, rang up. 'It's P. P.'

'*Who?*'

'Perry Perry. How are you doing?'

'Not great.'

He laughed. 'Welcome to the sodality. Listen, don't mind them, it's par for the course, baptism by unholy water. You're paying your dues.' He pronounced it 'Jews'. 'What are you doing this evening?'

'Getting jarred.'

'Grand. So why don't you do it here? Babs will give us a bite of supper.'

'Thanks all the same –'

'You will, I say you will. Hop on a bus to the Viaduct.' 'Testicles Viaduct' was corner-boy slang for Ballsbridge.

I said no, but he gave me the number of a house in Vavasour Square, off Bath Avenue, and I went because I wanted to. In his best days Perry Perry was never a giant – 'I'm a tall midget!' he joked, asking to be contradicted – but as an amateur actor, I had played in his comedy *A Ha'penny for a Fizz-Bag*, and now as a playwright I had crossed from my own world into his, no matter that he had been right in saying that his race was run. Even I, a greenhorn, knew that his plays were the equivalent of melted-down waxworks at Madame Tussaud's. They were no longer a staple of the Abbey repertoire. The fashion had moved away from cosiness and parish pumpery, and the same British critics who had once spelt 'Irish' with a capital 'O' were now beginning to hail new voices who – their cliché; I have plenty of my own, thank you – reaffirmed the 'eternal verities'. Perry's work was no longer anthologised or performed, except by amateurs whose rural audiences felt at home when the curtain rose on the living room of a Big House that had seen lordlier days or on a room behind a pub that was the web of a conniving village spider.

He and Babs lived in what was a Dublin dwelling house inasmuch as it pretended to be humble and which, as well as a number on the door, had a name on the gate. It was called 'Kansas', a peculiar name for a house. At the front it had one storey, with a few granite steps up to the hall door, but one had no sooner entered than stairs led down to a kitchen and, looking out on the back garden, a living room so cluttered that its door only half opened. Perry explained that they had moved into town from a good-sized villa overlooking the bay.

'We lived in Drane for a while,' Babs said, volunteering no more, but giving the name its proper pronunciation of 'Dreen', and closing the subject as if it were a door with a Yale lock. I all but heard the click.

'When was that, then?' I asked.

'Donkeys' years ago,' he said.

She gave him a look.

There were signed photographs elbowing for pride of place along the mantelpiece and on the surface of the upright piano, most of them in silver frames. I saw F. J. McCormick, Denis Johnston, Lennox Robinson, Lady Gregory and (of course) Hilton and Mícheál. One portrait had an inscription: 'To the Proud Peregrine from the Green Crow – Sean O'Casey.' While Babs prepared the bite of supper, he sat me down and opened two bottles of stout, pouring mine into a mug while drinking his own from an inscribed silver tankard – his trophy as guest of honour at an Arts Club dinner.

There were those who said of him that he was too nice a man to be a writer of plays. Others, even more cynical, watched for a glimpse of the cloven hoof. They were a long time waiting, for I was to discover that he was utterly without side or affectation. Those who knew him well said that he had never got over his delight at quitting his clerkship with the Ordnance Survey and writing for a living. He was a man who had found heaven on earth, and it showed; what was more, he liked to be liked. He worked at it, taking care to rub no one the wrong way. He was invited to sit on many committees because he could be relied upon to march to the sound of the loudest drum. He was given the supreme accolade of being 'a decent skin'. Dublin is not so much a city as a courtroom where you are judged from the cradle to the grave, even if your most spectacular feat is to knock the top off a boiled egg, and the drama critics hand out bonus marks for modesty. Perry Perry had a clean slate. He envied no one, and to some it came as a surprise that his best-drawn characters were schemers and blackguards. Perry, who himself would lie awake at night brooding over an unpaid milk bill, could smack his lips when writing of a villain who would cheat a widow of her pension.

When, quite out of the blue, a rag named *Irish Truth* made him the target of a long and hostile profile, he was bewildered. The occasion was the Abbey premiere of his new play. The anonymous author called him a fake, which he never was, and tore the play to shreds, alleging with a great show of Baggot Street erudition that it stole its characters and plot from *Volpone*. It was even implied, narrowly on the safe side of libel, that the badness of his characters was an echo of a hidden darkness within himself. The play, *The Party of the First Part*, was one of his weakest, which gave substance to the attack and encouraged others to contribute their gnat-bites. In Dublin, if you allow a man to render you a favour, he will be your champion for life, whereas if the reverse happens and you do him a good turn he will never cease to speak ill of you, and Perry Perry had been a friend to too many for his own good.

He was not used to hostility. He lost his nerve. His next play refused to be written, so he threw his hat at it and unwisely chanced his arm with a novel instead. As an author, Perry could not in any sense be thought controversial, but he belonged to a generation when, to find oneself keeping company on the banned list with Joyce, Frank O'Connor and Kate O'Brien, one needed hardly do more than put pen to paper. Perry's first novel, *The Gramophone on the Grass*, found a London publisher, but copies had no sooner made their way across the Irish Sea than they were seized by the customs. His offence had been to employ the expression 'Howth-men' in the sense that the Hill of Howth outside Dublin was reputed to be the haunt of homosexuals. He vowed to be more careful on his second time out, but *The Moon Sees Me* met the same fate because of a passage in which a parish priest allowed his eyes to dwell on the white flesh above his wizened housekeeper's black stocking-tops. It was an age when, for a book to be banned, a smut-hound had only to send a copy to the censors with an offending phrase underlined. By the time television had arrived to open the flood-gates of indecency and make censorship pointless, Perry's two novels were long out of print.

He and Babs had begun their married life in a red-brick terrace house in Irishtown, on the edge of Ringsend. Later, they moved to what the estate agents called a gentleman's residence on Widow Gamble's Hill in Monkstown. It was the kind of house in which one happily lives out whatever is left of one's life, but around the time the second book was banned they sold up once more and moved further away from town. This time it was to Drane, pronounced Dreen, where for all anyone knew and as if anyone cared, Perry fell into that state of paralysis known to writers as work-in-progress. Now they were in their fourth and, as it proved, last house, called Kansas.

Babs and he had invested their money well when times were good, and there was a fair, if dwindling, income from amateurs. He discovered a talent for speaking on radio, and he wrote and narrated a once-weekly programme called *In Them Days* which went out at 10.30 on Wednesday evenings. He reminisced about times past, as if from an armchair in his own sitting room. He became a fixture. When he died, of cancer of the colon, in 1972, he left £45,000, a goodish sum.

After the evening in Vavasour Square, I met him a few times a year, apart from at first nights. Sometimes it was an encounter on the street and 'You have time for a jar', and if I begged off he overrode me with 'Just the one, sure where's the hurt in it?' Meanwhile, my second play failed, like the first, but the third was a hit, although not at the Abbey. To Perry Perry, all my cygnets were no less than swans, and when *The Lock-Keeper* was a success he crooned that now I was at last on my way and unstoppable.

A few weeks after that third play had opened, he called me. 'Do you fancy a walk?'

'A what?'

'Stretch o' the legs. I thought I might wander out your way. Then maybe there's some place we could have a bowl of soup.'

The nearest we had ever come to meeting by appointment was the few times he rang up to ask why was I making myself a stranger, or was I afraid of wearing the paint off his hall door, was that it? He had never before suggested a walk, but I waited for him at an appointed time in McDonagh's pub from where I could see him hop off the Number 8 bus. We walked up the steep hill to the Burma Road, then crested the Back Meadow and dog-legged it to my favourite walk, along the Green Lane. These days, it is paved with balding asphalt; thirty-five years ago it was a mossy path that took you along the brow of the hill and beneath the jutting granite head of an eagle, carved out of a crag because two young men, long since dead, thought that the hill deserved it. The only sounds were the soughing of the sea on the White Rock beach far below and the soft whisper of our feet striking the moss. Half-way along, Perry sat on a bench that faced the mountains and had its back to the gorse.

'This will do,' he said.

Discovering that our walk had a purpose was one thing; getting him to say what the purpose was took until the first lights began to blink along the coast and it was nearly time to walk down to the Vico Road. He looked at the sea, not letting our eyes meet, and said, 'You're going to think I have a right smell of myself.' He shook his head as if coming to his senses and said: 'Ah no, forget it.'

Instead of teasing out whatever it was that ailed him, I nodded, said, 'Right, so,' stretching myself as if on the wing. The brutality worked, for he said as if coughing a crumb from his throat: 'Do you know who someone is after writing a book about? I mean, would you credit it, giving that fella a book, all to his bloomin' self.'

He used an overdone Dublinese that called a book a 'bewk'. He named a youngish playwright named Morgan Tubridy who was currently in fashion. Then he climbed back inside the skin of Perry Perry, who never had a grudging word for anyone. 'Well, the best of good luck to him. But no, I mean honestly –'

He interrupted himself with a silence and looked for a while at the yellow eye of the Kish lightship, seven miles out. When the eye had twice blinked back at him, he said: 'Some professor of ballsology out of UCD has not only gone and wrote a rig-a-marole about your man Tubridy, but he makes out that every word of every play he ever put down on paper was a sort of a . . . a . . . a . . . an anthology.'

'A what?'

'Ah, you know, you know.'

'Do you mean an analogy?'

A broad smile. 'The very word.'

Perry knew damn well what Perry meant. One had only to run an eye over his bookshelves in the house that was called Kansas in Vavasour Square to know that he was well read, but in the back street where he had been raised it was a mortal sin to be what he liked to call affectatious. He let his eyebrows go up in pretended surprise and for a moment he became O'Casey's 'shoulder-shruggin' Joxer'.

'Analogy, is that it? Oh, now that's a darlin' word . . . a daaarlin' word!' Vexation had made him lose his thread.

'Where was I?'

'Young Tubridy?'

'Ah, yes. Give you a laugh, but. There's this cod of a play of his about a married couple that's forever having to be dug out of each other, what with fighting like cats and dogs. Nothing pass-remarkable in that, says you, but this gawm from UCD uses a stack of tuppenny-ha'penny words to make out that the play is not about two ordinary people at all, at all, but a – a – a – what-you-said, about the Civil War, and that the pair of them are meant to be Michael Collins and de Valera!'

Perry laughed a bark of a laugh that caused the evening birdsong to go quiet. 'Well,' he said, 'at least nobody is ever going to write a book to explain the ins and outs of any play that *I* ever wrote. Jesus, no, they'd have their work cut out. I mean, take you, now. *You* wouldn't have any hand, act or part in such jack-acting. I mean, now would you?'

I said nothing, not then, but allowed him to talk until at last the would-I? took off its Hallowe'en mask and became an ashamed 'Will you?' I was glad that his face was lost in the gathering dark. He wanted a book, written by me about himself. He wanted proof that his plays were at least important enough to be pontificated about in words fit for hard covers.

It had become too dark to venture down the more than two hundred granite steps of the Cat's Ladder to the Vico Road. I said: 'Safer if we went back to the town by way of Torca Road.'

As I rose, he caught my sleeve. 'I mean I don't want anyone sucking up to me. I'd never have that, God no, not a yes-man. All the same, I mean, if anyone's going to write about me, I'd at least like a fair crack of the whip. And I'm only asking in case some bugger out of UCD ups and does to me what was done to Morgan bloody Tubridy. Have you me?'

'Sure, sure.'

In a moment, he would ask if I thought he was deserving of a book. Without waiting to tell an outright lie, I cursed him under my breath and said that yes, I would be honoured to do the needful. I added, with careful modesty, 'If you think I'm up to it.'

Which of course was the signal for him to stop short and say incredulously, 'If I think you're up to it!' He started walking again, paeaning my worthiness from the Green Lane to Torca Road, past the cottage where the boy Bernard Shaw passed his summers and down Ardbrugh Road to the railway bridge and the town beyond.

'But spare me the oul' blushes,' he said. 'I don't want it done until I'm six feet under and pushing up daisies. Just so long as I know that you'll be on the job.'

At this, a great weight lifted clear of my heart, and the rest was as downhill as the road we were walking on. If the book was ever written, then at least Perry Perry would not be around to sit on my shoulder, gently crossing 't's, dotting 'i's and unable to see a hair without splitting it. Then I thought of his wife surviving him. Writers' widows can be devils.

It was as if he had read my thoughts. He said: 'And you needn't go fretting about Babs being a botheration to you. She's never done saying that once I snuff it, she'll pop off, too.'

'That a fact, now?'

'Only the other night she said to me, "Sure, Perry, what for would I hang around without you and be a misery to myself and a burden to the world? No, I'll keep you company."' He cackled, fondly. 'You'd have thought she was going with me on a mystery tour. Wisha, poor oul' Babs.'

There were street lamps now, and I saw a tear come into the eye next to me. I was uncertain as to which comforting words would give least offence: whether to insist that his wife was good for years yet – and little did I know! – or to agree with him that no sooner had he fallen off the twig than, like Jill tumbling after, she would all but land on top of him. So I said, playing safe: 'Well, who knows? I could go before the pair of you.'

He said: 'Not at all.'

'And then' – it was said lightly, but I suppose I was nosing after secrets – 'one of these days the world will get a look at that stuff of yours.'

'Stuff?'

'The stuff that's in the National Library.'

He said: 'Where in this town of yours can we get a jar?'

The Catholics have always called it a town, whereas to the Protestants it is termed a village, but when it comes to drink we are ecumenical. I steered him towards Seamus Sheeran's on Coliemore Road. We ordered pints, and while we waited for them to draw he said with suddenness: 'That stuff wouldn't be any good to you.'

'What stuff? The pint?'

'The stuff that's in the library.'

'You what?'

'You wouldn't make head nor tail of it.'

Perhaps with hindsight I should now seize upon that moment for dramatic effect – after all, play-making is my job. Perhaps in the remembering I should endow him with a furtive look, a hint of what must not be told. There should at least be that click of a closed door, as when his wife had mentioned that she and he had previously lived in Drane. Instead, he all but yawned.

'There's five or six cardboard boxes, and all that's in them is vanity. Reviews, publicity stuff, first-night telegrams, letters. Rubbidgc.'

'Maybe there's a play there that no one ever heard about.'

'A play where?'

'In one of those boxes.'

'Well, there's no such thing.' He almost snapped at me in what was as close as I had ever known him to come to a show of temper.

'Sorry.'

He said, more to excuse himself than to chastise me: 'You're very inquisitive.'

'Well, what do you expect?'

'How?'

'If I'm to write that book you want.'

He was silent, thinking about it, then he clapped a hand on my shoulder and laughed. 'You're a queer harp.'

I said: 'I thought maybe that while you and Mrs Perry –'

'Babs, Babs.'

'. . . while you and Babs were living in Drane . . . How long was it?'

'I dunno. Four years, best part of five.'

'. . . that you might have been working on a new play.'

'Well, I wasn't. I couldn't. The truth is that I lost heart. There was two books of mine banned by the censors. And before that there was a – a – a class of an attack on me.'

'I know. It was scurrilous.'

'Thanks. Yeah, it was, and all of a sudden I was back of the neck. No one had a good word to say. So we moved.'

'To Drane.'

'Yeah. Thought we'd give ourselves a change of air. Get away from what your man Sean' – he meant O'Casey – 'called them, the slim-thinkers. But the house in Drane was too big for us, and in the winter, what with the salt from the sea, you couldn't see out the windows. Then Babs, and I wouldn't doubt her, said to hell with the begrudgers. More fools us for letting them hunt us out of our own town, which is what Dublin is, amn't I right? So we saw the house for sale in Vavasour.'

'Kansas?'

'Yep.'

'Funny name for a house.'

He gave me a wary look and said: 'Some mightn't think so.'

I changed tack and asked him: 'What about Drane?'

'How?'

'Do you miss it?'

'No, the people there were nice, but a bit, what's the word?'

'Clannish?'

'Peculiar, more like. And Babs didn't take to them.'

I thought of the look on his wife's face when he had first mentioned Drane, but all I was finding out was that someone there had perhaps rubbed her the wrong way, and so much for any mystery. I felt let down. Wanting to score off him, I said, sulkily: 'You must lead a very boring life.'

'Who, me?'

'I mean, are you saying that as long as you've been in the land of the living there's never been a skeleton rattling its bones?'

'You what?'

'No scarlet women in all your life?'

He laughed, pulled his pint towards him across the bar and gave himself a white moustache. He said, 'You're a desperate man. Scarlet women, how are you!'

'Not even a pink one?'

'Will you give over?' He uncurled a forefinger and wagged it under my nose. 'Any playwright who is worth half his salt puts his life into his work. You ought to remember that, young fella me lad.' I nodded and wondered where he had cogged it. The *Irish Digest*, maybe. He laughed and shook his head. 'Scarlet women! I'd run a mile. Anyway, that game isn't worth the candle. No happy ending for that kind.'

He had lost me. 'Excuse me?'

He crooked a finger and fired off a shot. 'Khrrr-hrrr.' He blew down the barrel of his Colt and holstered it. He sang quietly to himself: 'Little Joe, oh, little Jo-oe, oh where he is now I don't kno-ow . . .'

I said: '*Destry Rides Again.*'

A sundown of a smile spread across his face. 'That's right. With your one, Marlene Dietrich, stopping the bullet that's meant for Jimmy Stewart. A great fillum.'

He said, savouring the words, '*Destiny Rides Again.*' In its time it had been a deliberate malapropism used by the hard-chaws who sat in the fourpenny-rush seats up against the screen in such cinemas as the Shack and the Mayr-oh and the Ranch on Eden Quay. Watching his smile widening and the eyes that were miles away, it was impossible to know whether it was a mistake on his part or a joke.

Later, I saw him to his bus, and as its lights appeared he said, 'Pity they did away with the oul' trams.'

'Yeah.'

'Listen, great seeing you. And thanks for that.'

'Rubbish.'

He gave me a look as the Number 8 panted to a stop. It took him an effort to say 'Won't tell you a word of a lie. It upset Babs greatly.'

'What did? Do you mean Drane?'

'I wrote it all down, and then gave it to the library. I was glad to get it out of the house, I mean when it was done I read it to try and make sense of it. Treble bloomin' Dutch!'

He swung on board the bus platform like a two-year-old. That was in 1966. He died six years later when he was seventy-eight. Now that I have cobbled together and put a shape on what he wrote, there are days when I cannot make head or tail of it either.

Chapter One

Munchkin Land

Even without a war on, Drane was always a betwixt-and-between town. Unlike Dalkey to the north of it and Bray to the south, it had been behind the door when train and tram lines were handed out; and because of the time that was in it only doctors and such or people who were well-got were allowed to use a motor car. A bicycle or Shanks's mare was your only man.

The estate agent, M. J. Mulrooney, drove Babs and me to see Carvel, the house we had it in mind to buy. He said: 'It's seldom I'm out this way, so I'll have a dekko at a few other properties. I'll come back for yous in a couple of hours, okey-dokey?' He let out a sigh and said the name of the town to himself, pronouncing it as if there was shite running the length of it. 'Curse o' God Drane!'

I suppose it was on his mind that nobody was likely to get killed in the mad stampede to go and live there. It was a town that was on the way to nowhere except itself. Fair dues, there was a view of the sea at the far side of the silted-up little harbour, but I have always been a man who looks upon water as no more than water, and in Ireland we get enough of it from the sky to satisfy our deepest wonderment. Drane was twelve miles from the city and it might as well have been a hundred, for in those days – it was 1942 – there were still fields separating one village from the next. In the one blink of an eye Mr Mulrooney was driving us down an empty country lane and past the shops in Easter Street. I had a glimpse of the Picture House – *This Gun for Hire* was on – and after it was a jumble of pub, haberdashers, pub, paper shop, Our Lady's Hall, off-licence and pub. We turned left and were on Kish Road, with that same grey sea at the end of it.

'Look at that,' Babs said, nudging me.

In the front garden of one of the houses a middle-aged couple was sitting, the woman on a deck chair, the man on a rocker. He wore a striped blazer and a panama hat, whereas she was in summer whites with her arms bare.

'What about it?' I said.

'Do you mind, it's the month of April,' Babs said.

And so it was, so cold that you could almost see the goose-pimples on the woman's arms. Mr Mulrooney was driving slowly, keeping an eye peeled for Carvel, and it gave the pair of them time to catch sight of us. They smiled and waved; their faces lighted up, and through the closed car window I heard the woman call, 'Good morning!'

'Ah, but they're saying hello to us, aren't they nice?' Babs said.

I told her: 'They're head cases. Worse, they're wagoners.'

Carvel – somehow the name had a familiar ring to it – was an ugly, modern white brute of a house with a flat roof and four picture windows, two up, two down, facing the east wind. It had been tacked on to a fishermen's cottage, a relic of old decency which now huddled half out of sight behind it, maybe for shame. And yet, as we discovered, the entire dog's dinner was warm and cosy inside.

The owners were Judge and Mrs Garrity. They showed us around the house and sat us down with cups of tea in front of a turf fire, coal being a far-off memory. I had never seen a judge who so much resembled a judge that you would have thought him an impostor. He was wisdom in person, like old Dr Gillespie doling out the stuff in bucketfuls in *Calling Dr Kildare*. He had what you might call a mane of white hair, and his dark eyebrows would have swept crumbs from a table. He wore a Donegal tweed jacket over a brocaded mickey-dazzler waistcoat and had his eye-glasses on a wide black cord. He was the berries. With both hands he kept such a tight hold of the lapels of the jacket that he all but fell over when he let go of one of them to stir his tea. As for using both hands together, say to lift a slice of barm brack while holding on to his cup and saucer at the same time, well, I thought the tweed suit would unravel off of him.

Mrs Garrity was lamb dressed as mutton instead of, as is more customary, the other way about. Whereas the judge was in his late sixties, she had to be at least twenty years younger, but dressed as if she could not wait to catch up with him. She wore no make-up; her lips were pale and her hair was fine and fair, and yet, looking at the tight stretch of her skirt across her hips, a man who was a certain way inclined would not have kicked her out of bed. She sat quiet and let himself do the talking, until the teacups were empty and the barm brack gone, when she took Babs on a second tour of the upstairs. 'Women are more particular,' she said and gave me a little smile that said no offence. I thought: *Be still, my thumping heart.*

Once the women had left the room, the Judge risked letting go of a lapel. He put a finger to his lips and listened for the women going upstairs. When there was a creak, he poured out a hottener of tea for the pair of us, then took a flat half-pint bottle of Black Bush from his pocket and spiked the tea with two large ones. 'It is a whore of a day,' he said without winking.

He asked if I owned a motor car. I told him no on account of the Emergency, and he said that he hoped that Babs and I were walkers. He and his wife were selling up, he said, because their young lad was starting at Trinity in the autumn, and even cycling to the nearest railway station, at Killiney, would eat up too much of his day.

'Timothy is a good boy, Mr Perry,' he said.

'I'm sure,' I said, there to the tick with the snappy catch-answer.

He spoke to me about the town and the debating society and swimming club. 'Alas, this damnable war has curtailed our movements, little as they ever were. Some of the young bloods cycle out to a dance in Bray on Saturdays. And of necessity we are great filmgoers. At the Picture House, night after night, there is nary an empty seat. Do you go to the cinema, Mr Perry?'

'I was brought up on it.'

'Well, that is good, for, like it or not, here there is little else. We – my wife and I – are partial to a film if it is wholesome.' He had a distant look in his eye. 'I mean, with the good rewarded and the evil punished.'

Oh yes, I thought, *he is a judge all right.*

'In any case,' he said, 'the wireless reception here is abominable. It is rumoured – and mind you I am saying nothing – that a German person who works at the embassy in Dublin has been using some electrical apparatus to – what is the word? – to ah . . . what they do with eggs . . .'

'To coddle.'

'No.'

'Scramble?'

'Thank you. To scramble the signal. To prevent –' he made what was meant to be a comical face and nodded towards the front window and the sea beyond – 'English propaganda.'

'Ha-ha.'

'Might one enquire as to your field of work, Mr Perry?'

All my life long, no one has ever accused me of banging my own drum, so I told him as if I was no more than a milkman or a ticket-taker at Westland Row station that I wrote the odd play.

'*Odd*?' he said, the eyebrows rising till they all but polished the mantelpiece.

'I mean occasional.'

I waited, giving him a chance to say – and honest to God, many a one does say it – 'You mean you're *Peregrine* Perry, the *playwright*?', but it passed him by. And it was the price of me. I was on the move – maybe to the very house I was sitting in – because I wanted to be quit of writing and all that went with it, and here I was, with not a blush of shame in me, fishing for compliments.

The Judge said: 'Well, if it's solitude you want, you'll have no shortage of it here.'

I said nothing. There was no play or book in my mind to write, and the horizon showed no glow of either. What had been written about me in *Truth* had knocked the stuffing out of me. 'Get over it,' people said. Or, 'It's only a rag, don't give them the satisfaction.' I didn't dare tell them that what hurt me was not that it was all the rottenest of lies, but the skulking thought that it might be true. Maybe the guttie that wrote it was in the right and I had a poor excuse for a mind; maybe I was all easy sentiment on the outside and a bitter pill underneath. When I was a young chiselur at school, I lost as many fights as I won, and not a month passed but I got the strap from the Brothers. I smarted a bit, the same as when I had my ears boxed the odd time at home, but maybe I had been spoiled, for it wasn't until now, when I was forty-eight and read the muck that was thrown at me in *Irish Truth*, that I was ever hurt.

One day not long after, I said to Babs, 'I hate this house,' and quick as lightning she answered, 'So do I.' We were terrible liars. Everything we had best loved about the house on Widow Gamble's Hill became a reason for getting out of it. Once, I went too far and heard myself saying: 'Do you know, if we'd a had children they'd have moved out by now and the house 'ud be too big for us.' No sooner had I uttered such rubbish than Babs went into the kitchen, and I knew there was water-works. Another month and we were as good as on the move.

When the ladies came downstairs, I stood up and the Judge heaved himself to his feet by the lapels. Babs and I thought to go for a walk around the town until Mr Mulrooney came for us, and I promised to let the Garritys know in a day or two about the house. The Judge told us there was no hurry; there were good ghosts in Carvel, he said, and time enough to be rid of them, and at this there was a shadow across the window and the sound of the front door. A tall, fair-haired young lad of about seventeen came in.

'This is Timothy,' the Judge said. 'Timmy, say hello to our visitors, Mr and Mrs Peregrine Perry.'

The lad said, 'How do you do?' and shook hands; then he asked, 'Excuse me, sir, but would you be Mr Perry, the dramatist?'

I told him I was. A nice boy. I took to him.

Mrs Garrity said to him: 'Darling, I've tidied your room, but your books are as you left them. Now be a good boy and put them away.'

'Yes, mom.' Timothy kissed his mother on the cheek. He looked at me and said without as much as an honest-to-God blush of shame: 'Mom is my best girl.'

As I was trying not to gawk, the Judge said sternly, doting on him: 'Do as your mother says, mind.'

'Yes, sir.'

Timothy smiled goodbye at us and trotted upstairs. The Judge must have seen something in my face, for he said: 'Timothy has respect for his elders, and I think I may take a little of the credit.'

'The lion's share, dear,' his wife put in.

'No, no. But I'll have my due. There's not a day when he and I don't have a man-to-man talk, however brief.'

Well, that did it. I took a look at Babs to see if she had twigged, but the sort she was, she would have cried at Donald Duck, and she had been looking all dawny at the jack-acting of the three of them. Could they be having us on, I wondered, with their 'Mom' and their 'Sir' and the mugging and kissing and the kid saying that his ma was his best girl? As for the man-to-man talks, well, that gave the game away, for I had seen *Life Begins for Andy Hardy* only a week since at our own picture house, the Valhalla. And the old fellow in it – a judge, need you ask – was Lewis Stone, who always took a great part and was in nearly everything, and it came rushing at me that the name of the town where the family lived was Carvel.

It was a conundrum. On our way out, I thought to chance my

21

arm and said: 'Carvel . . . that's an original class of a name for a house.'

'Is it?' the Judge asked.

'I just wondered . . .'

He said: 'When we moved here the name of the house was "Bonnie Doon". Neither of us cared for it. We thought it a bit – words keep escaping me today – a bit twee, you know.'

'So how come you picked on Carvel?' He stared at me. 'If you don't mind me asking.'

Babs clucked at me and tugged my sleeve. 'He's so inquisitive.'

The Judge blinked like a man who had lost his way and said: 'Do you know, I haven't the remotest idea. Good heaven, now where *did* it come from?' He looked at his wife. 'Mother, do *you* remember? Where, now?'

She was half his age but never mind that, for there it was again: Lewis Stone as the judge, calling his missus 'Mother'.

Mrs Garrity didn't know either. She said: 'I wonder did we draw up a list? Was that it?'

The Judge said: 'Oh, I recall. Yes, to be sure, I blindfolded you, and you picked the name out with a pin.'

Mrs Garrity let out a laugh and gave his shoulder a slap that would not have winded a midge. 'He's a fright,' she said to us.

The Judge, seeing that he was on a winner, went for gold with: 'Yes, it was like pinning the tail on the donkey.'

Before the hilarity got out of hand, Babs and I said our goodbyes and walked across the road to the harbour wall. There were a few local men there, dressed in woollen gansies, leaning on the wall and spitting themselves dry into the sea. They nodded to us in a friendly enough way. 'It's a wonder,' I said, taking Babs' arm and moving her on, 'that they didn't say "Howdy, stranger."'

'What?' Babs said.

We walked for a while, then I asked her, 'So what do you think?'

'About the house? I dunno. What do *you* think?'

It was the old, old seesaw, and I knew she could sit on it until the seas ran dry. I said: 'Toto, I need an opinion. We're not in Kansas any more.'

She said: 'Don't call me names. What are you talking about? Are you mad?'

'I don't know whether I am or not. The three of them have me as demented as they are.'

'What in God's name ails you?'

'Nothing.'

'Perry, we'll do whatever you want. Whatever house we buy, you're the one who'll have to work in it.'

'I told you, I –'

'Or not work in it. Whichever.'

'Shush, now. Here's Fred and Ginger.'

We were drawing abreast of the garden where the middle-aged couple had been sitting on deck chairs. They were still there, still smiling. I said a little prayer: 'Dear God, please don't let them ask us to come in and set a spell.' Instead, the woman asked us if we were having a nice walk.

'We were viewing a house actually,' Babs the blabbermouth said.

The man said, 'Viewing? Oh, that would be Carvel.' He put the emphasis on the second syllable, American style. 'A nice house.'

'And nice people living in it,' the woman said.

'If they go,' the man said, 'we'll be sorry to lose them.'

'Not saying,' the woman said, 'that you wouldn't be an addition to us.'

'Oh,' Babs said, making a suitcase of the word, with all sorts of thank-yous and reciprocations packed inside it.

'We're the Hoseys,' the man said.

'Brigid,' his wife contributed.

'And Cyril,' himself said.

They were as good as the kind of acrobats you would see in the

23

Theatre Royal in town throwing hankies to one another.

Mrs Hosey said that if we bought Carvel we must come over in the evening for a glass of something and maybe a hand of cards. She looked comfortable and settled and more like a solo whist kind of woman, but she said, 'I'm very fond of a game of penny poker.'

'If Walter Pidgeon is not on at the Picture House,' Cyril said, winking at us and giving her a nudge of a look.

'Or Greer Garson,' Brigid said, returning his serve.

As we were moving on, Babs had a fit of boldness and said: 'Do yous not feel the cold, sitting there? I'm perishing.'

Mr Hosey said: 'Is it cold?'

His wife said with a shiver: 'Do you know, it's bitter.'

There was a honking from up the road, and we saw that Mr Mulrooncy was coming back and had spottcd us. Thc last wc saw of the Hoseys, she was folding up the deck chair, and he was humping the rocker.

'You broke the magic spell,' I said to Babs.

'I what?'

Mr Mulrooney looked like someone returning from a fool's errand. He was an honest man; he looked out at the town – the Picture House and the rest of it – and said: 'Well?' as if he already knew that nobody with a titter of sense would give up Widow Gamble's Hill to bury themselves in Drane. When I told him 'It's a definite possibility,' there was more magic, for he turned himself back into an estate agent.

He said: 'It's a very desirable property.'

He opened and closed his mouth like a man who had more to say but was deciding not to push his luck.

Chapter Two

Lucille le Sueur and other strangers

I might as well get it over with and say that when it came to films – or fillums, as we used to call them on Rope Walk in Ringsend – you would not find the beating of me. I recall one night, when me and Babs were not long married, that I heard a dog yowling in the small hours. Says I out loud in my best Hungarian accent: 'Listen to them! Children of the night . . . what music they make! But the dead travel fast.' Babs was not asleep like I thought she was. She said: 'You what?'

'It's from *Dracula*.'

'From where? Well, honest to God, Perry Perry, what age are you?'

In the dark I heard her laughing to herself. It was not a natural laugh; there was too much of it. The following morning over the stirabout she said, 'Dracula!' in a low voice and laughed again as if it was the best ever.

A person might think that it takes little to upset me, but I know what I know and, as Jimmy Cagney said in *The Strawberry Blonde*, that's the kind of a hairpin I am. I wasn't going to let even Babs, who was the best woman in the world bar none, get into that private place inside my head. I mean, if you don't want to share a thing, then you do what I did and put a padlock on the door.

It was like at school when you gave a fellow a nickname and he made the mistake of saying, 'Don't call me that.' Then you knew you had him. Babs had touched an inside part of me that was still a kid and, sooner than be made a jeer of, I let on to her that films were no more to me than shadows; so I put them to the far side of me. I gave the go-by to the lot of them: to Buck Jones, Ken Maynard and good old Randoloph Scott; Fredric March in *The Eagle and the Hawk*; Gary Cooper and 'When you want to call me that, smile'; Charles Laughton promising he'd hang the whole shaggin' lot of them to the highest yardarm; Philo Vance and Charlie Chan and Nick and Nora; Boris and Bela in *The House of Doom*; Charlie and the blind flower girl, or him doing the dance with the bread rolls in *The Gold Rush*; Wylie Watson as Mr Memory in *The 39 Steps*; old Marie Dressler, the heart of the rowl; King Kong on the skyscraper; Lilian Bond squeezing her tits in *The Old Dark House*; Stan and Ollie, dancing in front of the saloon; Victor McLaglen saying ''Twas I that informed on your son, Mrs McPhillip'; Herbert Marshall acting the eejit and telling a waiter that he wanted to see the moon in his champagne . . . Well, I mean, don't be talking.

Me and Babs went to the pictures two or maybe three evenings a week. It had been the same in the old days with my ma and da and the pair of them keel-hauling me – although 'clare to God I didn't need much hauling – to the Valhalla that was so close to us that if you were stony broke you could open a window and hear the picture, I mean what else had we? And it wasn't that Babs was jealous of Mary Astor being what she called a pash of mine, or of Marlene Dietrich, say, going on about how it took more than one man to change her name to Shanghai Lily. It was a while before I twigged, but I worked it out. It was the fillums themselves she was jealous of.

When I had a play of my own on, she was as proud as if it was herself and not me that wrote it. You would see her in the theatre bar beforehand and honest to God she was near falling out of her standing with nerves; and when it was over and we were home and dry there was a smile on her face that would meet itself around the back. But she knew that when the cards were cut for trumps the plays were a part of my life and not of hers. Well, she had to give me that much, but that was all she gave. It was Babs's nature that what she couldn't share she made little of.

Where was I?

The man with the brush and the pot of paint at the Robin Hood Hotel didn't look the least bit like Dracula; he was pushing forty, round more than long in the face and, sign's on it, well-fed. He wore a pullover that was as purple as Passion Sunday and told us that he owned the hotel. His name was Dermot Grace. I felt Babs looking at me when I gave him my name as Peregrine instead of Perry Perry.

'Ah, it's yourself,' he said. 'We're honoured.'

He already knew that we had bought a house in Drane. 'Your goodness,' he said, 'has gone before you. The whole town is a-buzz.' Well, me and Babs had spent all morning in the place, and there was the divil of a buzz to be detected.

Mr Grace – 'No, none of that,' he said, 'call me Dermo' – invited us in for coffee and led us to the residents' lounge. I was bracing myself for cobwebs and Methuselah's confirmation photo on the wall, but the chairs had flowery patterns and wrapped themselves round you. Dermo called out, 'Dympna, where are you?' whereupon a girl in a smart uniform looked in at the door and his way of ordering coffee was to make passes at her like the Great Bamboozalem.

When we were comfortable he said: 'Imagine. Peregrine Perry in person –'

'Perry, Perry,' I said.

'. . . coming to live in our midst! No disrespect, sir, but I can see that one day we'll have to move the horse trough and put up a fitting monument.' I must have looked taken aback because he said it again: 'No disrespect.'

Babs laughed. She already liked him.

I asked him: 'How did people know we were moving here?'

'How? Well, sir, and by the Lord Harry you have very little sense of your own significance.'

Babs laughed again, and it was a different laugh this time. She liked to see me being demoted the occasional peg, but there was not a ha'porth of harm in it.

'Chalk it down,' Dermo said, 'to the bush telegraph. And besides I have guests one floor up from us as we speak who can lay claim to the honour of your acquaintance. The Garritys.'

'Do you mean the Judge?'

'The same. He and her good self should have moved into their new home a week ago, but there's a twist somewhere up the pipeline – or is it down it? A problem about the deed of title. So their furniture is in storage and I have the pair of them until further notice.'

'Oh, the poor people,' Babs said.

'Not at all. They're in the Friar Tuck Suite and as comfortable as can be. And the sort of guests they are, we're in no hurry to see the last of them.'

It occurred to me that a compliment was due. I said: 'I'm sure that for them it's a home from home.'

'Decent man,' Dermo said. 'Thank you.'

'But why didn't they let us know?' Babs said. 'Maybe we could have postponed the move at our end.'

We could have done no such thing, and the pair of us knew it, so it was safe for me to agree with her and say 'Mm.'

'The Judge isn't that kind of person,' Dermo said. 'What he agrees to, he abides by.'

That was a good phrase, I thought; one for the notebook. Old habits die hard.

When the coffee came, it was not the fake war-time stuff but made from beans that were fresh-roasted, and there were biscuits with cream filling. Dermo had a good leg of someone. I asked him if he had owned the hotel for long, and he said that it was in the family. His grandda had built it.

'It was the Railway Hotel in those days, but what with the erosion from the sea they moved the line inland. Mind, we stayed open; we fought on. In fact, when I bought the cinema it was as a sideline, and the joke is that now the films do more business than the hotel.'

'You own the Picture House?' I said.

'Guilty.'

'Well, Perry,' Babs said, 'there's a nice surprise for you!' Like I said, she never missed a chance. Anyone would think I had a bit of stuff on the side, and she was aching to see me give myself away.

'Are you an enthusiast?' Dermo asked.

'Is he what?' Babs said. 'He's fillum mad. Aren't you, love?'

'Don't mind her,' I said. 'Babs has a bee in her bonnet.'

'Oh, have I?' she said. 'Go on, do Dracula for Mr Grace.'

'Dermo,' he said.

'For Dermo.'

I said nothing, but gave him a wink. He looked from me to Babs and back again, like he was uncertain how to take us. 'Oh, the Picture House is a great success,' he said, getting back on dry land. 'We're an independent, so we can show what films we like. And we have competitions every Saturday.'

At this I had to put the coffee cup down on its saucer before it started to shake. He might have been showing a starving man a sandwich.

'Do you mean a quiz?' Babs asked, in her element. 'Now you're singing his song. Ask him anything. Go on, do it.'

'It's cut-throat stuff,' Dermo said. 'Not at all what you'd call friendly. And the standard is high. None of your elementary stuff, my dear Holmes. None of your "Whose real name is Lucille le Sueur?" '

'Even I know that,' Babs said. 'It was . . . ah . . .'

'You're right,' Dermo said. 'Joan Crawford. Or in *The Great Ziegfeld* who was it sang "A Pretty Girl is Like a Melody"?'

'Go on, Perry, tell him,' she said, enjoying herself.

'I don't know.'

'You are the most appalling liar. Yes, you do so know.' She said to Dermo: 'He's letting on.'

Dermo looked disappointed. He said: 'Well, it was Dennis Morgan, only he called himself by his real name, Stanley Morner.'

At this, not for diamonds could I keep my mouth shut. I said: 'You're wrong. It was Morgan who appeared in the film, but his voice was dubbed by Allan Jones.'

'Begod,' Dermo said.

Babs looked as if she had drawn the favourite in the Irish Sweep.

'You'll be a great addition to us,' Dermot said, red with delight, whereas I was the same colour, but there's red and red. 'Yes, you will. You'll give some of our so-called sharks a run for their money.'

I said: 'That was a fluke. It's just something I happened to know.'

Babs gave me a look that had a blade in it. 'He's so disobliging.' She turned to Dermo: 'Ask him another one.'

He snapped his fingers. 'Do a bit of casting,' he said. 'A taxi driver.'

I said nothing, but names rattled through my head: Murray Alper, Garry Owen, Frank Jenks, Allen Jenkins, born Alfred McConegal.

'A butler, then,' Dermo said.

I thought of Charles Coleman, Robert Greig, Barnet Parker and Arthur Treacher. I shook my head. 'Sorry, I'm hopeless.'

'You needn't act the innocent,' Babs said, smiling. 'I have you taped.'

'Never mind,' Dermo said, throwing his hat at it. 'Anyway, a man of your eminence and all could hardly be expected to get up on a public stage. The people here are not as sophisticated as the kind you might find lashing out money to see a play. Sorry I asked.'

Our new friendship had hardly got started but it was cooling. While we were waiting at Bray station for the train home, Babs started to cry.

'What's up?'

'Nothing.'

'Come on, trot it out.'

'You're cross at me.'

'About what?'

'You know.'

Lying to her. 'I don't know.'

'You're very mean.'

'How?'

'You couldn't even be sociable.'

'When?'

She said: 'About fillums.'

I gave it to her straight. 'I don't like being made a jeer of.'

Her eyes became round. She could not credit it. 'Who made a jeer of you?'

Already I had said too much. When I made no answer, she went back to crying.

I said: 'The train's coming in. Now don't go making a show of me in front of people.'

'Oh, you needn't worry.' Now she was in a wax. 'I'll never talk to you again about your mouldy old fillums, good, bad, or indifferent.' She was so sincere that I began to wonder if maybe I was the person in the wrong.

There was a silence all the road home. We sat in the kitchen and I thought that people in other towns were listening to the Hospital Sweepstakes programme on the wireless, and your man with the plummy voice was wishing them 'Health, happiness and good fortune', whereas all we got was static, like as if the whole country was clearing its throat at us.

'Will I make us a cup of soup?' Babs asked, taking a tin out of the press. 'We haven't much. What about chicken and barley?'

'Sure,' I said, and to myself added, *And put an olive branch in it.*

I was wrong, for there was no soft soap. Instead, she said: 'Perry, I'm sorry. I didn't mean to make a mock of you. I won't do it again. I couldn't stand you being cross with me. Say you're not cross.'

Well, the old ticker all but melted. We didn't kiss and make up because we're not that sort and never were. I gave her hand a squeeze and that was as good as. I said: 'Now don't go starting me off because I'll be as bad as you are. Make the soup.'

She did, and I was delighted to see her happy and loving. A big smile came on her face.

'What is it?' says I, ready to share.

She laughed out loud. 'Dracula,' she said. 'You're a panic.'

Chapter Three

Love and Mary Astor

The worst part of the move was having to lug books out of tea-chests and upstairs to the back room Babs thought would do for my study – a den, the Yanks call it in films, as if they were lions in a cave digesting a misfortunate antelope. That was on a Saturday, and in the small hours the dream came, so bad that I shouted myself awake.

As usual, it was about New York. It was a city I thought I would never set eyes on, nor did I until well after the war, when a play of mine was put on in New Haven in Connecticut. Until then, all I knew of the place was from the films I saw, which were made over at the far side of America: a gangster picture, maybe, with the Dead End Kids being hooligans in Hell's Kitchen and with Pat O'Brien as the priest, or a film that was all Franchot Tone and white furniture and such, with men and their motts dressed up and dancing in night clubs. Codology, Babs called it.

Once a year or so I had the same nightmare. In it, I was in a New York that I had never seen in a film; I was by myself, hurrying to catch a ship that would take me home. I was half-walking, half-running down ordinary streets and now and then I could see the Statue of Liberty off in the distance; but more often I was looking into pitch-dark alleyways that seemed to belong to another place altogether, or maybe to another world, and I knew that I mustn't make a wrong turn into one of them or I was shagged. I kept wanting to go towards where the quays and the ships were, but the streets carried me the wrong way, past laneways where the ground was shiny with rain, with people in them who turned the dark white of their faces to look at me as I went past. The end of the dream was when all the streets had gone from me and there was nothing but the blackness of a laneway. I let out a shout that woke Babs.

'What in God's name ails you? You're dripping with sweat.'

'Bad dream.'

'I'm not surprised. All that pulling and hauling of books. Doing yourself a mischief. Here, get them pyjamas off of you.'

'Against the rules.'

'You wha'?'

'Total nudity, not permissible.'

'Are you mad?'

'Sorry,' I told her. 'Half asleep.'

Give her a crumb and she would make her dinner and tea of it. '"Total nudity",' she said. 'Oh, that's exquisite language. And "Not permissible", if you please! God, that's the best yet.'

When I'd got myself under the shower she made me put on fresh pyjamas and go back to bed. 'In the morning you can have a lie-in. I'll go to early mass by myself.'

About religion, we were not what you would call red-hot. We went to mass on a Sunday for no other reason than that we had gone the previous Sunday and all the Sundays before it. The first proper play I ever saw was *The Plough and the Stars*, with Fluther Good saying that we ought to have as great a respect for religion as we can, so as to keep it out of as many things as possible. That was a fair enough description of the pair of us. Donkeys' years ago in the confession box, I told a priest that I did something on my ownsome which is nobody's business and I will not put down on paper. He gave out stink to me, saying that if I didn't watch myself I would be a degenerate. 'Thanks for nothing,' says I. I had wanted a bit of comforting, and what he gave me was the hob of hell, so as far as religion went that was the end of it.

How and ever, after Babs had come home from her early mass she gave me breakfast in bed. 'Guess who I met at the chapel gate,' she said, and before I could come out with 'Greta Garbo'

34

she told me: 'Your man from the hotel that said to call him Dermo.'

'Oh, yeah?'

'And he says he's holding two seats for us for this evening.'

'What's this evening?'

'*Dodge City.*'

'I suppose you mean *Dodsworth.*'

'With Mary Astor.'

I let it pass and said: 'I have the rest of the books to move.'

She said: 'Can't they wait till tomorrow? You're a gentleman of leisure now. Nothing to do and buckets of time to do it in.'

So we went to the Picture House. Dermo Grace was on the steps, acting the head buck-cat, and with our tickets in his breast pocket. 'From this evening out you'll have to book,' he said. 'We're always packed to the roof.'

We walked in past a queue that was waiting, as I found out, either for the first-come-first served sixpenny seats up against the screen or the no-shows in the ninepennies and one-and-thruppennies. On Sunday evenings at the Valhalla in Ringsend there had always been a great buzz before the picture started. Maybe four or even six people would be in a cluster, chattering and colloguing like crows in April. Like a good many others that were doing a steady line, me and Babs did our courting at the pictures in out of the wet, and often we would go as a foursome with Babs's friend, Patty, and Patty's fellow, a head-the-ball named Jackie Conheedy. We went for the sociability as much as the film, and now and again the usher, name of Costello, would shine his flash-lamp across the seats as a warning to couples not to jump the gun and get dug in until the lights went out. There was noise and plenty of it, but nothing like at the Picture House in Drane that Sunday. It wasn't only people waiting to see a film; it was more of a hooley where everyone knew everyone else. There was gramophone music from behind the curtains – a tune called 'Moontime'; it's still in my head – that was near drownded by the bawling. One woman was enquiring, top of her voice, after a person that was sick, and another was shouting out a recipe for Dublin coddle. Jesus, I even heard one man giving the odds on a horse and doing a kind of tic-tac when he couldn't be heard. And it wasn't the sort of noise you would hear at the Valhalla from gurriers out of St Philomena's Mansions. By the look and dress of them, these were respectable people, same as myself and Babs. I could even hear the occasional Protestant accent. The people who stood up to let us squeeze by to our seats smiled and said 'Good evening.' One woman said, 'I hope yous like us.' And sure enough I saw the Judge and Mrs Garrity, who nodded to us.

The second the lights went out and the curtains opened, there was a peculiar sound. It was polite clapping, not the kind of Sunday evening carry-on that was more jeer than cheer. Even when the *Pathé News* started and the cock crowed, not one person imitated it. It was all about a fashion show and the blitz in London and a new way to use powdered eggs, and the English voice was the same whatever the news: quick and high-pitched, as if the commentator was having a class of a breakdown. The next film was the Laurel and Hardy; it was an ancient one where they go to the Rainbow Club and get drunk on what they think is a kind of red biddy, except that it's only cold tea and mustard. The audience laughed fit to be tied; they enjoyed it and it did my own heart good, for it was not the ordinary haw-haw laugh you would hear at a Charley Chase or the Three Stooges. It was not from amusement that came and went but from people being made happy. At the end there was more clapping, and a voice – one of the Protestants by the sound of him – called out, 'Well done!'

The big picture was *Dodsworth*. It was about this rich businessman who retires early because his wife wants him to. She thinks her life has passed her by in the days when the pair of them hadn't a penny to bless themselves with. Now she is after a second chance, a bit of adventure. Without putting a tooth in it, she wants to be young again, so, not to be disobliging, her husband takes her for a holiday to France and Italy and such. And if I go on about this, it's because it was the start of what happened to us in Drane.

The wife – Ruth Chatterton took the part – is a fool and ten times worse than a fool. No sooner is she in Paris than she falls for a right chancer who is only after her because she has the few readies. Her husband – Walter Huston was very good in the part – puts up with it for a while, then says that enough is plenty and sends the chancer on his way. Well, of course the wife is in bits and says she is sorry and all that, and the softy Walter Huston is, he believes her. Mind, the people in the Picture House were on to her. A lot of them were muttering, and one woman said: 'Oh, you rip, you.'

Well, to cut a long story short, doesn't the wife go and do it again. This time, she falls for an Austrian man, a count or a baron or something. Quality, anyway. She tells Walter Huston that she is in love and wants a divorce. She shouts at him: 'You're rushing at old age. I'm not ready for that yet.' It was good stuff, like. So of course the old muggins of a husband won't stand in her way; he says goodbye to her and all the best, and goes off by himself on his travels. Babs was so caught up that she even forgot to give me a nudge when who does Walter meet but my so-called pash, Mary Astor. She is a widow living on the isle of Capri, and the pair of them hit it off so well that he goes to live with her – for company, that is, in the same house, only with no andrewmartins; they are just good comrades the pair of them. You can see all the same that she is too good-looking a woman to be only a friend for long.

Well – need you ask – just when they're all snug and contented a letter comes from who else but Ruth Chatterton. It turns out that the young Austrian's old one has told her to feck off and leave her son alone, and so now the wife is left high and dry. And, the cheek of her, she wants Walter Huston back. 'She needs me,' says he to Mary Astor. 'Foolish and all that she is, I can't let her down.' The moan that went up at this in the Picture

House could be summed up by a woman that gave a banshee wail of 'Oh, the *eeee*-jit!'

Well, in the pictures men always go back to their wives, but this time we had a right lemoner in store for us. It so happens – ah, well, it's a film – that the ship the wife is taking to America stops near the isle of Capri, and Walter Huston says goodbye to Mary Astor and goes off to be a husband again and travel home with Ruth Chatterton. But wait; he is no sooner on board the ship than he has to listen to the same old carry-on of her where the world is out of step and she's in the right, and he sees that she is no different from the foolish and selfish woman she always was. He tells her: 'Love has got to stop someplace short of suicide.' At this, here was a gasp that turned into a roar that shook the Picture House. When Walter Huston left the ship and the wife screamed for him to come back, a woman shouted up at her from the ninepennies: 'The divil's cure to you!'

I thought to myself that in Drane they take films very seriously, for when Mary Astor got all excited and delighted at seeing him coming back and waving to her from a little fishing boat, the audience cheered and stamped their feet. But in the middle of it all, a voice from behind us said, 'No, no, no, no.' I turned to look and it was Judge Garrity.

After the lights had come on, Dermo Grace walked out in front of the screen and made an announcement that the semi-final of *Name that Star* would have to be postponed because one of the contestants was taken sick. A woman in front of me said to anyone interested, 'He's in Crooksling,' which was the name of a T. B. sanatorium. There was grumbling, but it occurred to me that *Dodsworth* had been more than enough for one evening, and in any case the 'The Soldier's Song' came on and them that had not been quick enough down the aisle and out of the door had to stand to attention.

'Did you enjoy that?' the Judge's wife asked us on the way out, and, 'Oh yes,' Babs said, 'did you not?'

'Well, I thought it was very much on the man's side,' Mrs Garrity said.

The Judge himself said nothing.

Dermo Grace was on the front step lapping up compliments like a priest after a sermon about hell and damnation. It had been full daylight when we went into the Picture House; now a half-moon was rising over the sea. When I think back on those days it is strange the quiet way an audience used to fan out from a picture house at the end of an evening, like small creatures in danger and with no roof over them but a sky. I say 'used to' because nowadays instead of walking home, hurrying but trying not to hurry, the furthest they walk is the few yards to the car park. Mind, it is rarely we go to the pictures now.

In Drane, people went home either this way or that along Easter Street, and the town was dark except for that half-moon. In the first place, it was war-time and wherever you went there were power cuts; in the second, in war or peace, there had never been much call the length and breadth of the town for a street lamp. Me and Babs were in sight of Carvel when Dermo Grace came hurrying to catch us up.

'Will you have a jar?'

'Excuse me?'

'A droppeen. Say you will. The Judge and myself are having a bit of a ding-dong –'

'Now, now,' the Judge said, coming up from behind.

'Let's say a difference of opinion,' Dermo said.

'Is that what it is? I wasn't aware that you had declared yourself,' said the Judge, always the exact man.

'And we thought,' Dermo said, 'that as newcomers Mr and Mrs Perry might be . . . ah . . .'

'Impartial,' the Judge said.

We walked to the Robin Hood, with Margaret Garrity linking Babs's arm – when it comes to being friends for ever, women can achieve in two ticks what takes men a lifetime. At the hotel, Dermo steered the Judge and myself, left wheel, into the bar, while Mrs Garrity and Babs went upstairs to the Friar Tuck Suite with a promise of cups of tea. Dermo ordered three large Hennessys.

'You will not get on the soft side of me,' the Judge warned him.

'I wasn't aware there was one,' Dermo said with a wink to me and a smile to him that could tempt a Jewman into a chapel.

The Judge turned to me. 'Sir –'

'Perry,' I said, all charm.

'Mr Perry, *sir* . . .' he said, with lines under it. He was in a wax and not at all the same man who had sold us his house; from the face on him, you would think he had been diddled and wanted it back. 'May I make so bold as to ask what you thought of this evening's film?'

I said: 'I really enjoyed it.'

'Oh,' he said, 'are we talking about enjoyment? Well, sir, if it comes to that, I too enjoyed it. And for all I know –' he prodded a finger through the ceiling and into the Friar Tuck Suite – 'my wife enjoyed it.'

'Well, then . . .' Dermo said and got no further.

'The subject is not enjoyment,' the Judge said, making the word seem like cat-puke. 'The subject is immorality.'

'What?' Dermo said. 'Do you mean the wife's carry-on?'

'Not at all. She was a deplorable woman. I hold no brief for her. The person I am speaking of is the husband. He leaves his wife to live with a woman who is probably no better than she should be.'

'If you'll pardon the expression,' Dermo said, 'that wife of his was getting her oats all over the map of Europe.'

By the look of him, the Judge did not pardon the expression. 'I mean,' Dermo said, 'the woman was misbehaving.'

'If she was,' the Judge said in a voice that belonged in the Four Courts, 'I detected no evidence.'

'Well, you know, you have to read between the lines.'

'Oh, do I?'

The large Hennessys were brought.

Dermo said: 'Let me explain. There's this thing in America, a kind of censorship codology that goes by the name of the Production Code.' He cocked an eye, raised his glass and said, 'Slàinte.'

'Your health,' the Judge said, as if wishing him double pneumonia.

'And it lays down what can be said and what can't be said in fillums. There's certain words that can't be used, like "damn" and "bugger" and the Holy Name and such. And you can't show double beds or women in their pelts or even in their underwear or stocking-tops. Honest. And if there's any badness whatsoever, it has to be punished. Maybe that's as daft as a brush, but it's the rules. It's like Marlene Dietrich stopping the bullet that's meant for the chap in *Destry Rides Again*.' I smiled when I heard him say 'the chap'. In those days it was our word for the hero, just like the bad fellow was always 'the bully'.

'She has to be killed,' Dermo said, 'because she's a whoor.'

At the word, the Judge looked as if it was himself who had stopped the bullet. Dermo had gone too far, and then he let himself down by tacking a 'Sorry' on to the end of it.

The Judge lowered the Hennessy to his insides without a gasp. Dermo, smelling trouble, said, 'You'll have another.'

'I will not,' the Judge said, getting up.

'Sit down like a Christian,' Dermo said.

In Ireland, the expression 'No' in the context of refusing drink had been obsolete since John Jameson and Arthur Guinness were in their prams. The Judge sat down.

I saw my chance and said: 'Excuse me, but I didn't ask to come here. But Mr Grace is right –'

'Dermo,' Dermo said.

'. . . There are rules and what's in them would fill a book. Certain kinds of carryings-on have to be punished. And in the film that's what happened to your one, the wife. The husband left her –'

41

'Exactly!' the Judge said. 'He left her, and in life that does not happen.'

'Well, I grant you that maybe it oughtn't to . . .'

'You misunderstand me. I did not say that it should not, but that it does not, and that is my objection. Marriage is indissoluble. A husband does not leave his wife.'

Dermo put his spoke in. 'Ah now, your Honour, come on. Look at Seamus Mangan up in The Dwellings. The whole town knows his wife ran off on him, and –'

'It does not happen,' the Judge said, full stop, end of sentence.

'It did in tonight's film,' I said.

'Exactly. And how do we know that the woman would not have changed her ways?'

'That one? Catch her!'

'*But how do we know?* Mr Grace, Mr Perry, I am both a filmgoer and a student of human nature. I know what happens and what does not happen, what is permissible and what is not. This evening's film . . . this *Dodge City* . . .'

And have you met my wife? I thought.

'. . . is a dangerous travesty. People – our people – should be shown life as it is, not given bad example. Mr Grace, are you trying to corrupt them?'

Dermo said: 'Saving your presence, I think it's you that wants to corrupt them.'

'How dare you?'

Dermo was on his home turf and so could say what he liked. He laughed, so loud that I wondered if he was peluthered. 'Yes, that's your game. Oh, by the hokey, I have you taped. You want to corrupt us all into ignorance.'

'Ignorance?' the Judge roared.

'Innocence, then,' Dermo Grace said.

It was like a sudden calm. The Judge smiled and all but smacked his lips. He said, 'Corrupted into innocence. Yes, that's good, that's fair enough.' His smile even included me. 'Yes, I accept that.'

'Do you, now?' Dermo sneered.

The Judge took the risk of letting go of one of his lapels and pointed a finger at his waistcoat.

'Yes,' he said. 'Guilty.'

Chapter Four

Breezy

The inquest into the drowning of Angelica Looby in a slurry pit was held in the ballroom of the Robin Hood Hotel. Back in '39, the first thing Dermo Grace had done after his father died in spite of drinking two bottles of John Jameson every day for his health was to give over the old man's practice of renting out the ballroom for Sunday night hops. Truth to tell, there had been little enough hopping done; thanks to the parish priest, Canon Turmoyle, in the days when he was hot in his leather, it was all Victor Sylvester and strict tempo.

'The da had one foot in the door of the poorhouse,' Dermo told me. 'If he'd lived another year I'd have been reduced to gutting mackerel below on the pier. This is not a dancing sort of town.'

Nor was it, although with no competition from the hotel there were certain chancers who thought they were on the pig's back by promoting half-crown hops at the town hall. There was jitterbugging, and they brought in bands from the city, with famous singers that no one in Drane had ever heard of on account of the wireless reception was so brutal; but before the year was out, the interlopers were as poor as Job's ass, with their names published in *Stubbs' Gazette*. As for the ballroom at the Robin Hood, it was used after funerals for friends of the corpse to tell the obligatory lies in, or for the occasional wedding breakfast, or else it was utilised same as today for a coroner's inquest.

Babs said she had a shelf to paint, and that in any case she

44

could find out from the bread man all she needed to know about sudden death without leaving the comfort of her own home. Funny woman. Of course Dermo Grace had a front-row seat at the inquest, not on account of he owned the hotel, but because wherever you looked he was laid on like the gas. After the verdict the women trotted off home to get the dinner ready, and the men went either to stand at the harbour wall or for a pint in the hotel bar, which, thanks to the bold Dermo, wore a sign that said *Rick's Cafe*. I was heading home when he caught at me and said: 'Stay and have a jar. Want to talk to you. Bit of biz. Back in two ticks.' He was gone before I could answer. I knew the bit of biz he had in mind; he wanted me to help him dream up new film competitions for the Picture House.

In the bar, there was a pint waiting for me, compliments of Mr Grace. Rick's Cafe in Drane was not the kind of place where men wore snazzy white dinner jackets, had a hurt look in their eyes and said, 'The Germans wore grey, you wore blue.' As for women, in those days they did not go into pubs, at least not in a small town. The seats and barstools had leatherette cushions with the stuffing coming through the tears, and on the door leading to the jacks, someone or other – not Dermo, who was too neat in himself – had daubed in dribbly black paint 'Little John'.

Men were standing at the bar. Being a blow-in in the town, I was not invited to be part of the colloguing, but at least voices were no longer dropped when I came in. That may have signified a kind of probation, or it might have been because there was no argufying about the inquest; instead, the talk was the usual goster about the war and the German bombings across the water in Limeyland and last Saturday's match at Lansdowne Road. There was nothing pass-remarkable in that. A town looks after its own, and scandal is not for runners-in, but to be enjoyed decently at home, with curtains drawn and keys given a double turn.

Dermo came in, looked at my glass and said, 'You'll have another.'

'I'm in trouble enough already. Dinner is on the table at one.'

'Then I'll run you home. Come on.'

Trotting alongside him, I took sheets of paper from my pocket. 'I jotted down a few ideas for the competitions.'

'Sound man. Wouldn't doubt you.'

'You'll need a few lantern slides.'

'No trouble.'

'And still photos. Stuff you can cut out of *Picturegoer* and *Picture Show*. You can –'

And there I stopped. It was seldom with the war on that I saw the inside of a motor car, much less the outside of one like Dermo's. I nearly fell out of my standing when we came down the front steps and at the end of tyre marks across the lawn and a flower bed there was a 1938 two-seater Jensen with an AEA licence plate, number 299.

I said: 'Where the hell did you get that?'

'Do you know cars?'

'That's an English plate.'

'Yeah.' He was pleased with himself.

'And so how come you can run a car in war-time?'

'Maybe you think I'm not entitled?'

I could see that I had ruffled his feathers. I said, and put a shrug into it: 'Dunno whether you are or not. If you want to know me, come and live with me.'

The Jensen started with a roar that sent seagulls up and squawking. Gravel played 'The Harp that Once' on the bars of the front gate.

I said: 'I'm sorry I can't invite you for a bite of lunch. Babs still calls it dinner, you know.'

'Oh, yeah?'

'And the ration will stretch only so far.'

What I could have said but didn't was that it was Babs herself and not what was on the table that would stretch only so far. She had a sister who was married to Adolf, as we called him, a

German pork butcher in Fenian Street, so when it came to eating well we were laughing, but in a film whenever someone said, 'Stay for dinner', Babs would unfailingly let a snort out of her. Whether it was called dinner or lunch, we ate it at home and on our ownsome, unless family came on a special Sunday, and then it was high tea with bread and butter, cold ham, a lettuce leaf and scallions. The pair of us were what you would call comfortable but, with our kind of upbringing, the only knees ever put under a table were our own.

Dermo shouted to be heard over the engine. 'Thanks all the same. Actually, I cook for myself.'

'You're coddin'.'

He said: 'Don't look so surprised. I'm red-hot. There's many a good man has sold himself into servitude for the sake of a rasher-and-egg breakfast.' That put him back into a good humour. He laughed and said: 'Here, hold tight, I'll show you what she can do.'

He changed down into second, the bucket seat pucked me in the small of the back and we shot, half-snarling, half-singing, through a web of lanes and hedges and on to the Bray road, screeching around the Big Tree at Loughlinstown and past the Bride's Glen, then up a 1-in-5 hill that filled the world with sky as if we were looking for Messerschmidts.

Dermo pointed at a farmhouse that was under the oxter of the smelter chimney at Ballycoras. 'That's where it happened,' he said.

'Where what happened?'

'Where she did herself in. Your one. Angelica Looby.'

At the Golden Ball he did an about-turn and started home by more laneways, this time past Rathmichael. Our nearside tyres were in and out of the little Shanganagh River, watering the gardens beyond, and the pint I had had at the Robin Hood was threatening to pay its respects when we whipped around a blind bend and passed a post office van with the width of a senna pod between us.

Dermo slowed and said: 'Hello, look who's ahead of us.'

It was the Judge's wife, Margaret Garrity, on foot and making heavy weather out of carrying a full shopping bag. She had heard the cough of the Jensen passing the van and was pressing herself against a hedge. Dermo changed down until the car ticked like a new clock.

'Magser,' he said, and I was shocked at the familiarity, 'you're a bold woman.'

She said, very proper: 'Excuse me?'

'Did I not tell you, loud and clear, that whenever you want to go to Bray or anywhere else I'll run you there and back? I suppose you walked all this way from the bus?'

Instead of answering, she nodded to me with 'Good morning, Mr Perry. As you can see, my husband and I are still here.'

Dermo said: 'Hop in. Sit on Perry's knee.'

She said: 'Oh, no.' It was as if he had asked the Blessed Virgin for a bar of a song.

I swung myself out of the seat and said: 'Look, I'll hoof it, I'm nearly home,' although I was no such thing. For the next minute the three of us might have been singing in an opera, with me doing Faust and the honest-I-don't-mind obbligato, Mrs Garrity going pink in the face and warbling like her namesake, Marguerite, that oh no, she couldn't possibly, don't ask her, and Dermo with horns sprouting out of him, waving his forked tail and going 'You will, you will, you will.' Next thing, she was in the car, saying to me, who was out of it: 'He's a kind man,' and to Dermot, 'Yes, you are, you are so.' With that, they were off, the pair of them, in a cloud of exhaust that was like hell-fire, leaving me, the sap, with no more than the agreeable remembrance of her legs as she swung into the car.

It was five past two by the time I got home, and Adolf's pork sausages were shadows of their previous selves. Babs was a reasonable kind of woman, which is to say that she would vastly prefer me to have to walk three miles home than to drink three pints. I was looking at a plate of mashed spuds studded with sausages that could sink a pocket battleship when she said: 'What about the inquest?'

Before I had time to answer, she said, 'Read that,' and flicked a business card in front of me.

> *Come one, come all,*
> *No Job too Small*
> *Chas. and Sonny Looby*
> *Slaters and Repairers – Estimates Free*

A red line had been drawn through the *Chas.*

She said, 'This was put in our letter box two weeks ago, the day after we moved in. It's not very mannerly, is it?'

'What isn't?'

'Crossing out a person's name just because they're dead. Especially when the person is your own flesh and blood. I think it shows a want of nature.'

I said: 'Look, about the inquest –'

'I mean,' the madwoman said, making herself crystal thick, 'the proper thing to do would be to get new cards printed. Amn't I right?'

The dried-up pork sausage fell off the end of my fork and all but cracked the plate.

She said: 'Can you not answer a body when you're asked? What happened at the inquest?' She put me in mind of a tram running on two sets of lines at once. 'Was it suicide?'

'No such thing,' I said.

'Go to God.'

'It was "Death by Misadventure".'

'Huh.'

'Huh yourself. Anyway it wasn't a man that died. It was a woman.'

'I know it was. Who said otherwise?'

'Then what's all this carry-on about a name being crossed off?' I squinted at the card. 'Charles Looby?'

49

'He was called Chas,' she said. 'And he was her husband. He died first. He fell off the chapel roof.'

Maybe she caught the knack from me, but Babs could have written an Act One curtain line that left an audience goggling. She waited a split instant before the house lights went up for the interval and said: 'That was the morning Canon Turmoyle had his stroke.'

Once upon a time, Laurel and Hardy were in a film that had Ollie all dressed up to marry the boss's daughter, only what does Stan do but bring him a jigsaw puzzle for a wedding present. Well, and need you ask, the pair of them can't leave the shagging thing alone; they start trying to put the pieces together, and in the heel of the hunt the entire wedding is up the spout and so is Ollie. Well, it was the same with me trying to make head or tail of what had happened to Angelica Looby. She had been found in a pool of slurry on her da's farm up at Rathmichael, and excuse me, I didn't give a rat's fart if she fell in or was pushed, or what happened to Chas Looby either, or the canon, come to that, no disrespect to his cloth.

Fact is, I was going potty from idleness. After that whoor's melt, whoever he was, tore the skin off me in *Irish Truth* and all the other begrudgers joined in, like as if they were ferrets that got a smell of blood, I swore that I would eat clay before I gave them or their bastarding sort a second chance. Well, as the saying goes, 'Never say "Never".' One minute you think you're for the boneyard, and the next you're whistling 'It's a hap-hap-happy day'. All of a sudden, I missed not doing a good day's work, then strolling down to the coal harbour in Dun Laoghaire and dropping in at the Trawlerman for a jar and a jaw. In Drane the only diversions were the Picture House in the evenings and a walk in the daytime, either up the town and along the length of Easter Street, or the other way, around the headland and back by the Robin Hood.

That was then, of course; nowadays, when scenery is all the

go, you would not know the place. There are people who would steal the pennies off a dead pope's eyes just for a view of the sea and to wake up every day to the smell of rotted seaweed; and if they could not find a genuine run-down Georgian house to live in, they had one built to order. I drove out to Drane the other day and what had once been the Robin Hood Hotel was still there, as big and bold as ever, but now it had the look, mud-coloured and creamy, of last year's birthday cake. A sign on the gate said 'Kish View Luxury Apartments'.

Well, never mind about now. After our first few days in Carvel, I knew in my bones that our move to curse-o'-God Drane had been a mistake. Maybe it was just to pass the time that I got it into my head to ferret out what had happened to Angelica Looby, or it may have been a way to keep from blaming Babs for not telling me I was barking mad for dragging her out of the house on Widow Gamble's Hill. One thing I did not dare to do was let her suspect that I wanted to renege, not after giving up all her friends and good neighbours for my sake. So I filled in the odd half-hour by sifting through dustbins of rumours. In the end, all I got for it was the name of being a poker into other people's business. I never saw the truth although it was gawking at me.

The Loobys were brothers; that much was for sure. Chas was forty-one, a dark, short, thickset fellow with little to say. He was going bald and had an old scar half buried under an eyebrow. Sonny – for Nicholas – was eight years younger than him, tall and wiry and as jokey as the other was sour. They lived in a terrace of council houses called The Dwellings. When the war was threatening, there was a slump in the building trade and the brothers had to take whatever work was going. Then Sonny went to England to find a job. ('Not at all,' Babs told me, as if she was a dummy, Charlie McCarthy, maybe, perched on the knee of the bread man. 'Chalk and cheese. Him and his brother were Kilkenny cats. They couldn't get on, so one of them caught the mail boat.')

Word came that Sonny, beyond in Cheltenham, had joined the RAF. By then, Chas, who was living on his ownsome, had started doing a steady line with Angelica Ring, a farmer's daughter from below the smelter at Ballycoras. She was a dark girl, wide in the hips and with a big good-natured smile. Everyone in Drane had a nickname, some of them not very nice, and she was called Breezy; the reason being that she would cycle down to go with Chas to the Picture House without ever tucking her skirt under her out of decency; instead, to the delight of the corner-boys and the scandal of the old ones, she let it hang over the back of the saddle so that the least breath of wind lifted it. Breezy, yes. It was by all accounts not a name you used without – what's the word? – without punity in Chas's hearing.

After a year or so of pawing at one another the banns went up and Chas and Breezy got married. The surprise of the wedding day was when who else but Sonny, fresh off the mail boat, turned up for the breakfast wearing an RAF uniform under his overcoat. It would do your heart good, so I was told, to see the pair of them. They were not the kind to go in for hugging and mugging, but the handshake between them would have drawn tears from a stone. Then Sonny took off his overcoat, and at the sight of the uniform there was a gasp and a shout from someone of 'Get a rope!' Canon Turmoyle said: 'Now, now, men, a joke is a joke.' Whether it had you in kinks or not, Sonny sat sweating with the topcoat on him until the secretary of the local branch of the St Vincent de Paul had found him a blue suit. With all the excitement, the poor bride, dolled up in her ma's wedding dress, had been put in the ha'penny place, but Angelica was an old softy and took it in good part. As for Sonny, he said that he was home for good and had been invalided out of the air force.

Babs: 'No such thing. He was one of them deserters.'
Me: 'How do you know?'
Babs: 'Because I know.'
Me: 'Who from? The bread man?'
Babs: (tongue stuck out).

It was business as before for the brothers – they even took on an apprentice, an impudent young know-it-all by the name of Ger Hegarty. Sonny moved back into The Dwellings with Chas and Angelica and paid his whack as a lodger, while she kept house and cooked for the brothers and herself, and not a grumble out of her. The three of them went to the pictures together, with her sitting in the middle. You would have said they were as happy as Larry.

'They never missed a night,' Dermo Grace told me a week or so after the inquest on Angelica, when the pair of us were sitting in the empty Picture House with our eyes watering from the smell of disinfectant mixed with the blue staleness from the previous night's cigarettes. 'And still and all,' he said, 'aren't the pictures great? You can have a life of misery, with nothing ever happening except your wife giving you lackery, and for a measly bob or a ninepence look what you get. Look at the places you can go to. And you can be anyone you like. What about last Sunday evening and *Young Mr Lincoln*? Up there on that screen!'

'That was good,' I granted him.

'Good? *Good?*' he said, getting worked up. 'You can even get killed and come back to life again.'

'You what?'

'Where else can that happen to you? Did you not see that film last week with Chester Morris? The one where he's a know-it-all and his jack-acting gets the girl's kid brother killed. Then he reforms, like, and takes the place of the fellow she's engaged to. This guy is supposed to drive a truck full of . . . you know, nitro-whatever-it-is, only Chester Morris socks him on the jaw and takes the truck out himself and –' Dermo gave an imitation of a truck blowing up with Chester Morris in it. 'No, what I mean is, you put yourself in his shoes, and then you go and get killed, but you come back again the following week in another fillum, and there he is again and there you are, with not a feather out of either of you.'

'Tell me about Angelica,' I said.

'Who? Oh, she was as mad for fillums as Chas and Sonny were. Worse. She ate up every picture I put on the screen. If it was Ginger Rogers in *Bachelor Mother* she would go home laughing. And, oh my God, you should have seen her at *Goodbye, Mr Chips* when Greer Garson snuffed it. "You're making a show of us," Chas said when it was over and she couldn't stop bawling. Mind, he was not giving out to her in any sense. I mean, he doted on her.

'"Oh, Breezy will cry all the way home," Sonny said, at which Chas drew out and hit his brother a belt for himself in the face.'

'Do you mean there was a fight?' I asked.

Dermo grinned and said: 'Oh no, you don't.'

I said, acting the innocent: 'Don't what?'

He said: 'If you're making out there was bad blood between the brothers, then try again. Sonny just stood there on the steps of the Picture House sticking his tongue out to catch the blood from his nose. "You mind that dirty mouth of yours," Chas said, and put his fist behind his back as if he was afraid it would do more mischief. That was him, wanting to burst you one minute and great with you the next.'

I said: 'This is a cod of a yarn.'

'I was there. I heard them. I saw them. And the very next evening, the three of them were in the ninepennies as usual. It was a film called *Manpower*, with George Raft and Edward G. Robinson as two men – pals tried and true, you know – working high up on what's-it-you-call-'em, pylons. And the pair of them are wild out about the same bit of stuff. Your woman, you know: Marleen Dietrich.'

'And they fight when they're high up,' I said. 'And one of them falls and is killed.'

'Oh, you saw it?' Dermo said.

'Matter of fact, no, I didn't.'

'Good guess, then. Spot on.' He gave me a long look. 'What's your interest, anyway? I mean in Angelica, R.I.P.'

I felt my ears burning. 'Nothing.'

'Something to put in a play, I suppose.'

'There's no fooling you!' I said.

'I have you taped,' he said, sure of himself. 'Do you know, and if you ask me, I don't think poor Angelica had the remotest about why Chas hit Sonny that puck in the gob. The innocent sort she was, I doubt if she ever knew about the nickname.'

'"Breezy".'

He lowered his voice. 'Yeah.'

So suddenly that I gave a start, Dermo stood up and his tip-up seat banged and made an echo. He stubbed his cigarette out in the ashtray on the back of the seat in front and put the butt into his half-full packet of Gold Flake. 'I'm very tidy in myself,' he said, 'and the cleaner has been and gone.'

I followed him into the aisle and he pushed the emergency door open to let the sea air in. He held it to let me out and said: 'Look, I know you're a decent skin, but leave it. The poor girl is dead and gone, and that's the end of it. You were at the inquest.'

'"Death by misadventure".'

'Whatever.'

I asked him: 'What about her husband? Chas, was that his name? The one they say fell off the roof.'

Dermo was getting vexed. '"They say . . . they say." What is it you're asking me? Did he fall or was he pushed, is that it?'

'I suppose no one'll ever know.'

'*Everyone* knows.'

'Do *you*?'

'Certainly I do. What day is today? Wednesday? Grand. So the Carnegie Library will be open, and you can look it up. Try the *Bay Tidings*. There was a full verfeckinbatim account in it of the inquest on Chas Looby. That would have been . . . when?' He made a show of counting on his fingers.

'Cool down,' I said.

'Three weeks ago – or was it four? – before yourself and Mrs P. came and honoured us.' He grinned like a Hallowe'en mask. 'No, wait . . . wait. Don't bother looking it up. Not at all. Ask your missus.'

'Babs? What does Babs have to –'

'Sure. Why not? She's the brainy one.'

'I asked you what –'

'Goodbye, now.' He did not say it but half-sang it. He let the emergency door slam shut again, with himself back inside the Picture House and me standing outside and fit to be tied.

At home at teatime I made an excuse to bring up the subject of the inquest; not the one on the misfortunate Chas, but on Angelica. I wanted to ease it in, like; Babs listened until I thought her neck would dislocate. 'What brought that on?' she asked.

'Nothing,' I said, and the halo looked well on me. 'I was talking to Dermo Grace about that inquest, and how the coroner wasn't going to let the girl's people be put to shame. "There is no evidence whatever," he said, "as to how the unfortunate young lady entered the slurry pit. She could have slipped and fallen." And I heard a voice behind me muttering "Decent man." That was when he told the jury to bring in the verdict of Death by Whatsit.'

'Whether she fell in or jumped in,' Babs said, 'at least it put a stop to the gossip.'

'What gossip was that?' I asked.

'You're so innocent you'll never see purgatory,' she said. She raked over what I already knew: how, after the inquest on Chas, the whole town had it that Sonny and Angelica had been carrying on. What spoiled the story, though, was that when Sonny flaked off back to England, Angelica neither went with him nor after him.

She moved out of the The Dwellings right enough, but where she went was home to the farm at Rathmichael and was seen there feeding the animals and doing the milking.

Her da, howsomever, used to drink of an evening with a young guard out of the barracks at Kilternan and one day happened to mention that your one, Angelica, had taken it into her head to shag off. 'All week,' he said, 'I haven't seen hide nor hair of her.'

'Did she go bag and baggage?' the young guard asked him.

'You wha'?'

'I mean, did she take her clothes?'

'Not a stitch,' the da said. 'What do you want to know for?'

'Because I'm thinking,' said the young guard who, unlike the majority of policemen, was of a literary bent, 'of the curious incident of the dog in the night-time.'

And, need you ask, that did it. They searched. They found her, and she was in the slurry pit.

'Ah, the creature,' Babs said.

It was then I got to the meat of it. 'And what about your man, Chas?' I asked.

She looked at me. 'What would I know about him?'

'He fell off the roof.'

'Well?'

'He fell off the roof,' I said again, 'and landed in front of the canon, who was walking in the chapel yard and saying his office.' Which – or need I draw a drawing of it? – was what accounted for the stroke.

'Well?'

I told her straight out: 'Dermo Grace said you'd know all about it?'

'*Me*?'

'He said to ask you, seeing as how you were the brainy one.'

And I declare to God, the woman smiled, taking it for a compliment. She cleared my plate off the table and brought it to the sink humming a bar of her favourite song, 'I'll be your sweetheart'. She said, chastising herself: 'No, I oughtn't to. It's a sin to make light of it.' Then, with her face lit up: 'Honest, was that what he said? Me? Brainy?'

'Well, do you know or don't you?'

'The whole town knows,' she said. There was slyness on her face. 'Do you mean *you* don't?'

Like I say, I knew her of an old date. She would tease and squeeze, making me out to be a thick until I was all but begging her to say what had happened to Chas Looby. But how could she know? How could anyone know? Like Thomas Moore said in *The Minstrel Boy*, a roof's a fine and private place.

'He said to ask me?' I had wound her up and now she would go on for ever. She gave me a look that was two parts pity and one of patience. 'Perry, it was in the paper.'

That was what Dermo had said to me. 'Try the *Bay Tidings*.' I got up from the table and started out of the room. 'Where are you going?' she asked.

'Thought I'd take the oul' dog for a walk,' I said.

As I took my topcoat down from the rack in the hall I at least had the satisfaction of hearing her say: 'We haven't got a d–'

The Carnegie Library was open two evenings a week until half seven and all day on Saturdays, and the newspapers and *Dublin Opinion* were chained to a reading table near the door. The *Bay Tidings* came out twice a week, and what with the shortage of newsprint and the shortage of news, all it had to say was hard put to it to fill four pages. It took me no time to find an account of the inquest on Chas Looby. There was a headline across the front page: DRANE MAN'S FATAL FALL.

It was all there, about the overcast day that was in it, and how the slates on the chapel roof were greasy from the night's rain, with a south-west wind blowing in gusts, but I had to read it all three or four times before I caught on to whatever the whole town, Babs included, had twigged and I had skimmed over. I read how Sonny had turned up for the inquest and had drink both with him and on him. He started to cry when he told how he saw his brother slip and fall. The coroner ticked him off for being ossified, but said he would make allowances. Then the apprentice, Ger Hegarty, gave evidence that he had been on the far side of the roof when he heard Chas let out a roar.

Coroner: So you did not actually see the accident?
Witness: As good as.

Coroner: Never mind 'As good as', and you will address me as 'Sir'. Did you or did you not see what happened?

Witness: I heard it.

Coroner: 'Sir.'

Witness: . . . Sir.

Coroner: You heard it, but you did not see it because both the deceased and his brother were out of sight at the far side of the church roof?

Witness: Aye. They were.

Coroner: I have already warned you –

Witness: Sir.

Coroner: And you have heard the evidence of Nicholas, otherwise Sonny, Looby, who said that his brother had lost his footing and slipped on the wet slates.

Witness: (*A nod*)

Coroner: (*to the Clerk*) Make that an affirmative. (*To Witness*) And would you say that was plausible? (*No reply*) I mean, in your opinion is that what could have happened?

Witness: Oh, sir, that roof was very treacherous. And it was blustery.

Coroner: One more question. You have said that you 'heard' the accident. What was there to hear?

Witness: I heard what I heard, sir. I heard Sonny, saying –

Coroner: You mean Nicholas Looby?

Witness: Yes, sir; him, sir; Sonny, sir. I heard him and Chas across the chapel roof, clear as I hear yourself. And the last words that were said was Sonny saying to Chas – real sociable, like – was how it was breezy out.

The witness was then excused.

Chapter Five

The Standing Ovations (1)

Try as I do to be sociable, I have rarely succeeded in hitting it off with a woman who has a moustache, be it ever so faint.

When Monica Mundow came to the door of Carvel it was clear that I was never likely to be high up on her list of great favourites. Within the space of a second, she caught me first of all looking at her ronnie and then not looking at it, and the second look was worse than the first. She gave me a February of a smile and said: 'Oh, it is the great man himself!' employing what in years to come would be known as an Edna O'Brien voice: shy and innocent and sure God help us, all I am is a girleen.

Quick as a flash, I said, 'Good afternoon.'

I had seen her often in the town, wearing a long Donegal tweed cloak that flowed behind her – I thought of poor Angelica – as she pedalled a Rudge bicycle that was the height of a horse. Once when I let a cackle out of me, Babs asked, 'What's that in aid of?' 'Nothing,' I said, thinking of your one in *The Wizard of Oz*, saying, 'I'll get you, my pretty, and your little dog, too!' On the doorstep, she was at closer range, and what I had taken to be a stray lock of hair blown across her face by the wind turned out to be a permanent feature of her upper lip.

She said, 'Might we have a word, O master?' and waited to be invited in. There was a clatter from the street below, and I saw the other part of the 'we': a smallish baldy man making a dog's dinner out of parking two bicycles at the foot of our steps. 'Monica Mundow,' she said, taking hold of her left tit as if fearful that I might shake it. The smallish man came up the steps two at a time. He looked familiar, too. 'Slow coach, slow coach,' she sang in a voice with little bells in it. Then she introduced him. 'My husband, Sinjin Mundow.' It would be a while before I twigged that his first name was St John.

'From the bank,' he said deferentially.

I recognised him then as the assistant manager of the local branch of the Bank of Ireland. Seeing him now in a corduroy suit that was as baldy as he was, you would have offered him the lend of a shilling without expectations of ever seeing a penny of it. I let out a warning call of 'Babs, we have visitors,' and asked them to come in. There was the grinding of a chair being pulled back in the breakfast room, and Babs came out whipping her glasses off and with a bright woman-of-the-house smile glued in place. It was October, with an east wind from the sea, and the pair of us had been reading in front of one bar of an electric fire. Now, however, we showed the Mundows into the living room where Babs had weeks before arranged a little mountain of turf briquettes in the fireplace, more for show than glow. She gave it a look as if it was a furnace that had gone out on her and said: 'Peregrine, what are you thinking of?' I was Babs's Perry when the sun shone, but I got the full Peregrine, meaning 'Don't get a whiff of yourself', whenever the east wind caught her in the small of the back and uninvited visitors put in their interference, such as now. Nothing personal. 'Put a match to that, like a good man.'

Monica Mundow took one of Babs's hands in both of hers and said: 'Sinjin and I are in the Standing Ovations.'

Her husband smiled and uttered an 'Ahem, ahem' that came out as 'Aha, aha.'

Mrs Mundow – or the Madame, as we would learn to call her – said: 'I think what Sinjin, the bold creature, means to say is that he and I *are* the Standing Ovations.' She crinkled her nose at him, causing her moustache to do a little two-step. 'You are, you are. Bold.' She might have been giving him an affectionate poke with a meat-skewer.

'Ah, the local am-drams,' I said. I had seen a printed card in the window of Jemima's the newsagent's to say that the Standing Ovations were looking for new members for their Christmas presentation of *The Great Waltz*.

'Amateurs, yes, if you so choose to call us,' Madame said, not best delighted.

'Yous will have a cup of tea,' Babs said. 'Just in your hands.'

'No, no, too much trouble,' Madame said.

There is a certain etiquette about being offered a cup of tea. If you were to say with great sincerity, 'Thank you no, I absolutely will not,' the translation would be, 'I will, but coax me.' On the other hand, if you replied, like Madame, that it was too much trouble, then that was not only a 'yes', but you were asking for a fig roll as well. Babs said, 'Trouble indeed, sure what else have we?' and went off to the kitchen to scald a teapot and use up the last of our ration of half an ounce of tea per person per week. Madame sat in front of the fire with Sinjin standing behind her, the pair of them like your grandma and grandda all in sepia. A nest of scrunched-up paper was cajoling the briquettes into a blaze.

'Yes, the Standing Ovations,' Madame said. 'There are certain people – and sure God love them and pity their ignorance – who think that with such a name we must have a great opinion of ourselves. But I always say that what we call ourselves is a class of an ideal to be aimed for. Have you me?'

'I have,' I said.

'An aspiration.'

'Um.'

'And next week casting will begin for our new production.'

'*The Great Waltz*,' I said.

'Do you hear, Sinjin?' she said. 'Our fame goes before us!'

He lilted a bar from 'Tales from the Vienna Woods'. 'De-dah, de-dah, de dum, dum-dum!'

I thought of the film, one of my favourites, with the drive in the woods, and the squeak – eek-eek-eek – of the carriage, the clop of the horse's hooves and the tooting of a horn-player on the back of a passing stagecoach, all coming together to make up the tune. 'That'll go down well in Drane,' I said.

'It will,' she said.

'Like a dose of salts.'

'We'll do it,' she said. 'Never fear.'

She gave me a look that dared me to go another inch, and at that moment Babs came back.

'I forgot,' she said. 'It's gone the glimmer-time.'

The way things were during the Emergency, the gas came on for cooking or for fires at certain hours in the day, and in between these, it was diminished to a trickle of flame you could not warm your hands on. 'If we give the fire a few minutes,' Babs said, 'we could boil a kettle.'

'Not at all, nonsense,' the Madame said. 'We'll just – how does the saying go? state our business and be off.'

'They're doing *The Great Waltz*,' I reminded Babs. 'Not to be missed.'

'Aren't you a pet,' our visitor said. 'Mind, dare I say that we had hoped for more from you than mere attendance. You would be a great addition to us on the other side.'

'After death, do you mean?' I said.

She said to Sinjin: 'He would make a cat laugh. It is no wonder his plays are popular.' Then to me: 'I meant on the other side of the –'

'Foots?' I said.

'Pardon me?'

'Footlights.'

'Oh, excuse my abysmal ignorance. You will join the Ovations, yes, you will, say you will. Are you not a great man of the theatre?'

'That's very kind of you,' I said.

'Well, at least there are them that say you are,' the bitch said.

I knew I would have to give her a plump and plain answer that locked and barred the door she was looking for. Mind, I like am-dram people; they are the heart and soul of the theatre, and they would be the first to say so. Often when I see them doing a play of mine I wish I had the courage of Lennox Robinson who went to a performance of his own *The Far-Off Hills* and was asked to say a *cupla focail* – the obligatory 'few words' – from the stage afterwards; and with the heart of a lion he got up and said to the audience, 'Did you see what they did to my beautiful play?' Well, whenever I am called upon, I hop like a hare on to the stage in front of the cast and damn my soul with mendacity. I think of the royalties; I tell myself that the theatre is the place for lies, whether in a play or out of it; I tell the actors they are great and that the most hopeless dud amongst them is Mícheál Mac Liammóir and F. J. McCormick squashed into one.

To Monica Mundow I said: 'All I ever did in the theatre was write plays, and I've given that up. I've retired. Full stop. I'm done with it.'

She was quiet for a few seconds, and I gave Babs a look, warning her not to put her prate in.

The Madame said: 'That sounds very final.'

I said: 'It's meant to be. Sorry.'

She tried a dab of soft soap. 'Well, living here as you do among the – what will I call them? – the ho-hee poll-o-hee, maybe you would do us the honour, famous man that you are, of being our patron. Just your name on the programme, that is all, and then you need not discommode yourself by coming next or near us.'

I had set myself to work out what 'ho-hee poll-o-hee' could mean, but then had a vision of a programme with my name printed between Jno. Clohessy, Beer, Wine & Spirits, and McKeon Bros. – Dublin Bay Dover Sole. I thanked her and the Standing Ovations for the great compliment, but repeated that my days in the theatre were over. I was not to be tempted; otherwise, where would it end? I might even go back on my word and write another play, God forbid.

The smile on her face was so thin that she could have shaved off her moustache with it. She could do no more now than take herself home, and Sinjin along with her, and have it all over the town that we were too frigging mean to offer them a cup of tea. Her eyes went from me to Babs, and I never saw the rabbit punch coming when she said: 'Well, you won't say no to us, will you, Mrs Perry?'

'Excuse me?' Babs said, impersonating a beetroot.

Mrs Mundow told Babs that joining the Ovations was a great way for a blow-in in the town to meet new friends, and maybe Babs could do this and that behind the scenes. Maybe she could lend a hand with the costumes for *The Great Waltz*, or there was always call for a prompter with a good clear voice. And speaking of voices, maybe she could even appear dressed in finery as one of the chorus ladies in the ballroom scene.

'Oh, my God, no, don't ask me,' Babs said, laughing, and now her face had the darkness of a red goose-gob. She was a shy, unsociable woman with a terror of standing out from a crowd. Even at a bit of a Sunday hooley around a piano and among friends, she would not respond to a noble call, and, as for her setting foot on a stage, don't talk to me. I could have told Mrs Mundow to save her breath for charming birds out of trees. She opened her mouth, but no further word came out, for Babs said 'No' and kept saying it, 'No, no, no, no, no, no, no,' shaking her head and smiling all the time. It was as if she was refusing a cup of tea that she was gumming for.

Ten minutes later, the Mundows took themselves off. I could hear the clatter of the two bicycles, then Babs laughing goodbye from the steps, then more guff from under the moustache, answered by another ra-ta-ta of 'No's like hailstones on a roof. Babs came back into the living room, where I was shifting the briquettes out of the grate before the fire took. The war-time had made misers of us.

"The cheek of them,' she said.

'How?'

'You know how. Wanting me to get dressed up in someone's granny's hand-me-downs and be a – a – a – laughing stock.'

'Give over,' I told her. 'I think they got on the right side of you.'

'No such thing.' She gave me a long stare. 'Are you mad?'

*

A week later and all at once, like greyhounds when the traps went
up, everyone was telling everyone else that the evenings were
drawing in. In the house we lived in, we needed no reminding,
for the wind had swung to the east. It was a bitter wind that
would all but blow you off the front steps and lifted and banged
the knocker until your nerves begged you to tie it down. The
same easterly told us why the Drane fishermen built their
cottages with the front doors at the side, facing away from the
sea. At Carvel there was or had been such a door, giving on a
laneway – a grand parking place for motor cars, I thought, if the
war ever ended. The door had been bricked up since old God's
time, and I got the idea into my head to undo what must have
been done without thinking. I had strength enough for the job,
but bugger-all skill, so I got a young lad named the Shagger
Sheehy to help me.

One day, me and him were going at it middling hard when a
voice behind me said, 'Bravo, sir. I see you're doing what I
should have tackled years ago.' I looked around and there were
the Judge and Mrs Garrity, arm in arm. He was wearing a tweed
overcoat and hat, a muffler and black boots you could see your
face in. The way herself kept him, he might have stepped out of
a bandbox, and I looked at his clothes first and his face second
because whenever the pair of them came in sight I felt a twinge
of guilt that went against reason. It was as if me and Babs were
interlopers, what with us being in their house, while they were
full-time boarders at the Robin Hood.

'Yes, that's the remedy,' the Judge said. 'Use the front door for
appearances only, and make it weatherproof. That east wind is
purgatorial.'

Purgatorial. A nice word, I thought; you could dip your
bread in it. 'True for you,' I said. 'It goes through the house like
a side.'

'Like a . . .?'

'The thing you cut grass with,' I said and felt myself going red.

The nearer to the River Liffey a young lad grows up, the oftener a 'th' slips out of him that sounds like a 'd'. 'A scythe,' the Judge said. 'Just so.'

'The wind is so bitter,' Mrs Garrity said, getting her spoke in.

I invited them into the house for a cup of tea and a chinwag, but the Judge answered 'No' with such ferocity that the usual you-will, you-will etiquette went by the board. His wife said, 'James,' in a low voice.

'Forgive me,' he said. 'We lived in this house for so many years that it would go hard with us to come into it as strangers. Perhaps one day when we are settled into a new home.'

'I have you,' I said.

'Fond memories,' Mrs Garrity said.

She gave me a nice little smile that flustered me. To tread water, I remarked that they could hardly be better off than where they were, snug as bugs in the Friar Tuck Suite at the Robin Hood. 'And is there any news of the new house itself?'

'That's over and done with,' the Judge said.

He looked at his wife and she looked at him. Then the story came out between them in dribs and drabs, with neither one wanting to tell it. What was clear when it was put through the strainer was that there had been some kind of hookery. The deeds of their new house were all a cod; and the so-called owner was only a cute whoor. The transaction was up the Swannee, and the Judge was suing to get his deposit back. 'Never, never go to law,' the pot said, destroying the kettle's character.

'So we're leaving the hotel,' Mrs Garrity said.

'If we stay any longer,' the Judge said, 'we would be objects of local ridicule. The corner-boys would have a field day.' He gave a look at the Shagger Sheehy, who was standing, listening, with a dripping trowel in his hand.

'And there's the expense,' his wife said. 'Generous and all as Mr Grace has been to us.'

'Now, Mother,' he said, looking more like Lewis Stone than ever. 'What is or will become common knowledge is one thing and can't be helped. Our private affairs are something else again.'

She said in a near-whisper: 'Excuse me.'

He said: 'We have found a house to rent out by Shanganagh. It isn't, dare one say, our kind of neighbourhood, but as our friend Mercutio said, "'Tis enough. 'Twill serve."' When it comes to plays, I thought to myself, he knows all about your man Shakespeare, but sweet feck all about Peregrine Perry.

The Judge made a woeful attempt at a smile. 'So now we must go all the way back to number one.'

'Square one, pet,' Mrs Garrity said.

'Square one, yes.'

They went off linking arms again, down the road, and I felt sorry for them and was all the sorrier because I wanted Babs and me to be out of Carvel as bad as the Judge and his wife wanted to be back inside of it.

'Will we go?' Babs said.

A postcard had come from Monica Mundow. It was addressed to Babs and invited her to a private showing of the MGM film, *The Great Waltz*. At the bottom the faggot had written, 'Do come. No obligation!!'

I said, 'That Mundow one is dangerous.'

'How?'

I had no answer. Instead, I shook the card at her. 'You're invited, and I amn't. Why?'

'Because you were so short with her, why do you think? No, not short at all. Next door to rude, that's what you were.'

I said: 'What the hell is she up to?'

In the end, I agreed to go, partly out of curiosity and also because I was fond of the film in spite of itself. It was what the mammy, God rest her, would have called an old come-all-ye, with people getting up on tables and putting words like 'I'm in love with Vienna' to tunes they had never heard in their puffs. Or your man, Johann Strauss, composing 'Tales from the

68

Vienna Woods' before dinner time, and having an all-girl orchestra playing it in time for high tea. And 'Look,' a fellow says, pointing. 'It's Carla Donner, the famous opera singer!' I mean, as if a woman who was famous had any need to be called famous.

I had seen the film more than once since it came out six years before, in 1936, and what I remembered best was not the story but the telling of it. Most of all, there was the bit early on inside Dommayer's cafe, with Johann's orchestra playing its first concert and the place all but empty, while in the square outside there were people drinking beer or playing chess or fighting with swords or enjoying the evening air sitting at windows or in a rocking chair. And Herman Bing was Dommayer – my God, I remember him; he was a little German with curly black hair, always excited, and he could hiss his esses until they were like the trolley of a tram spitting against the overhead wires – and he threw open the cafe windows and shouted at the people in the street: 'For nosssing you will lissssen!' And then you saw that all of a sudden the beer mugs were lying empty on the table, the chess pieces were overturned, and the rocking chair was to-ing and fro-ing, with nobody in it. And of course where was everyone but waltzing in Dommayer's and singing songs about Vienna that they could never have heard since Jesus was a carpenter.

I had no wish to lay eyes on the Mundow woman ever again, and shame on me for saying that my heart gave a jump of joy when the Picture House came in view and I saw that the rip was on a pair of crutches. Everyone who went in stopped for a word with her; you could hear the sympathy from across the street, and I guessed that they were all members of the Standing Ovations. 'Wet leaves,' I heard her say. 'The wheels went from under me.'

The Madame was not thrilled to bits to see me. 'Oh, you brought himself, I see,' she said, as if I was one of the leaves her bike had skidded on.

'Is it not all right?' Babs asked, letting me down.

'I thought,' I said, 'that you might find room for one of the "ho-hee poll-o-hee".'

'Wisha, don't belittle yourself,' the Madame said. She tried to step back, crutches and all, to get a good look at me. 'Oh, but you would have been a great addition to us. You could have been the Emperor. I can see you with medals and the white mutton-chop whiskers. A fine Christmas tree of a man. Am I not right, Sinjin?'

It was only then that I noticed him. He was handing out a pencil and what looked like a penny copybook to every am-dram member who went up the steps of the Picture House.

'But what in the world happened to you?' Babs wanted to know, maybe to steer the subject away from whiskers, even mutton-chops.

'Don't ask, don't ask,' the Madame said with a sigh.

'The bicycle.' Sinjin lobbed the word at us over his shoulder.

'How the mighty are fallen!' his wife said with a terrible laugh that took the joke out of it. 'I seem to be fated not to play Carla Donner.'

That was a lemoner for me. At the thought of Mrs Mundow acting the part of a gorgeous blonde bit of stuff who could sing the birds out of half the trees in the Vienna Woods and get the long underwear off Johann Strauss, both at the same time, I all but fell out of my standing. By the time I could shake the image from my head, the Madame was saying that she had found a replacement. 'A discovery of mine,' she said. 'That's her there with her mammy.'

I looked and saw two women. One was of middle age; the other was in her twenties and tall with fair hair. They looked lost and stood out of the way of the am-dram crowd who went past, gawking at them without saluting.

'A very nice little soprano voice,' the Madame said, 'only she lacks what you might call a Star Ingredient.' With one hand she steadied herself against me and used the other to pull Babs to her with the handle of her crutch. 'She's English, you know.'

'Oh?'

'It gives her the necessary hint of foreignness.'

There were maybe forty people inside the Picture House by the time Sinjin had shut the curtains behind the stained-glass panels in the street door. It was then I noticed that Babs had been given a copybook, with the name 'Frau Hofbauer' written in block letters on the cover.

I said: 'What's that in aid of?'

'Shhh.'

'Oh, for God's sake. Don't tell me they've roped you in to –'

She whispered. 'I'm only lending a hand just for today.'

'Well, for the love of –'

But by then the new Carla Donner and her ma were finding a place to sit, and the MGM lion was doing its roar.

The picture had been on a while before I twigged what was happening. I heard a woman say in a complaining voice: 'They talk so quick.' She was shushed, and when I looked along our row I saw that she was scribbling like mad into her copybook and saying 'Jesus' under her breath. In fact, they were all at it, Babs included. Every member of the am-drams had been given the name of a person in the film and was copying down whatever that character said.

After the first half-hour, when Miliza Korjus had sung 'There'll Come a Time', the lights came up and the film stopped. There was a sound like Boris Karloff dragging his club foot in *Tower of London*, and Mrs Mundow came down the aisle, shwump-and-thump and dot-and-carry-one, and plonked herself in front of the screen.

'Wasn't that great?' she said. 'Well, fillum stars and all as they are, they won't hold a candle to us. And now we'll have a little rest.'

Someone spoke up and asked if she had e'er an old pencil-sharpener, and of course when Sinjin supplied the needful, everyone wanted one. 'And don't worry if you missed some of what was said,' Madame told her actors. 'Just write down the sense of it, and later on Sinjin will find the words when he is making up the script. Sure we will be well away.'

The film went on again, and when it was over Sinjin collected the copybooks. 'Don't forget now,' Madame told her members, 'there will be a second showing in the afternoon at two o'clock sharp, and that will be our last chance to write it all down.'

As everyone stood up to leave, Sinjin whispered to her.

She gave a little cry and flung her hands up. 'Oh, excuse me, I have a colander for a brain. I want to extend the heartiest of welcomes to Miss Sunny Day who will be taking the part of Carla Donner.' She gave a dainty little handclap that a bat would not have heard, and said, 'Welcome to Drane, Sunny, and to the Standing Ovations.'

On the front steps, she crutched over to Babs and me, all smiles. 'So did the Master enjoy it?'

'It was massive,' I said, 'same as it ever was. But I have a question. Do you not know that *The Great Waltz* was a stage musical to begin with?'

Her smile went on a crash diet. 'Thank you, yes, I do know, and what of it?'

'What I mean is, it's published. You can buy the script, so there's no need for this carry-on, I mean is there?'

'The musical play,' the Madame said, 'is a rubbishy rig-a-marole about the father and son, with the old Johann being jealous of the young Johann, and the pair of them carrying on. I read it, and it would give you the sick, so it would. No, we will do the story that is in the fillum. Sinjin will write it out for us, the same as he always does. No better man.'

She made to take herself off as fast as the pin in her broken ankle would let her. 'The same as he always does?' I said. 'So what about paying the royalties?'

'The roy-let-ies?' she said in let-on amazement. 'What would we pay the like of them for?'

'For using an author's work,' I said.

Maybe she forgot who I was or what I once did for a living, but it was what she said then that my dislike of the woman turned to hate. She uttered the worst insult that a writer can ever hear.

'Oh, my dear man, and God bless your innocence, we never pay roy-let-ies.'

Chapter Six

The Standing Ovations (2)

There was a small room in one of the two cottages at the back of Carvel that Babs liked to call her sewing room. Most of what was in it was rubbish: old framed photos of sepia people, fat suitcases that yelled: 'Whatever you do, don't open me!'; a caddy for Mazzawattee tea, rattling with the keys in it that fitted no lock; a cracked vase full of honesty; and a chapel-shaped Philco wireless set – if you plugged it in, there were lit-up names on it like Hilversum and Luxembourg – and, thanks to what I called the *Übergruppensturm*-gobshite up on the hill (and I will get to him later on), all we ever heard out of it instead of Big-Hearted Arthur and Henry Hall was what sounded like electric phlegm. But you could call it a sewing room, for sure enough by the window there was a table with a treadle and a rusty Singer machine.

The only sewing Babs ever did was to put a button on a shirt or darn a heel, but one day a tin of machine oil appeared on the scullery shelf, and next I heard the clatter of the old Singer. I didn't need to be Nick and Nora Charles to know what she was up to. Maybe the Madame had found an honest-to-God job for her with the Ovations, or it might have been the old cow's way of aggravating me. Whichever, I gave myself the private satisfaction of asking no questions and did not even stoop to taking a sly dekko into the sewing room.

'You're going to murder me,' Babs said suddenly one evening.

'Only if you go into the am-drams,' I told her, laughing, then saw that there were two contrary looks on her face: one that was afraid of me giving out to her, and the other, behind it, that told me she would have her own way if it was to be the end of her.

'It'll only be for two evenings a week,' she said and then took a swallow. 'At first.'

'What does that mean?'

'It'll be all over before Christmas.'

'That's what they said about the war.'

'It's not a joke!' She gave me a look I had not seen before, with anger in it; then she was calm again. 'It's like what the Madame said –'

'The what? The who?'

'. . . Mrs Mundow, the day she came here. She said that I might help to fill up the stage in the ballroom scene. For decoration, like.'

There were any number of roads I could go down. I could put a saint's face on it and pretend to be glad that she had found a way of making new friends; or I could whinge about being left on my own for half the week without even the wireless to listen to unless I went up the hill and strangled Erich von Stroheim; or I could go into the sulks. I was a great sulker.

Or I could say again, and I did say it, that Babs would be helping to do a writer out of money he was entitled to. She answered, and it was not her I was listening to but the Mundow rip: 'Him? Sure he's an American.'

'Who is?'

'Whoever wrote the words.'

'How do you know?'

'So chances are he has enough money without wanting more.' She gave a little laugh. 'A pity about him.'

I said: 'I think I'll go out and come in again.'

She said, cool as you like: 'Do. You should take your bike and go for a spin.'

'Right. I will.'

Picture us, Babs at the back end of the hall and me at the front door, and if we were not having a row, that was as close as we had ever come. I had my hand on the catch of the door when she said: 'And there's something else.'

'Jesus, now what?'

'Don't take the sacred name.'

'So what else is there?'

She said: 'It's Sunny Day.'

I was honest to God so brimming over with rage that I opened the door and looked out into the pitch dark. 'It's night-time. What are you talking about?'

She said: 'Don't act the eejit. I mean the Sunny Day who's doing Carla Donner in the play, only someone is going to have to put her up just for a few nights every week –'

'Who is?'

'Shhh.'

'Do you mean *us*?'

'Tell the neighbours, why don't you?'

This was the woman who would not invite a person in for a piece of cold ham and a leaf of lettuce unless she and them had been in the same womb. She looked back over one shoulder and then the other, as if Sunny Day had already snuck in and was on our stairs, heading for bed in a flannelette shift. She crooked a finger at me, and said, 'Come here.' Out of curiosity, I went a step or two.

'What?'

She whispered, 'She leapt over the wall.'

The world changes, and I dunno if the expression is still in use, but when a girl changed her mind about being a nun, they used to say that she had leapt over the convent wall. There is another old saying: 'If you want to know me, come and live with me,' and it took Sunny, when she was lodging with us, to tell us her own story. I let on to Babs, just by way of putting her under a compliment, that I was vexed at having a stranger in the house, but the idea of having a different face to look at and a different voice to listen to appealed to me. And I have to say that when she came to us for three days in the week Sunny was no trouble at all, except that first thing in the morning you would hear her in our spare room driving the birds demented with 'One Day When We Were Young'. Once, she sang something else and when I asked her what it was she trotted out with 'It's "Klange der Heimat" from *Die Fledermaus.*' 'So it is,' I said, snapping my fingers.

The Mundow woman's way of doing *The Great Waltz* was to rehearse the chorus, Babs included, in the ballroom of the Robin Hood every Monday and Friday. She took the principals at home in her own house on the three days in between, and on those evenings at seven Sinjin would call to Carvel to collect Sunny and leave her on our doorstep again by half ten.

At first, I had no notion why she came to stay with us instead of at a B and B or at the Robin Hood itself, but we found out on the first day at breakfast. Decent girl, she had not turned up empty-handed, but with a quarter-pound of Lyons' tea – four weeks' ration for two people – and half a dozen eggs. Babs went raving mad and fried the whole six of them, with sausages from Adolf, the pork butcher in Fenian Street. And so there we were in the breakfast room, Babs in her housecoat, me with a collar and tie on so as not to offend decency, and Sunny, all frilly and flimsy.

The beginning of her story was that her old fellow was a big-wig of some kind beyond in London. 'Is he in politics, maybe?' I asked her. Instead of an answer, she looked down, shy-like, at her plate. At least, there was that much of a nun in her, I thought.

'Don't be so inquisitive,' Babs said.

One thing was certain: whatever her da was or did, he was important enough to get his name all over the front page of a certain Sunday rag because he had sent Sunny and her old one out of England to where they were safe from the air raids. He was not a true-blue Brit, the paper said. And the ma – I hope yous are ready for this – used to act in films back in the silent days, and that gave the same muck-merchants even more to chew on.

'What name did she go under?' I asked, all innocent and don't-you-know. 'There might be a photo of her in one of my film books.'

Sunny just smiled and shook her head.

There is nothing for the devil to lick his chops about if a married man has to put a napkin across his lap at the sight of a mott at breakfast time with half her bazoom showing – it's a sight you would see at the pictures, with your woman, Jean Kent, acting the tart. I mean, what's a few months in purgatory? But unnatural desires are something else again, and I never saw a sight so deserving of hell without the option as a strand of Sunny's fair hair all but dipping into one of her fried eggs.

I remembered her mammy from the morning she came with Sunny to see *The Great Waltz* in the Picture House. In 1942, it was like another age since the end of the silents; and yet there were only fourteen years in between, and a fine figure of a woman she still was. Sunny told us how the pair of them had come over from England by the Holyhead mail boat and went to live with an old aunt in County Westmeath in one of those big houses that would give you pleurisy just to look at it. How the convent happened was that after a while the ma went home to spend a few weeks with the da in London, and Sunny was left on her ownsome, with the nearest village four miles away and so small that they had to take it in turn to be the local loony. She all but went potty from the loneliness. Well, one misfortune hides behind another, and to cap it all the old aunt got sick and died on her. So the doctor arranged for the local nuns – I think they were called the Little Yellow Sisters of the Sick – to take her in and feed her with beef tea and stirabout until the ma came back from Limeyland. That was all there was to it. 'I was never a nun,' Sunny said. 'I wasn't even what they call a postulant. Is that a word? I mean, if we're anything we're C of E. And the newspapers were horrible. There were pictures of Mummy and me, and there were lies about how I had – oh, it was a disgusting expression! – jumped over the wall.'

I was delighted to see that Babs had gone red.

'And then,' Sunny said, 'the journalist started to follow Mummy and me. They were wherever we went, all the time waiting for us. So I could hardly stay at an hotel; I mean, could I? They even tried to get information out of Madame Mundow, but of course she wouldn't tell, not even if they tortured her.'

An agreeable picture came into my mind of two *News of the World* reporters with tweezers working on the Madame's moustache.

'And *you* won't breathe a word, will you?' Sunny said.

She gave me an imploring look that made me – a person who could not pull the skin off a rice pudding – yearn for reporters to come to the door so that I could throw them down the front steps.

'Not a bit of us,' Babs said.

'Where's your mammy?' I asked. 'I mean, where do you live when you aren't here with us?'

Sunny knew how to keep a secret. It was as much as she could do to say the one word, 'Ballsbridge'. So that was that. When I tried a different tack and asked her why she was set on appearing on a stage in Drane – a town which God wouldn't look at twice – she told me that her ma had always set her heart on seeing her go into films. 'That's why I'm doing this,' she told us. 'Mummy says I need the experience. Always make your mistakes, Mummy says, out of sight of the public.'

'You picked the right place,' I said.

'Mummy says I could be another Jessie Matthews,' Sunny told us, being very hot on what the mummy said. 'Do you know Jessie Matthews?'

Before I could answer she was out of her chair and through the door, singing as she went:

> *He dances overhead,*
> *On the ceiling near my bed*
> *In my sight,*
> *All through the night.*

I all but heard my heart thud with love or near enough, and as Babs and me were gawking after her she was floating up the stairs with:

> *I try to hide in vain*
> *Underneath my counterpane,*
> *But there's my love*
> *Up above.*

We heard the door of her room clicking shut. I thought that whatever else about her, she knew how to make an exit.

A few days later, a courier came from the British Embassy, no less, with a package for Sunny. She was all excitement when she unwrapped it, and small wonder, for it was a 16-mm print of *The Great Waltz*.

'You must have a great leg of someone high up,' I said, fishing again.

She made no answer, but put a finger to her lips. 'We won't tell the Madame about this,' she said. 'This is mine.'

'From your da?'

She gave a careful little nod. 'But how am I going to get the machine for it?'

That was easy, for there was a 16-mm projector in the Picture House, and Dermo Grace gave us a lend of it on the q.t. That evening, when Sunny got home from her rehearsal, I rigged up a screen that was one of Babs's sheets from the airing cupboard. I threaded the film, the three of us sat like kids on the sofa in the front room, and off we went.

It didn't matter that we had seen it only a fortnight since.

Sunny sang all the songs along with Miliza Korjus, and in between she cried buckets, even though it was a cod of a yarn. In it, your man, Strauss, is married to this nice girl named Poldi, who is as dawny as if she had come down in the last shower. Then he goes and falls for the opera singer, Carla Donner, who is a bit of a rip, and they decide to do a bunk and sail off together on the river Danube to Budapest or such. Well, Poldi twigs what they are up to, and there is this woman-to-woman scene with Carla Donner being all superior and calling her 'my dear', but instead of giving out stink to them, Poldi gets noble and gives them her blessing – 'I know the blessing I'd have given them!' Babs said. So the pair of them – the bold Johann and Carla Donner – start off for the steamer, only now it is the opera singer's turn to get noble. She sends him back to Poldi and sails off on the ship on her ownsome, singing 'One Day When We Were Young' at him from the top deck.

'It's not fair,' Sunny said, drying her eyes.

'What isn't?' I said.

'Her sending him back to that boring wife of his.'

I don't rightly know what hackles are when they're at home, but I could see that Babs's were doing the Indian rope trick. She said: 'Well, Sunny, if you'll excuse me for saying so, I don't see that being a wife means that a woman has to be boring.'

Sunny started to go pink. 'Babs, I didn't mean that –'

Not to let them break up the happy home, I said: 'Look, never mind about who is boring and who isn't. They couldn't go off together because it's against the rules.'

'The rules?' Sunny repeated, drinking this in.

It was what I had explained to Judge Garrity after seeing *Dodsworth*. 'There's what they call the Production Code,' I said, 'and every film has to toe the line. There's things that are back of the neck – I mean, that aren't allowed – and the worst one of these is for a man to leave his wife and run off with another woman and live happy ever after.'

'I saw a French film once –' Sunny said.

'The French are like rabbits,' I told her.

That night in bed, Babs prodded me. 'Listen.'

'What?'

'Music, are you deaf? She's downstairs playing it again.'

'Playing what?'

'Wake up. She's playing the fillum.'

Where the Standing Ovations were concerned, Sinjin was the Madame's dogsbody. Not only did he write the scripts, he worked the lights, painted the flats, dressed the sets and patched the tears in the backdrops, and in the weeks before the show went on he put up the placards in the shops and pubs and went from house to house selling tickets, a different street or laneway every evening. One of her nibs's ideas was that he should take Sunny with him, all got up as Carla Donner in a dress with a neck on it that was not so much glad as delirious. One thing about her, she was not shy. She would appear at a front door, smile and say: 'Won't you please come and see me in *The Great Waltz*?' Well, need I say, the tickets went like hot barm brack.

'That one,' Babs said, 'would go out in her skin.' Which was a thought to put into a man's head.

One evening, Sunny had great news for us. There was a rumour – untrue, as it turned out – that the Madame had taken the Gaiety Theatre in Dublin for a Sunday evening after the play's three-night run at Drane town hall. Our lodger was thrilled to bits. She said, and her eyes might have been candles: 'I'll be a star.'

I said: 'Sure you will. And between Drane and the Gaiety you'll have every scandal rag in England trailing after you. Just what you wanted, isn't it?'

'Oh, Perry, don't be cross with me,' she said. 'This will be the *right* sort of publicity.'

So there I left it, but on the following Monday evening there was news of a different kind. With the first night only a week away, Babs went out to her rehearsal at half seven as usual, but was home at nine.

'You're early,' I said.

'The rehearsal was cancelled.'

'In that case, you're late.'

'A few of us went into the lounge to have coffee and talk about it.'

'You have a Good Friday of a face on you. Talk about what?'

I knew it was more than just gossip, because she was too excited to hem and haw and wait for it to be teased out of her. She said: 'Madame Mundow broke down in front of us. She went into floods of tears.'

'Get off.'

'I was there, honest. She was teaching Miriam McCrum how to turn on her left foot. She was saying, "No, dear, on your *other* left foot," and then without a word of warning she started sobbing and shaking. Dermo Grace had to be sent for, and he took her home in his motor car.'

'God almighty. And I suppose Sinjin was there with the smelling salts?'

'Are you mad?' Babs said conversationally. 'Wasn't Sinjin the cause of it? Listen, come up to date. The Madame turfed him out.'

'Do you mean out of the rehearsal?'

'I mean she shagged him out of the house. Their house at home.'

It was like being hit twice in the pit of the stomach, once by what she said and again by hearing her saying 'shag'.

I said, 'You've lost me.'

She said, putting every word in a little coffin of its own: 'On. Account. Of. His. Carrying. On.'

'Do you mean he's taken to drink, is that it?' I was spoofing as I said it. In Drane, there was nothing pass-remarkable about a man going on the gargle; it happened sooner or later. What always caused the tongues to wag like the winner at a dog show was when he took the pledge.

Babs shook her head. Only guessing the half of what was coming next, I said: 'Not carrying on with a woman? Not *him*? Now come on, not him? With the baldy corduroys and the alopecia?'

She nodded, and I laughed out loud at the idea of Sinjin Mundow, doing the dirty on his rip of a wife. 'Fetch and Carry', they called him in the town. There were even rumours that whenever he dared to look crossways at her she beat the tar out of him.

I said, already believing it: 'I don't believe it.'

She said: 'And what's more –'

'No, what I mean is, what kind of a woman would fall for the likes of that yokc? Did she escape from the Home for the Bewildered?' I was enjoying myself. 'Or maybe she has a spare head, is that it?'

'No, she only has the one head on her,' Babs said. 'And it belongs to Sunny Day.'

She waited. Her eyes went through me. I don't know what I looked like, but inside what I felt was jealousy first of all and, on top of it, rage. I think I said: 'Well, the little rip.'

Babs said: 'And you, you poor gawm, thought the sun shone out of her.'

I managed a shrug. 'I might have thought she wasn't the worst of them,' I said, giving her a ha'penny worth of truth. Then: 'Look, it's a joke, isn't it? You're taking the Micheál.'

She sighed, being patient with a thick. 'The Madame sat on the floor because the good leg had gone from under her, and she told us the whole thing. You'd a thought her heart would break. All about Sinjin and Sunny Day. And the name of the little rip's family isn't Day at all. It's Knight.' Babs gave a laugh that I never knew she had in her. 'Sunny Knight!'

I said: 'Well, she can find new lodgings for herself from this out.'

'What?'

'She's not staying here. Not in this house.'

'Oh, yes she is,' Babs said. 'We're not going to take the blame for making what's bad worse and maybe having the play cancelled.' (I thought: *If she says that the show must go on I'll open a vein.*) 'What anyone has been up to is none of our business, and it'll only be for another week. So you'll say nothing to her, not a word, and nor will I.'

There was no defying her. All I could say, under my breath, as if it was a curse, was: 'Sinjin Mundow.'

'Oh, stop your ullagoning.'

'I mean, but why him? What the hell is the attraction?'

'Don't ask me,' she said. 'I don't know. Does any woman ever know?'

I went to bed that evening wondering if she was being personal.

Next morning, Sunny arrived, as she did every Tuesday, in a car with a CD plate, and with her she had what had become her weekly present to us, half a dozen fresh eggs. She looked so innocent, same as ever, that angels could have taken lessons from her. If there is such a thing as a sign of adultery on a woman's face, I could not see it. She chattered away while Babs boiled the eggs for our breakfast, and when mine were put in front of me I sliced the top off one of them as if it was Sinjin Mundow's head.

Babs tried to make conversation; then she said: 'What's the war news?' which was less than tactful. After a minute, Sunny got up from the table. 'Babs, could I have a word?' To me she said: 'Excuse us.' She went out and up the stairs.

I said: 'I think I'll go for a walk when I'm done here.'

Babs followed her, turning at the door to watch me cutting a slice of bread into soldiers. She said: 'She hasn't put you off your eggs anyway.'

'What?'

'You haven't a word to throw to a dog!'

I went out thinking that if the Hill of Howth at the far side of Dublin Bay had disappeared into the sea, then somehow the blame would have found its way to me.

It was too cold for walking, so I spent an hour in the Carnegie Library where I looked through a book of paintings by your man, Renoir. One of them was of a naked woman, nice and pink and plump, and some art lover had changed her nipples into eyes that were looking crossways at one another. When I got back to Carvel, who else but Sinjin Mundow was on our doorstep talking to Babs, and she was telling him that if he waited a few minutes Sunny would be out to him. The downstairs blinds were drawn – a sure sign that *The Great Waltz* was on in the living room, and I could hear her telling every tree in the park and every leaf on the tree that she was in love with Vienna. Whatever else had been said between Babs and her while I was out, Carla Donner was still going strong.

Sinjin nodded to me as he came down the steps. 'I thought I might take Sunny for a walk,' he said.

'Ah-hah.'

'I have any amount of free time now,' he said. 'Did you know I've been suspended from the bank?'

'Ah-hah?'

'Monica did what you might call the dirty on me with Head Office, so I've been given the shove. They're death on any kind of scandal, you know.'

'Ah-hah.' I was giving him a memorable conversation.

'Silly woman. She was only cutting her own throat. I mean: after all, I'm the breadwinner.'

I said 'Mm?' just to be versatile.

'Anyway, they can keep their job. First thing on the Sunday morning, Sunny and I will be off to London. It's all arranged, and because of the war and the call-up there's no shortage of vacancies for bank staff, so we'll do very nicely, thank you. Sunny is such a dear girl, you know.'

I gave him a witty smile.

'Meanwhile, we'll carry on with the play as if nothing's amiss. Business as usual, eh? After all, the show must –'

I was already up the front steps like a whippet.

Babs was waiting in the hall. 'Sunny was crying,' she said. 'She thinks you're black out with her on account of Sinjin, but I told her that it was all in her imagination. So don't you go making me out a liar, do you hear?'

'Yes.'

'I mean it. I asked her what she was going to do, and she says that the show – Don't walk away when a body is talking to you.'

The show did go on and, as usual, Sinjin's name was in the programme as *Asst. to the Producer.* And fair dues, he was a Trojan; he had opened up the town hall and got a team of helpers to make it fit for an audience to sit in. He hired arc lamps and spots, a couple of floods and banks of lights and down the side-aisles there were paraffin heaters. He did the stage manager's job and, as if that was not enough, served coffee and orange drinks in the intervals. And by now, the Madame had swapped her crutches for a stick and was hopping around eating compliments as if they were milk chocolate whirls. Of course the whole town knew about the break-up with Sinjin, and she was so saintly that it was plain she hated him.

As for the play itself, there are two kinds of lies told in the theatre. One is when you see what is such a dog's breakfast that you would give your soul for the floor to open under you; and still and all you are ready to swear black is white that what you are looking at is the berries. Well, no matter; that is only common politeness, like when a comrade of yours writes a book and you review it for the *Ballybollicky Tribune* and say, 'Tolstoy, go home.'

The other lie is the reverse of this; you see what you know in your heart is good, but you shoot it down and blackguard it, and that is something else. It is the sin against the Holy Ghost or, to use the Irish name for it, begrudgery. So I have to bite the bullet and say that the Madame did a smashing job with *The Great*

Waltz. It was a credit to her. The orchestra was only a piano, a violin and a viola, but she filled the stage with colour and dazzle. The costumes had the audience oohing and aahing – and Babs, by the way, was there in the chorus, twirling around like she was a dancer in a proper theatre in town – one of the Royalettes, maybe, or a Queen's Moonbeam.

Oddly enough, the only real let-down was Sunny. She wasn't bad, mind. Away from a theatre, she could walk into a room, and every other woman in it would want to go home early. But when she was on a stage, it was as if there was plate glass between you and her. I remembered the Madame saying, and I thought at the time it was only cattiness, that Sunny lacked a Star Ingredient. It was true.

At the end of the play, the audience roared and the Standing Ovations lived up to their name, for all of the front two rows were on their feet applauding. Mind, even in those days, that was a trick that had hair on it; for when the front seats stood up those behind them were obliged to do the same or else sit and look at a panorama of arses. Sunny, taking her bow, blew kisses at the audience. Her ma was there, of course, in a fur coat, and I met her at the reception afterwards. Stretching the truth an inch or so, I told her that I had been a great fan of hers in the silent days, and she said wasn't I kind, which was my ration for the evening.

Sunny came up to her, dragging Sinjin after her and saying, 'Mummy, here he is. The man I love.'

The ma was a tall woman, which enabled her to look down on him in every sense. She gave him a 'How d'you do?', not expecting an answer. I assumed that she had already gone into the women's dressing room after the show and said 'Darling, you were marvellous' and such, but now Sunny said: 'Mummy, I don't think they liked me.'

'They adored you.'

'They didn't.'

Sinjin said: 'Don't be silly, love, they did.'

Sunny's ma gave him a north-easterly of a smile and said: 'Darling, whether they liked you or not, the day will come and not so very far into the future, when you will say to yourself, "Who cares about little people? The main thing is: the camera loves me."' At which she pointed herself at the door. It had a sign that said *Exit,* where a man in a peaked cap was waiting. 'Oh, dear, I think I see my driver.'

She gave me a small nod; Sinjin got bugger-all. Sunny said to him: 'I'll see Mummy to the car. And don't worry, darlin'. Soon she'll love you as much as I do.'

'Work that one out,' I said, making his night for him.

The play was declared a great success, the best ever, and on the Saturday evening me and Babs walked our lodger to the town hall for the last performance. The arrangement was that Sunny and Sinjin would meet the morning after on board the nine-o'-clock mail boat. It was three and a half hours to Holyhead, from where they would take the Irish Mail to London. 'So when do we lose you?' I asked.

'Tomorrow morning at seven,' Sunny said. 'If you're up.'

'We will be, never fear,' Babs said.

'Oh, but I'll miss you both,' Sunny said.

She stopped there on the public road and hugged us. I felt the wet of her tears on my cheek, and that all but started me off as well. Foolish as she was, she had a good heart, or so I thought. I felt fatherly towards her, and it was high time.

After the play there was a cast-only party in the bar of the Robin Hood. Sunny excused herself, saying that she had an early start in the morning. I saw her bidding a butter-wouldn't-melt goodnight to Sinjin, who was hard put to it to keep his hands off her, and I noticed that the Madame was the only person in the room not turning to look at them. Barring myself and Babs, it was the last anyone there would see of Sunny, or of Sinjin either.

It was going on for twelve when we got home, and there was a light showing under Sunny's door. We went to bed and as I was nodding off I got a jab. 'There's a car,' Babs said, and sure enough I heard the soft sound of a motor. During the Emergency a motor car was a rarity in the daytime and trouble after dark when it meant a policeman, a priest or a doctor, so I went to the window and took a squint. It was the same black car that brought Sunny to us every Tuesday morning and collected her first thing on Fridays, only now the driver was carrying her suitcase down the front steps, with her following.

'What's happening?' Babs whispered from the bed.

'She's doing a bunk,' I said.

'Go to God.'

'Come and look.'

'The little bitch,' Babs said.

I heard the soft, rich click of the car door, and she was gone.

There was no sleep for either of us after that. We looked into Sunny's room for maybe a goodbye message, but there was shag-all word from her. I got the Primus working, and Babs made tea for the pair of us, and we had a couple of Mariettas. We talked about Sunny and Sinjin as if they were runners at Leopardstown and we were studying form about possibilities, and the hot favourite was that they had gone off together on the quiet, maybe to catch the Fishguard boat from Rosslare. There was always the possibility that the Madame, gammy leg and all, might have had some sort of a lemoner in store for them in Dun Laoghaire at the mail-boat pier.

'So, that's it,' I said. 'They were too cute for her.'

'You're right,' Babs said. 'Still, she might have said a proper goodbye.'

Then the doorbell went, and it was Sinjin.

He was in a bad way. 'Is she here?'

'Pardon?'

'Sunny. Where is she?'

Babs caught him by the lapel of his coat and dragged him into the hall. 'Come in here and be quiet. And don't go calling us liars, because we aren't. She went half an hour ago without a word to either of us, and I don't know where to.'

'Belfast,' Sinjin said.

'Where?'

'She's going to catch the boat at Larne. It says so here.'

He was waving a sheet of notepaper at us. I switched on the hall light and held the note up to it.

Dearest Sinjy. By the time you read this, I will be on my way to the boat that goes from Belfast. For more than a week now I have thought of you and me and have not had one wink of sleep –

'For God's sake,' I said, by way of throwing him a crumb of comfort, 'she snores. We heard her.'

'Read the letter,' Babs said.

. . . not one wink of sleep with worry. As much as I love you, I cannot break up a happy marriage . . .

'Happy?' Sinjin said. 'O Jesus.'

. . . So it is up to both of us to do the nobble thing. [I thought that it was not a bad word, no matter which way you spelt it.] *We cannot go against the rules, so it is best that we part. I will always love you. Sunny.*

We gave Sinjin a cup of tea and sat with him. Then Babs went to bed, and I took out a well-hidden bottle of John Jameson. 'For snakebite,' I said, doing my Gabby Hayes imitation.

'Yer durn tootin'!' he answered.

There was that much life in him. I was impressed. 'So what will you do now?' I asked him.

'I still have two mail-boat tickets in my pocket,' he said. 'I can get a refund on one and use the other.' Before I could tell him not to be in such a rush, he said: 'I'm done with the bank, and the bank is done with me. I'm not going to stay here and be a laughing stock.'

'What about the Madame?' I asked.

'Who?'

'She might take you back.'

He shook his head. 'Every cloud has a silver lining,' he said.

He went by the morning boat, and we got a Christmas card from him a week later and again the Christmas after. Years and years went by, and I heard that he was what they call a floor manager for the BBC, and sure enough I saw his name on the screen. The Madame left Drane a few weeks later and opened a school of acting in town. She did well, so I am told.

I never heard of Sunny ever again. Not a whisper.

Chapter Seven

The Good German (1)

'Do you want to join the fillum society?' Dermo asked.

'I didn't know there was one,' I said.

He gave a little crow. 'So who says we can't keep a secret?'

'Why does it have to be a secret?'

He had offered to drive me into town. He said he had business to do, whereas I was longing for a dawdle down Grafton Street or across the cobblestones of Trinity; or there might be an old butty of mine in Neary's or Tommy Lennon's around from the Abbey. And there were still pubs in those days where you could signal to the curate to lift the latch of the snuggery, and a butty of yours would look up from his paper and say 'I couldn't agree less'; and it took a minute for you to cop on that he was replying to an assertion you had made to him six months ago. It is always nice to be missed.

'Did you ever hear tell,' Dermo asked as he drove, 'of a French fillum called . . .? Ah, now give me half a minute . . .'

'Peculiar name for a picture.'

'Dry up.' He made a horse's collar of pronouncing the name, not that I would have done much better. The film was called *Le Jour se Léve*.

I said: 'Matter of fact, I did hear tell of it.'

He laughed. 'Begod, there's no end to you.'

It was in one of my film books. By all accounts, it was not exactly a cure for the glooms, but there was an actress in it with a one-word name, which was Arletty. I loved her. There was a photo of her coming out of a bath with most of the top half of her exposed; and although she did not have what is often referred to as a fine pair, I remember thinking that even if she had been dressed from neck to foot in a bell tent, the film censor would have banned her. It was the look on her face – no, I mean in the eyes, which were dark with mortal sins in them, and they came between me and my sleep for more nights than a full moon ever did.

'Yes, I heard tell of it,' I told Dermo, 'but I never saw it.' In those days, and even in a city the size of Dublin, there was not much call for foreign films.

'I put it on at the Picture House,' Dermot said.

'You liar, you,' I said, in admiration.

'For one night only. A bloody good fillum, even though in the end the chap shoots himself.' (Like I already said, a thing that Dermo and me had in common was that when we were growing up 'the bully' and 'the chap' were our names for the bad fellow and the good, just as going to the pictures was called the fourpenny rush.)

I asked him: 'How did you get hold of it?'

'Pardon me?'

'I mean with the war on.'

'That'd be telling,' he said.

'You'd make a secret,' I told him, 'out of threading a needle.'

'And it was a washout,' he said. 'If I had stood up and shouted that there were bananas on sale down at the harbour, new in from Yassa-yassa-land, the Picture House could not have emptied quicker.'

'It didn't do well?'

'In a way it was a mercy that it was in French,' Dermo said, 'because if it had been in English and you could have understood every word of it, you still couldn't have heard it. The corner-boys were shouting "Take it off" and throwing half-sucked sweets. I lost patrons that night, and they would never have come back if it wasn't that in our town the pictures is all there is.'

He took his hands off the wheel, the right counting on the

94

fingers of the left. 'There's no wireless, no whist drives, no dances, neither old-time nor modern, no plays except for the am-drams twice a year – and they're kaput since Madame Mundow packed it in.' He switched hands. 'No lectures about pre-Christian remains – and if you ask me we're still pre-Christian – no summer regattas ever since the Catholic Sea Scouts' boat was scuttled – I was showing Gary Cooper in *Souls at Sea* at the time, and –'

'Jesus, will you get on with it?' I said, as he came within an aim's ace of hitting a Terenure tram.

'. . . and all they have in the entire year is the Corpus Christi procession the Sunday after Whit, with the priest in his gold threads walking under the canopy that was like one of the prairie schooners in *Covered Wagon Days*. Well, they say it's an ill wind, because at least that's when the fillum society was born.'

'I'll join,' I said. 'How much?'

'A guinea for six shows. But not a word.'

'Are you putting on blue films, is that it?'

'May God forgive you.' He was genuinely shocked.

'So what's the big mystery? Film societies are legal, I know they are.'

'Maybe.'

'What does that mean?'

'Talk to you later.'

He dropped me outside the Shelbourne, and we arranged to meet there at five. I walked around the Green and looked at the ducks, then strolled down Grafton Street and used the last of my clothing coupons to buy a bed-jacket for Babs for her birthday. The day was bitter, so I went into Neary's for a hot whiskey, and Paddy Kavanagh the poet was there, walking up and down with his arms folded and clearing his throat with a noise that might have been a hacksaw on tin. He was the man who wrote 'Threshing Morning' and 'On Raglan Road', and you marvelled that there was room inside his skin for both the mean nature of a bogman and a spirit that God himself collogued with.

I had once saluted him and been nodded to in return. Saying an uncalled-for good morning is like sending a Christmas card – you are obligated to repeat it for life – and today I half-smiled and said to him, 'Ha'sh old weather.' He gave one of his *Hrrrumps* and looked through me. I foolishly stood and said, 'Peregrine Perry,' and what I got for an answer was: 'Oh, excuse me, I thought you were John Millington Synge.'

A pint-drinking waxwork at the end of the bar let out a snigger. Another specimen said, 'Sound man, Paddy.' I got the hot whiskey down me in one scalding gulp and went out hating Kavanagh and wishing he was back to hell in Mucker where he came from. There was sleet falling, and still my ears burned at having let myself be hunted out of Neary's. I could have gone into the Bailey, but my gumption failed me; I was afraid, would you believe, that maybe a barman would be short with me. So I hoofed it to O'Connell Street, butting my head against the sleet, and went to the Capitol to see Joel McCrea in *Sullivan's Travels*. It was a good enough film, but at first all I could think of was Neary's and Paddy Kavanagh and the few begrudgers coming between me and my day in town.

By and by, I let the film take hold of me; it was about a film director, who discovers that pictures have the power to make people laugh and forget whatever ails them. Which, of course, is only the half of it. Picture houses give people a spare life to live in case the one they have turns out to be a dud, which is often the case with some. Present company excepted, I need hardly say.

After the Joel McCrea it was sleeting, and the wetting I took trudging from O'Connell Street to the Shelbourne made me bad-tempered again. The Jensen was among three or four cars parked outside the hotel, and a couple of gawkers were peering into it and foostering with the pull-down roof. One of them reached in and prodded the leather, and the doorman said: 'Now, now, wait till yous win the Sweep.' He knew me of an old date and touched his cap. 'Afternoon, Mr Perry.'

There were two men sitting in the lobby. They could not have been other than plainclothes men; for one thing, they were too big for their chairs; for another, only their breed could turn a suit of clothes into a uniform just by wearing it. The look they gave me as I went past would have caused milk to turn while it was still in the cow. The two old maids in *Mr Deeds Goes to Town* said that in Mandrake Falls everyone except them was pixilated; well, plainclothes policemen the world over thought that everyone except themselves was a blaggard and the filth of the earth. 'We'll get you yet,' their look said. Probably their mothers got the same look from them when they slid out of the womb.

Dermo was in the Horseshoe Bar in the company of a man he introduced to me as Hansy Mueller. Hansy wore gold-rimmed glasses and a bow tie he had tied himself, and had thin straw-coloured hair. He liked to be liked; he jumped up and made a pump handle of my hand as if he had been waiting all day for the intro. It occurred to me that if he was lit, sinister-like, from under his chin, he would look as if he was pulling the nose hairs out of poor old Albert Basserman in a war film.

'He doesn't speak much English,' Dermo said.

'Excuse me, I speak blooming good English,' Hansy said.

'He never misses an evening at the Picture House.'

Hansy smiled. 'Is true.'

Right enough, I had noticed him there many a time. Now that I could hear him as well as see him, he had an accent that would make Conrad Veidt sound like a Kerryman. And here I ought to say that the 'z' key on my typewriter is stuck and has to be pulled loose with pincers, so I will not try writing 'ziss' and 'zee' for 'this' and 'the'. Which ought to be good news all round.

Dermo ordered a large Scotch, which was set in front of me. Out of turn, Hansy slapped down the money for it, picked up the glass and clamped my hand around it. I asked him: 'You live in Drane, do you?'

'Oh, yass. Is nice place.'

As I was putting that opinion through a sanity test, Dermo said: 'Hansy works here in town.' He gave me a look. 'At the Kraut embassy.'

At the word 'Kraut', Hansy laughed so heartily that all on his own he could have filled up half of a German joke book. He gave Dermo a push in the chest and called him an *Aufruhr*. He looked at me for confirmation. 'Yass?'

'I told him once that he was a riot,' Dermo said. '*Aufruhr* is his word for it.'

'Oh?'

'And also he says that I am a Kraut,' Hansy said. 'And a Jerry and a Boche, and what else? Oh, yass, a goose-stepper. And what is not nice, a Nazi. I am never a Nazi.'

He had raised his voice, and the two plainclothes men looked around.

'Easy,' Dermo said.

Hansy looked at the pair and waggled his fingers. '*Guten Tag*, Dick. *Guten Tag*, Doof.' The men looked away again.

'Dick and Doof is the German for Stan and Ollie,' Dermo explained.

'Yass, Dick *und* Doof,' Hansy said, and I realised that he was a bit squiffy. He caught sight of my face. 'Dermo, I think your friend does not like me.'

Which offended me, seeing as how it was the truth, which is not what a man comes into a pub or a bar to hear. 'Well, I don't know you,' I said.

'Maybe it is that you don't like Germans,' Hansy said. 'Maybe you have a preference for the English.'

I said: 'I don't give a tinker's damn about either of you.'

'Now, now,' Dermo said.

'Good!' Hansy roared. 'Neither do I, so we can be friends.'

Dermo pretended to look at his watch. 'I think we ought to be making a move for home. Hansy, are you right?'

'I am hunky-dokum,' Hansy said. I would have laughed, only I was too tight of arse to recognise him for a decent man. 'But I will not leave here until you and your friend agree that we will have a drink at Heimat.'

'Excuse me?' I said.

'It's where he lives,' Dermo explained. 'It's the name of the house.' As if afraid that I might refuse, he said: 'Say you will.'

'I don't mind,' I said. 'I have a crow to pluck with this gentleman.'

'He wants me to fuck a crow?' Hansy asked.

'*Pluck* a crow,' I told him and got no further because he said: 'Has this to do with the rationing of food?' and laughed himself into a fit that sent the second half of the German joke book for its tea.

At first, the Jensen drove out from town towards Drane. We seemed to have the road to ourselves, then at Temple Hill we heard the first few notes of 'Deutschland über Alles' on a klaxon. 'Jesus,' I said.

'It's a joke, it's a joke,' Dermo said.

Hansy passed us, waving from the window of an armoured car that called itself a Merc. Not to lose him, Dick and Doof in a black Vauxhall stayed on his tail, shoe-horning in front of us and obliging Dermo to brake.

'They're Special Branch men,' Dermo said. 'Hansy is not allowed out without them. Wherever he goes, they go.'

'Are they spying on him?'

'We're a small country,' Dermo said. 'So they're a little bit of everything.'

Heimat was a low-built Georgian lodge at the top of a steep hill that marked the westward edge of Drane. Until today, all I had ever seen of it was the front gate where a uniformed Garda stood whatever the weather, and because of the winding driveway the house itself was invisible from the road. The policeman saluted and pushed the gate open, and as we went in we saw him take a field telephone off its cradle. On the climb up to the house, Dick and Doof had vanished into nowhere. I looked at Dermo who said, 'Trick photography.'

As he swung off the driveway and rearranged the landscaping, I asked him if there happened to be a Mrs Mueller.

'A Frau Mueller, you mean,' Dermo said. 'Oh, she exists, so I hear tell. Only she was hardly here with him when she decided that Drane was a kip.'

'Sound woman.'

'So she fecked off to wherever home is. That was early in '39. Himself – Hansy – he's different; he loves it here, can't get enough of it.' He yanked at the hand-brake with a sound like Patrick Kavanagh clearing his tubes. 'And if you're so brassed off with us, what are *you* doing here?'

I nudged him as Hansy appeared at our nearside window. As he did so, there was a stream of light and the front door of Heimat was opened from the inside. A dark late-thirty-ish man with a blue chin and wearing a white jacket said, 'Good afternoon,' in an Irish accent that was as perfect and standard-English as my own.

Hansy said: 'Sean, you know Mr Grace.'

'Always welcome, I'm sure, sir,' Sean said to Dermo.

'And this is Mr . . .?'

'Perry,' I said. 'What I mean is, Perry Perry.'

Sean did not blink. He took our coats, and when he felt the shoulder of mine, he said: 'This won't do at all, sir; it's soaked. I'll hang it next to the Aga.'

'I'm only staying a minute.'

'With respect, sir, that's what they all say.'

As he started away from us with the overcoat, Hansy called after him: 'And Sean . . .'

'I'm ahead of you, sir,' Sean lobbed back at him and went out.

'Am I not the luckiest man in the world?' Hansy said. 'Dermo, remind me. Please, what is this so comical name you call my Sean?'

A voice came back from the stairs that led down to the

kitchen. 'He calls me Jeeves, sir. Well-intentioned and no offence taken.'

Dermo said to Hansy: 'Still, I'm sure you miss your good lady.' He added, smarmy bugger that he was, 'And of course vice versa.'

Hansy gave what threatened to be one of his laughs. 'Marthe does not miss me,' he said. 'She has the Führer.'

There was a log fire blazing in the living room. What I was already aware of was that for the first time since the clocks had gone back five months since, I was getting a bit of warmth into myself, and I could have bathed in it till I was a prune. At home, if I as much as shivered, Babs gave out to me, saying that I was a cold creature. But unless you had winter clothes on you from an old date – from before the Emergency, that is – whatever you put on was like wearing a net.

Hansy poured whiskey for the three of us. 'In a minute,' he said, 'Sean will bring us some *Frankfurter Würstchen*. Very nice, to be sure.'

'He's a wonder,' Dermo said. 'Where the hell did you get hold of him?'

'Not in hell, my dear Dermo,' Hansy said, 'but in *Himmel*!'

I was ready for another of his laughs, but instead he turned to me and gave his side-table a bang of his fist. 'And now, my new friend, before you take food in my house you must tell me about this crow of yours.' Before I could do more than stare at him, he said: 'And be vorned that here I do not allow talk of politics or the war. Not because I am a good diplomat, you understand, but because I am a very bad diplomat. Now why is it that you give me this look in the Shelbourne?' He made a Lugosi of a face at me.

Live and let live, I always say, but the Germans have no shagging manners. I tried to make his foreignness an excuse for him asking me the kind of straight question that goes hunting after straight answers. All the same, I did not put a tooth in it, but came out with it: 'It's what you're doing to the wireless.'

He said: 'The *vire*less?'

Dermo said: 'Perry . . . ah, Perry.'

'I hear tell,' I said, 'that you have some device or gadget or yoke that scrambles the reception so that all anybody for miles around can hear is sweet shag-all. So if you will excuse me, you have a bit of a nerve saying that you don't allow any talk here about the war.'

Hansy looked at Dermo. 'Sker-ambled? Voss is this sker-ambled? Is he mad?'

Dermo was highly embarrassed. 'Where did you get that cod of a yarn?'

I said: 'It was told to me as solemn fact.'

He said: 'You what? Sweet Jasus, man, don't you know enough yet to be aware that you live in the best bloody country in the world, but that here what they call a solemn fact is the equivalent of a rumour?'

My instinct told me that I was on a 100–8 loser with a sprained fetlock. As for Hansy, he was not only at sea, but half-way to Holyhead. He started by getting his 'w's under control with 'What is he talking about?' and went on to 'He blames me that here there iss no vireless?' For a finale, he said: 'Maybe he thinks I am like the Herr Doktor Frankenstein with a vurkshop in the basement?'

By then the odds had gone to 100–1. I could hear myself beginning to bluster.

To Dermo I said, 'So a solemn fact isn't a fact at all. It's only a rumour?'

'Absolutely!'

'And what if something really is a solemn fact? What do you call it then?'

'Nothing.' Dermo crossed his legs at the knees, looking like a priest that had an answer for everything. 'In Ireland, if you come across a fact, it means you're in England.'

Hansy said: 'You think I would destroy my own radio? That I could live mittout what I cannot live mittout? Beethoven, Brahms, Schubert, Schumann, Lord Haw-Haw?'

That made sense. I hoisted the white flag and said: 'Well, what *I* miss most is *ITMA*.'

Hansy asked: '*ITMA*? Is a medicine?' and Dermot roared 'Yes!' and I said I was sorry for being such a bollix and put my hand out to Hansy. As if that was a signal, Sean came in with two tureens. One had tiny boiled sausages in it with German mustard on them; the other had thin slices of ox tongue in vinaigrette.

'*Wunderbar*,' Hansy said. 'It is *Ochsenmaulsalat*.'

'Bless you,' Dermo said.

'*Danke schön*.'

'No, I meant *Gesundheit*,' Dermo said.

Sean set out plates and napkins embroidered with eagles and put logs on the fire. Dermo and I wolfed the food as if the time was nine o'clock and a famine was due to begin at five past. 'Sean cooked it,' Hansy said proudly.

'He taught me,' Sean said to us.

'So who,' Dermo said, 'gave you that cod of a yarn about Hansy buggering up the wireless?'

'Judge Garrity did,' I said. 'It was on the first day Babs and I ever came here.'

'A judge told you,' Dermo said. 'And you, you sap, believed him.'

'Oh, my God,' I said. My mention of Babs had put into my head what I had forgotten: that she was at home, sick with worry, looking at the clock and making a balls-up of her knitting. I jumped up. 'I have to go. She'll murder me.'

'Who will?' Hansy asked.

'His wife,' Dermo said. 'Who else would?'

'Use the telephone.'

'We don't have a phone,' I said. 'It was disconnected when the Judge moved out.'

'I will fix that,' Hansy said. 'Sean . . . *bitte*.'

And I wouldn't doubt him, but true as God the same Sean took a notepad from his pocket and gave it to Hansy who scribbled in it and handed it back. *Jeeves, how are you!* I thought.

'The same Judge Garrity,' Dermo said, not letting go of the subject, 'is why the fillum society has to be such a secret.'

'I keep telling you,' I said. 'It's legal. He can't stop it.'

'Oh, can he not!'

'It's a private club, so how can he?'

'Easy,' Dermo said. 'Only show a fillum where some Frenchman gets into bed with a bit of stuff, and his worship will bring a charge saying that it's in breach of a criminal law against obscenity.'

'Oh, come on.'

'Well, indecency then. And yours truly would end up being dragged off to do six months hard in the Joy. Do you think anyone here in the town would stand up for me? Not that lot. "We want no foreign filth!" And dare you show a war fillum that has Krauts – sorry, Hansy – massacreeing civilians and calling them *Schweinhunds*, and next thing we'd be up on a charge of contravening the Neutrality Act.'

'Oh, yass,' Hansy said, nodding his head and shaking it, both at once. 'The German embassy would be very angry.' Adding a P. S., he said: 'If they knew about it.'

'And Judge Garrity would put on a black cap and call it his painful duty,' Dermo said. 'I mean, shag it all, where's the harm? Twenty or so people, sitting in a room at the Robin Hood and seeing what they're not let see elsewhere.'

'So why do you take the risk?' I asked.

'I love fillums,' Dermo said.

The hotel was only a ten-minute stagger downhill from Heimat, and Dermo insisted that the night air would clear his head. Hansy said that he would drive me home in the Merc. I said: 'Not at all. I'll walk.'

He said: 'No, *bitte*. There is some-sing I vish to show you.'

He insisted, and by now there was a new policeman at the gate, which put me in mind of how late it was and that Babs would either take my sacred life or cry her eyes out until today was yesterday. It served me right, I thought, for spoiling her. I was so broody that I did not notice Hansy turning down a side road. Then the Merc began to bump along and we were in a steep laneway with no paving except flagstones.

'It's the wrong way,' I said.

'I vant that you should see some-sing.'

Oh, Christ, I thought, *I want to go home.*

At the side of the flagstones and maybe a hundred yards apart were what looked like three small forts of grey stone. Every one had a padlocked door and a sign with a lightning flash and 'Danger – Keep Out'. Hansy stopped, with his headlights on one of them. In the distance, I could see the lights of Dublin.

'Perry, my friend, do you know vot that is?'

'No, I don't. Tell you the truth, it's so ugly I never looked.'

'And as for me it is so ugly that I did look. Now come out for a moment and listen.'

I cursed under my breath and got out of the Merc. Now I could hear a low throbbing sound from a motor of some sort.

'What is it?'

'These three buildings are vot is called pumping stations. You know vot that is? They send the vawter –'

'The what?'

'The vawter vot you trink and vosh vith. They send it up the hill to the houses there. One of these is my house . . . Heimat. You understand?'

'What about it?'

'While we were talking this evening, I have been listening, but also I have been using this.' He tapped his forehead. 'The motor that drives this pump is worked by electricity, yass? *Und* now let us suppose that there is no confessor . . .'

'No what?'

'To keep it quiet. Not to cause the interfering.'

'Do you mean a suppressor?'

'Ah, sank you. Or maybe there is a suppressor, but it is –'

I finished it for him. 'Broken.'

105

He moved back to the car, and in the dark I could feel him smile. I thought of the crackle from the old wireless set in what Babs called her sewing room.

'Now I sink I take you home,' Hansy said.

The porch light was on in Carvel, and I saw the front curtains give a jerk as Hansy slammed the driver's door of the Merc. 'I sink you vill not need your keys,' he said.

He was right. I said goodnight, but he came up the steps all but taking the heels off me. Through the pane of stained glass at the side of the front door I could see Babs coming into the hall. Her hair was in curlers. She whipped the front door open.

'Where in the name of God were –'

She saw Hansy and came to a full stop.

'This is the Frau Perry?' he said. 'But she is more beautiful than you told me. Vy do you unter-exaggerate?'

Well, after that he could do no wrong and, come to that, neither could I. He had the knickers off of her, metabolically speaking, in two minutes.

I wish now I had never met him.

Chapter Eight

The Good German (2)

If I tried to write down the things that ought to be as simple as pie but which I make a holy hames of, we would be here all night. At the head of my list would be tying a bow tie, not walking in cat pooh, making my own bed, mending a puncture, changing a typewriter ribbon, playing whist and telling lies to Babs. When I went to Dermo's film society for the first time, she was kitten-curious; so, knowing that she hated all kinds of card-playing except penny poker, I cutely thought to kill two birds with the same stone by telling her that Hansy was teaching me whist.

'I'm only doing it,' I said, 'to oblige him.'

She gave me a look, then said, 'That'll be nice for you,' and off I trotted to the Much the Miller Suite of the Robin Hood.

That first film was called *Masquerade in Vienna*; it was a comedy made in 1934, and I thought that Anton Walbrook was great; a heart of stone would have melted when he was shot and wounded for doing the right thing for once in his life, and the girl, Paula Wessely, said to him, 'You silly, silly fellow.' And the little mystery was solved of how Dermo got hold of films for the society. It turned out that Hansy used the German embassy to bring in pictures such as this one, and he had an army friend in Paris who liked films more than fighting and sent him 16-mm copies of French pictures. There was no dubbing or subtitles to these; instead, everyone was handed a leaflet in English that told the story, like at the opera. Not knowing a word of the lingo except '*Bonjour*' and 'Charles Boyer', you would want to be as mad about films as we were.

Now and again, Dermo showed an English or an American war film which in the nature of things was banned by the censor. His new season in the autumn of 1942 opened in style with *In Which We Serve*, and everyone, Babs included, thought it was the best film ever. It made her cry buckets, and yes, she was a member of the society by then, and in so saying I am putting the cart of my story before the ass.

To go back to the April of that year, there was the sound of Hansy's klaxon as he turned up to drive me to *La Grande Illusion*, and Babs called out to me to wear my scarf. 'Ne'er cast a clout till May be out,' she said, following me down the hall and ready to lasso me with a grey muffler. She whipped it around my neck, dipped two fingers in the holy water font by the door – it was a habit from an old date – and flicked a few drops at me.

'What fillum is on tonight?' she asked, all innocent, and I, like an eejit, answered, 'A French one.'

I suppose I went red and tried to put the cat back in the bag. 'What I mean is –'

She said: 'Oh go on. Boys will be boys.'

I said: 'Who told you?'

She said: 'No one told me.' She laughed. 'A secret, in this place? What April shower did you and Dermo Grace come down with? And poor Hansy, yous have him as bad as yourselves.'

As I went down the front steps, she waved to him in his Merc. Hansy had been a great favourite of hers ever since that first night. She called him an oul' pet, and to put the icing on the cake he had our phone reconnected inside of a week. He had a sense of humour like a two-ton feather, and this evening to remind her that he was teaching me to play whist he stuck both his hands out of the car window and pretended to shuffle a pack of cards.

'You can quit that lark for a start,' I said, as I got in beside him. 'The jig is up.'

'The vot?'

'She knows about the film society.'

'*Mein* God,' he said, getting bilingual.

'And don't look at me,' I told him. 'I didn't say a word.'

As soon as we got to the Robin Hood, I told Dermo, who was handing out mimeographed pages about *La Grand Illusion*.

'And she says the whole town knows,' I said.

'Would that include the Judge?'

'I haven't the remotest.'

Dermo looked worried. He licked a thumb and peeled off two of his leaflets.

'Sank you,' Hansy said, refusing to take one, 'you forget that I speak *sehr gut* French.'

'Do you?' I asked.

'Oh, yass. Just like I speak English.'

Over the years I saw *La Grande Illusion* more than once and got to know whole bits of it by heart. Maybe I learned to understand it better than the kind of know-it-alls who would spout codology and give out to you that it was a film against war. Their sort were like the woman who once tapped me on the shoulder in the Grafton Picture House, when I was laughing out loud at Buster Keaton in *The Navigator*, and said, 'Oh do hush, please. This bit is symbolic.' No, to my mind what *La Grande Illusion* was about was that it was not a man's country that mattered to him but the class of people he was born into, and if you disagree with me then fair enough and a pity about you. Back in that April of 1943 we were not ready for such a film. In the kind of pictures we went to there was the bully and the chap, and either the chap won in the end or he sacrificed himself for his country or because the girl was too good for him. Whatever he did, it made no differ; the bully always lost. That was the rule, but in the film I saw that evening at the Robin Hood, there was neither chap nor bully, so riddle me that.

There are those who say that half of the Irish people were neutral on the side of Germany, and that the other half were ditto on the side of the Brits. But here is another conundrum. What did 'half' mean when it was at home? Did it mean that out of every two people who lived on this island one of them was for the Brits and the other for the Jerries? Or was it that every Irish person was in two minds, with one part of him against England because she was the old enemy – Perfidious Albion, my da used to call her – and the other part against the Germans, because the Nazis were rumoured to be a pack of mean lousers?

After the war was over and England had won, there was cheering, but nothing that would deafen you. When we saw the pictures of the concentration camps, there was a kind of disappointment, as if Hitler had been an odds-on favourite and then had let us down by playing dirty. In *Destry Rides Again*, your man, Jimmy Stewart, had a saying that went 'I knew a feller once', which was the signal for him to spin one of his yarns. Well, *I* knew a fella once as well; he was from a family of red-hot republicans and over a pint, I asked him what side he had been on during the war. He gave me a very superior class of a look and said: 'We were neutral.'

'I know that,' I said, 'but inside of your private self which ones were you for, the Jerries or the Brits?'

In my foolishness, I thought that if I knew him it might help me to know myself as well but for a minute I thought he was going to turn his back on me. He said: 'Maybe you like digging up the past and throwing it in people's faces. I don't.'

With that answer, which was less than none, he did turn his back as if I was a kind of sleeveen and a go-by-the-wall.

Dermo and Hansy came home with me after *La Grande Illusion*, not for the pleasure of my company but to sweet-talk Babs into singing dumb about the film society. She told them not to bother their barneys shutting the door of an empty house. She had heard about the film society from a woman named Maddie Dignam, a holy Mary who owned the hot bread shop in Easter Lane and every day spooned beef tea and slander into Canon Turmoyle, who was still a zombie after his stroke.

'If she knows, the town knows,' Babs said.

'You ought not to talk to the old b.,' I told her.

'Such a fuss,' she said. 'All you're doing is putting on the kind of rubbishy fillum that would give a body the sick.' Then, and without drawing breath, she wanted to eat her cake and have it. She said: 'So why can't *I* join?'

Dermo shrugged and said there was no longer a reason for keeping her out; but meanwhile and just for safety's sake, she should not breathe a word to the Garritys. So I forked out another guinea, and she was no sooner in than she was complaining that it was a bore and a waste of money. She was born contrary. I told her that being a film society it was *supposed* to be boring, but there was no point in talking commonsense to her.

Once we were into the month of May there was more on our plate than going to the pictures. When the evenings had got a proper stretch we gave the bicycles an oiling and went for spins to the Dargle Valley and Enniskerry, or for a dip off Killiney Strand, or to Dun Laoghaire pier to listen to the Artane Boys' Band – the sadness of the brass is with me still – while we watched the Holyhead mail boat go out. Once, Hansy drove us to Glendalough in the Merc, with Sean acting the part of chauffeur and then rowing us across the lake and hooshing us up into St Kevin's Bed, but the best treat of all was when he and Sean showed us his boat, the *Liebelei*.

'It is the name of a play by Schnitzler and of a film by Max Ophuls,' he told us. 'A film that is *wunderbar*, but *sehr tragisch*.'

'German?' I asked him.

'*Nein!*' He shook his head so fiercely that it nearly fell off. 'From Wien.'

'Is that where you're from, Hansy?'

'I? No, I am a native of *die Welt*.'

'The world,' Sean said, proud of him.

It was not much of a boat, more a little *putt-putt* of a thing, but it had a cabin where you could sit in from the waves and the weather. It was moored in Dun Laoghaire harbour and he took us out in it. Sean had brought life-jackets and deckshoes, and I could tell that Babs was shaking with fright, only she would not

111

let herself down in front of Hansy. I mean, he was a man who had called her beautiful.

I was a bit uneasy myself, looking at the green water and knowing how much more of the stuff was under us. As we got near the harbour mouth there was the sound of a ship's siren and the scream of seagulls. The mail boat – the *Princess Maud* – moved out from the Carlisle Pier and, as it went by, Hansy waved and shouted '*Wiedersehen!*' Passengers waved back. To us, he said: 'Poor peoples! They are going to the place of bombs and vor, and ve stay here. *Hurra! Hurra!*' He steered the *Liebelei* across the steamer's wash so that we buck-jumped and crunched. Babs screamed from fright and excitement.

'Now,' Hansy said, shouting over the cries of the gulls, 'we go to look at our town from the sea and maybe catch a fish which Sean will cook for our supper. Can you cook *Makrele*, Sean?'

Sean had to yell to be heard. 'Dunno. I can if it means mackerel.'

Hansy gave him a thumbs-up sign and was given one back. The pair of them knew damn well what they were up to, for not only was there a tangle of fishing lines in the boat's locker, but Sean had brought along a can of live bait. We left the harbour and crossed Scotsman's Bay, then chugged past gardens running down to the sea and a view of the Loreto convent with nuns on the rocks in striped bathing costumes from necks to ankles.

Then: 'Oh, look,' Babs said. 'There's Carvel, as plain as plain. Look, Perry, it's our house.'

It was Carvel, sure enough, and Hansy winked at me. It did him good to see her so happy. We drifted off-shore, seeing the town in a picture-postcard way and making out the church, the town hall and the Picture House. I found myself wishing that the place looked half as scenic facing from Easter Street across the silt of the harbour and with the tide out.

When the Wicklow Mountains came into view, Hansy spun the wheel. 'Now vee do our fishing,' he said and headed out to sea.

'Be careful,' Sean said. He pointed at a vessel a short distance off. 'The Irish navy.'

I laughed. 'Go to hell.'

'It's true.' He shouted at us over the chug of the engine. 'First, the Brits gave us motor torpedo boats so's they could keep an eye on the coast. Then they wanted them back to go to Dunkirk and gave us a few minesweepers in their place. Then we got corvettes. We had three or four of those, and next we bought a couple of trawlers. That's one of them coming to have a look at us.'

'Trawlers? What good are they?'

'Begging your pardon, you'd find out if you tried to out-run them. They go like the clappers.'

And sure enough the vessel – and it was a trawler – was getting bigger every few seconds, and soon we could make out the name *Naoibhe Gráinne* on her bow and see the green, white and orange flag on the stern. Sean made a sign for Hansy to ease back on the throttle. The sea was a sheet of glass.

'Remember the three-mile limit,' he told him. 'Keep well inshore from her.'

'Maybe they'll think we're spies,' Babs said.

'They might.' Sean gave me a half-smile. As well as I had come to know him, there was nothing between us as familiar as a wink. Then he said: 'Well, mocking is catching. They're coming alongside.'

'Oh, Mother of God,' Babs said.

'I'll take the wheel,' Sean said.

Hansy had begun to look pasty. Sean took hold of the wheel and kept us down-wind of the trawler, with not more than a man's height between us. Four men in uniforms and peaked caps looked over the side. They were smiling. One called to us: 'What are yous after?'

Before I could say 'U-boats', Sean, the sensible man, answered: 'Mackerel.'

'You don't want those,' the captain said. 'Dirtiest fish in the sea, and anyway they're not running. Would you be interested in a few Dublin Bay herrings? The real thing.'

'Don't tempt us,' Sean said.

'Here we go, then,' the captain said. 'A present from the Irish navy, where every man's an admiral!'

One of his crew swung an arm and Babs screamed as a necklace of maybe a couple of dozen herrings, strung on a cord, splattered on the deck at her feet. The captain or commander or whatever name he went by saluted and shouted 'Good luck,' and the trawler swung away from us. We waved back, and Hansy had savvy enough not to shout '*Danke schön.*'

That evening at Heimat we had *Hausfrauen Art*: herrings, salted, with onions, apples and tomatoes in a sour cream sauce. Hansy said that Sean should sit with us at the table, which was a great exception, and afterwards, while Babs said 'Oh, no,' 'It's too much trouble,' and 'Honest, you're awful,' Sean wrapped what was left over of the fish – enough for a full dinner – in silver paper for us to take home. It had been a great day.

One Sunday evening in May, Babs and myself were walking on Dun Laoghaire pier when she said: 'Oh, God forbid. Say it's not them.'

'Who?'

'Hilton and Micheál . . . are you blind?'

The pair of them, arm in arm, were strolling towards us: Tweedledum and Tweedledee, only different. Hilton Edwards was short, baldy and pink with a nose that could have cut a ribbon to open a flower show, and he spoke with a slurp; Micheál Mac Liammóir had a cat's smile and wore a wig like a black tea-cosy. He was in his full war-paint for a summer's day, blue eye-shadow and all.

'Don't look!' Babs said.

She dreaded being made a show of. While Hilton, in plus-fours and carrying a silver-topped cane in his free hand, looked like the proper English gent, Micheál was what in all seriousness a certain Dublin producer of plays called a bit too flam and buoyant. He was half-way between precious and priceless. People walking on the pier looked at them, nudged and smiled. They were as much a part of Dublin as Nelson's Pillar. We were starved in those days for more than food and tea and clothes to put on our backs, and Hilton and Michael – we called him by his English name – gave us a ration of the plays of Shakespeare and Shaw and Ibsen. Some made out that if they were honest-to-God homos, then in the words of Noah there was room in the ark for two of everything, and more luck to them. Others, and bad scran to them, said that their carry-on was only for show, a cover-up for what was worse, or else they would have been tarred and feathered years before, and a good job, too.

'Oh, God, don't let them see us,' Babs said that day on the pier, and of course they did. Michael stopped with a jerk that all but pulled Hilton off his feet. 'My God,' he said in a great purr of a voice, 'it is darling Perry Perry and the Blessed Catherine Mary.' Nobody knew, at least we never did, whether it was from just acting the jennet or out of badness that he called Babs by that name. He kissed her on the cheek and left twice as much of his make-up on her than she had of her own. Hilton called me his dear fellow and said that I was sorely missed in Epidaurus, whatever that meant.

It was only a case of hello and goodbye, which meant ten minutes of listening to words pouring out of Michael, all in one breath without comma or colon. 'You must come to one of our Sunday evening at-homes,' he said. 'Remind me, Hilton, on what day is the next one?'

Being an Englishman, Hilton had no time for codology. 'It will be on a Sunday, Michael, as you have very correctly said. We are at home every second Sunday.'

'Do you tell me?' Michael said.

'Because on weekdays we work. In the theatre.'

'The thee-ayter, yes. Hilton calls it work,' Michael told us, shutting an eye that was like a blink from the Kish lightship, 'and

I call it friv-ol-it-y.' To the day he died, he did not know what a throwaway line was. He would chop long words into bits and wrap them up in coloured paper, pink for girls and blue for boys. 'We will send you an in-vit-ay-shon. Where is it you live?'

'Drane,' I told him.

'Drain, yes,' he said, fondling the word so as you could get the smell of it. ' "That which we call a rose, By any other name would smell as sweet." Hilton, dear Hilton, advise me, am I quoting from the First Quarto or the Second?'

'You are quoting from Juliet, my pet,' Hilton said, sucking back a noggin of dribble, 'and people are receiving a Shakespearean performance from you without paying for it. Now come along.'

He kissed Babs's hand, and Michael gave her face another coating of Leichner No. 3½. We watched the pair linking arms again, as they continued their saunter. Babs shook her head and made a *yech* sound.

'What's up?'

'If you don't know, don't ask.'

'I wonder if they'll invite us.'

'For God's sake!'

Babs was a wonder. In three short words, she managed to say that there would be no invitation, and that if there *was* an invitation then it would be the waste of a stamp, for neither of us would set foot inside the house on Harcourt Terrace. We were not their sort.

As we were cycling home, she was still grumbling. 'I was never in my life so embarrassed.' When I made no answer, she said: 'Don't sulk.'

'I'm not.'

'I hate that kind of people,' she said. 'Calling one another "Dawwh-ling" and such.' In her mouth, the word sounded like a curse.

I said: 'There'll be people there I haven't seen in going on for a year. I wouldn't mind a bit of chat. And what's more, it'd be

116

good gossipy chat. We don't see that many of the theatre crowd, you know.'

She said 'Aww, wadda-wadda,' the same as to a babby.

I pedalled harder and drew ahead of her. By the time she caught up she wanted herself and me back the way we had been. She said: 'You know we couldn't go anyway. I mean, how would we get home?'

That much was true. With the petrol shortage, there was no finding a taxi driver who would take us from town all the way to Drane late at night, and then drive back empty.

'I suppose you're right,' I said.

'Anyway they're not going to invite us,' Babs said. 'Not in a fit. Will you get that through your head? They're just full of old talk.'

'Inevitability' is what Joxer Daly would have called a daaarlin' word. Critics have a great time with it; they use it to make a comedy or a farce look respectable, and often they shove the word 'Greek' up against it. Now there is a stunner for you. 'Greek inevitability'. It was something we not often came across in Ringsend National School, and the only Greek we knew ran a chipper in Thorncastle Street; but after Babs and me met Michael and Hilton on the pier, I had to give myself another think. I had set foot on the wrong train, and it was non-stop.

Like I say, that was on a Sunday, and on the Tuesday the invitation came.

Chapter Nine

The Good German (3)

There were empty seats at the Picture House because of the good weather, but Dermo had not a feather out of him. He stood in his usual position at the top of the steps and said hello to everyone by name. He looked at the sky – after the strain of being without a cloud all day it had softened to Wedgwood – and said: 'It'll rain. See if it doesn't.'

There were certain films that never failed to draw the customers. One of these was *The Four Feathers*, which he put on so often that jokes were invented:

'Did you hear they're building a new picture house in Drane?'

'Honest?'

'Oh, yeah. It's to show *The Four Feathers* in.'

'Bloody funny.'

There were red-hot republicans whose blood went on the simmer at the mention of the Seven Hundred Years of English Tyranny; but whenever *The Four Feathers* was on they went home thinking they were Harry Faversham being a credit to his regiment and decimating the Fuzzy-Wuzzies when he was not escaping from the Dervishes. On the Saturday after Babs and me had met Michael and Hilton on Dun Laoghaire pier the same film had been brought back 'by Public Demand', this time with what Dermo advertised as a 'Great Surprise Picture'. In spite of the fine weather, there were young mickey-dazzlers outside wearing raincoats with the belts not buckled but tied in a knot the same as the trench coat Alan Ladd wore the previous week in *The Blue Dahlia*.

'You wait till their chrissies turn up,' Dermo said. 'Every one of them with the hair over one eye like Veronica Lake.'

'What's your surprise fillum?' Babs asked him.

'Ah, that would be telling,' he said.

'No, what is it?'

'Tom Mix in *Cement*.'

'You're so smart. Well, we're sick of *The Four Feathers*.' She turned to me. 'Aren't we?'

I said: 'Oh, am I here, too?'

'Hansy is inside,' Dermo said. 'He's holding two seats for you.'

And so he was, waving to us from the middle of the one-and-thruppennies, with empty seats all around him. As usual, a crackly gramophone record was on and the tune was 'Moontime'.

'Don't invite him back to the house,' Babs warned me as we went up the side-aisle. 'I've nothing to give him.'

'Hansy doesn't mind,' I said.

'*I* mind.' That was her; never to be put under an obligation.

We had not seen him all week, but our news was easily swapped with his. Babs and me had been nowhere that a bike could not take you, and Hansy and a party from his embassy had been to a play at the Gaiety; or, rather, two plays in the one programme: *Tsar Paul* with Hilton and Michael in Bernard Shaw's *The Man of Destiny*.

'Any good?' I asked out of politeness.

'It vos like Mozart,' Hansy said.

'Great.'

'No, no, vot I mean is that ven the Emperor heard a piece by Mozart, he said to the composer, "There are too many notes in your music." Vell, when I hear some-sing that is written by your Herr Bernard Shaw, then I say: "There are too many vords in your play!" Ehh-heh, ehh-heh.' The last bit was the sound Hansy made when he came out with what he thought was funny.

'Very good,' I said.

'I do not much like the theatre,' Hansy said. 'I sink I prefer what I see up there.' He pointed at the curtains that were between us and the screen of the Picture House. 'But in the play I saw, that man who vos Napoleon, that Herr Mac Limerick, vos very good.'

'Mac Liammóir, you thick,' I said. By now we were so great with each other that I could pin the occasional insult on him like a medal.

'Now be polite,' Babs said. The mention of Michael's name reminded her. 'And did you answer that invitation?'

'No, but I will.'

'Well, do it when we get home. It's only manners.'

'You are invited?' Hansy was nearly as inquisitive as she was.

I said: 'It's a kind of what we call an at-home. Your idol Mac Liammóir is having a few people in.'

'So?' Hansy was impressed. 'And you know this man?'

'It's Dublin. Everyone knows everyone.'

'More's the pity,' Babs put in.

'And the Herr Mac vill be there?'

'Sure. It's his do and Hilton's. It'll be a regular orgy.' I gave Babs a grin. 'Won't it, pet?'

'Whatever it is,' Babs said in a voice that was as flat as a breadboard, 'we're not going.' Then, in case that might have made her sound a bit of a b., she said: 'We can't get a taxi home, so that's the end of it.'

'Do you vant to go?' Hansy asked.

Whatever ailed her would not be tamped down, and she would have the last word if it killed her. 'Oh, do we not? We're dying to! Aren't we, Perry?'

She did not know Hansy well enough to see the simpleness of his nature. The sort he was, he heard her words, but the jeer in them went past him.

There and then, 'Moontime' came to an end; there was the sound of the needle skidding on the record; the curtains opened and the 'surprise' film came on the screen. First we saw the

Paramount mountain; then a groan went up at 'William Boyd as Hopalong Cassidy in *Twilight on the Trail*, with Brad King and Andy Clyde'.

'It's a rotten old cowboy,' Babs said in disgust. Michael and Hilton's at-home was already forgotten.

Hansy was a dog worrying a bone. He said: 'But that is not a problem. You give me the address and I vill come and pick you up at vottever time you vish to go home.'

'Home from where?' Babs said.

'And there is to be no refusal.'

'What? Oh, no. No, Hansy, I was –' As half-empty as the Picture House was, someone shushed her.

'So now you vill go!' he said, raising his voice.

I laughed; I thought it was a howl. She snapped at me: 'You're so blooming smart.'

When 'Hopalong Cassidy' was over and Hoppy had caught the crooked foreman she took hold of Hansy by the sleeve. 'Now be a good man and –'

He said in a voice that would break your heart: '*Mein Liebling*, you vill not say no to me ven I vish so much for you to be pleased? *Bitte?*'

She said to me: 'Tell him no.'

'You tell him.'

'I can't.' It was nearly a wail; she could refuse him nothing.

I gave an imitation of Cinderella's fairy godmother and said, 'You will go to the ball! You will go to the ball!'

She might have been a parcel tied with coloured string. It was settled.

The evening ended when Harry Faversham had given back the last of his four feathers and made it up with Eithne in the summerhouse – actually, I would have stuck her feather up her backside for not thinking better of me to begin with. Babs was in the sulks all the way home, not taking a lift from Hansy and walking ahead of me with her head butting the sky, but next morning she said with a face on her:

'What time is Hansy to call for us after this blooming old whatever-it-is?'

I said: 'What about eleven o'clock?'

She said '*Eleven*?' as if that was all hours.

Babs could be the best woman in the world, but no one had ever taught her to do a climb-down, no matter that during the week she had begun to look forward to our evening out, with the drive home in the Merc at the end of it. In them days, the only times we were likely to act the royal family in a motor car was to go to funerals. And need I say that Hansy not only wanted to take us home from the do, but to it as well. We said no to that, and so he drove us to Dun Laoghaire where there was a taxi rank for the mail boat passengers, and he only stopped the Merc when I threatened to jump out.

We took a cab to Harcourt Terrace, and the party was what you would expect, with most of the guests flying the colours of either Sodom or Begorrah, as the Gate Theatre and the Abbey were called. Hilton and Michael made sure we mixed. 'This will emph-at-i-cal-ly not do,' I heard Michael say when he came upon a group colloguing in a corner. '"You blocks, you stones, you worse than senseless things!" If there was an audience watching you, they would by now have asked for their money back. For God's sake move around, my darlings. *Mo-o-ove*! *Minnn-gel*!'

The chat was good. People asked me if I was writing a new play – 'Yes, you are,' one said when I told him no; 'Does the Liffey run backwards?' – and Babs was gossiping with women who, like herself, were a bit left out of it. At ten o'clock there was a buffet supper, and in the stampede to the kitchen the ones who were actors left their hoof prints on the backs of the ones that were not. There was beef done in a wine sauce – Michael had a long French word for it – with carrots and onions, all of it dished up with rice, and a young actor – a discovery of Hilton's named Marius Corby with golden hair that God would have been hard put to it to invent – had made the sweet, which was bread-and-butter pudding. 'God help us, I think it is bread-and-margarine pudding,' Michael said in a wailing voice, like a Connemara woman keening for her drownded son.

I was bringing a plate to Babs when Hilton touched me on the shoulder and said: 'Dear boy' – and the nerve of him with his 'boy', for I could have given him three years and walked barefoot for another two – 'we do not want to lose either you or her charming self.' He gave one of his wateriest slurps. 'But against the evil moment, have you arranged for transportation? Most of our guests are bussing it or tramming it or are within walking distance, and I fear that if you require a taxi –'

'We don't,' I told him, 'A friend is collecting us.'

'Oh, joy. Then say not another word. I am presumptuous.'

'He's a diplomat. A great admirer of Michael's.'

'Oh, how thrilling,' Hilton said, with jealousy slobbering out of him. 'Mickey, do you hear?'

'An admirer of mine?' The room was full of talk, but you had only to mention Michael's name and he was on the spot, quivering like a pointer dog.

'The friend who's picking us up,' I said, 'saw you the other evening in *The Man of Destiny* –'

Michael did a little twirl for joy. 'Hilton, you preposterous creature, do you hear? I have a *fan*.'

'Oh, a great fan,' I said, like a born crawler.

'Mercy upon us,' Michael said. 'And at what time are we to look upon this barometer of good taste?'

It was hard to know if he was making fun of me or of himself or of Hansy, who was still to appear. He said: 'All that is left of our supper is grrrisss-ell. But I shall tell darling Marius – he is to be my Laertes, you know – to put the poor remainder of our bread-and-margarine pudding in a safe place. We must offer my admirer hospitality.'

I said, 'Hansy is only coming to give us a –' but he had already gone ballet-dancing off.

On the stroke of eleven the doorbell went. Michael shot out

into the hall like a greyhound leaving a trap and came back holding Hansy by the arm and – and I near fell out of my standing – talking German to him, thirteen to the dozen. 'It is only *Plattdeutsch*,' Michael said to me, corner of his mouth, as they went past. Hansy gave me a helpless look, and the golden boy, Marius, was there to the tick guarding a plateful of the bread-and-whatever pudding with his life. Babs came in and asked, 'Was that Hansy?'

'He's doing all right,' I said. 'Leave him.'

The time came for the last buses and trams, and the party began to quieten down. There were goodbyes, and cold air came in from the street with every slam of the hall door. I had not been to a Second Sunday for years, but nothing had changed, and towards midnight Hilton still sat in a wing chair by the dying fire and held court. He had the kind of actor's voice that pulled a room to him. I suppose he had a smell of himself, but he was good value. There was maybe a dozen of us left, sitting on the carpet; Babs was next to me, and across the room Hansy looked as if he had died and gone to heaven. He moved to make room for Marius.

As usual, Hilton began as if he was nattering to just the one person, and then a running loop was thrown around all of us. He began with: 'Michael and I are great filmgoers on afternoons when we are not in rehearsal. We were at the moving pictures the other day. I forget what film it was.'

One or two of us looked at Michael, expecting him to put in his prate; instead, he pointed a plump finger to remind us of who had the floor.

'It was a thing with bows and arrows and portcullises,' Hilton said, 'and there were two young women in front of us. I heard one of them say, and it made excellent sense, that in costume films you could always tell the hero because his tights did not wrinkle at the knees, whereas the villain's always did, and the bagginess increased as one went down the scale of iniquity from Sir Guy of Gisbourne and the High Sheriff of

Nottingham to a brutish henchman of the fourth class.'

His listeners laughed and some clapped their hands to egg him on. Hansy looked around him; he was maybe catching no more than one word in five but was thrilled to be in the middle of it.

'My own problem with the silver screen,' Hilton said, 'is its predictability.' I took a dekko at Michael; he had his eyes closed and was tasting the word 'pre-dic-tab-il-it-y' as if each little bit of it was cream chocolate. 'You are all aware, I am sure, that in the year Nineteen Hundred and Ten the recently departed Dublin corner-boy, James Joyce, was briefly the manager of a picture house.'

'The Volta,' someone put in.

'Thank you, dear heart,' Hilton said.

'In Mary Street,' the same voice said.

Michael looked at the know-it-all through two thin circles of eye-liner and said in a roaring whisper: 'It suddenly occurs to me that the Grand Canal is at the end of this short thoroughfare. And it is *six . . . feet . . . deep . . .'*

We all looked at the interrupter, who had gone the colour of a brick.

Hilton went on: 'And it was the same scrofulous James Joyce who wrote "Reproduction is the beginning of death." Now I wonder if he found that pearl of sagacity in one of his silent films at the . . .' He looked into his audience with cod curiosity. 'Was it the Voltage, dear boy?'

After the snigger had died down, he said: 'In any event, the truth of it holds good today. Only let the hero of a moving picture have a close friend who marries and becomes a father, and woe betide that person. His biological function is over. He is done for. If he is a policeman, he will be shot dead in the line of duty; if he is a zoo-keeper, a lion will eat him; if he is a clerk, a pen-nib will be thrust through his heart.

'And there are others who are almost as surely doomed. The spurned fiancé – a dullard, of course – is one of them. He is now redundant. In the Holly-wooden world, sex is the opposite of justice, for it may neither be done nor seen to be done. It has been replaced by the shorthand device of a kiss, closely followed by the National Anthem. And yet, sex and sex alone is what films are about, and the wretch who has been cast aside is destined for oblivion.

'Only compare this nonsense with the theatre. Ah now, the theatre is the work of artistes! It is achieved with a painter's brush and a sculptor's thumb.' Hilton used his own thumb to make a curve in wet clay that we could all but see. 'Whereas, the cinema . . . well, what is it, except poor shadows and lines drawn with a ruler and a T-square?'

I wanted to tell him, but did not dare put my spoke in, that what he called the predictability of films was part of what some people liked. It made the world safe for them. It was like going home. When you saw the same street corner or the same cat on a wall, you knew where you were.

Hilton went on for maybe ten minutes, ticking off what he called clichés, starting with the half-breed woman who on account of some law or other could not be let marry a white man, and ending with the young soldier who goes into a battle with a picture of his girl back home – he was always a certainty for the chop. 'All of them doomed,' Hilton said, 'for oblivion. And then, when you think you have run the whole grisly gamut,' he said, 'along come the *new* clichés.'

'Oh, my God,' Michael said, clasping his hands as if more was too much. It was his way of whipping Hilton's audience into the home stretch.

'Think of war films. They may be kept from us by the censor but we read the fan magazines to which you are so devoted. Aren't you, Mickey?'

Michael blew him a kiss.

'And I speak not of storm troopers or Nazis or common-or-garden traitors, but of the collaborators whose conscience takes them along the knife edge between good and evil. There is your new cliché for you. All of them are doomed, just as are the so-called Good Germans.'

At this, he caught sight – if he had ever lost it – of Hansy.

'My dear fellow,' Hilton said with one of his best splutters. 'No offence is intended. None in the world. I apologise most abjectly.'

Hansy was as good-natured as ever. 'Is not needed,' he said.

'And I spoke not of actuality,' Hilton said, 'but of the world of cinema and the ghastly stereotypes it imposes on us. Damn MGM and those deplorable Warner Brothers and the elves of Elstree and the rest of them.'

'But you know,' Hansy said, as mild as milk, 'some of us are not bad people.'

'Which is exactly what I am saying,' Hilton said. 'The wretched picture houses have so much to answer for. But the multitude, the masses, they will not pay their dollars or their pounds sterling to look at a good German. To them there is no such animal.'

He looked at his watch and said, 'Good heavens.' It was the signal that his star turn and the at-home itself were over. Everyone – at least them that wanted to be invited to Harcourt Terrace on another Sunday – said their goodnights. I waited while Babs went up for her coat – she had left it in a bedroom off the first landing. She was back inside of a minute.

I told her: 'I can't find Hansy.'

'*I* found him.'

Her face was death, not even warmed up. She staggered against me.

'What is it?'

'Get a taxi. I want to go home.'

'We're *going* home. Where's Hansy?

'I don't want him. I want a taxi.'

Her voice was high. People were looking at her.

I said: 'There aren't any taxis. Are you mad? What's up with you?'

Next thing I knew, Hansy was on the stairs following her down. She went past me, out into the open without a goodbye to our hosts. I was going to tell Hansy that she wasn't well, then I saw by his face that whatever ailed her, he was part of it. Like her, he went out without as much as a yes, aye or no to Hilton or Michael. He opened the rear door of the Merc, and she got in without looking at him.

I slid in beside her and asked: 'What the hell's wrong?'

She shook her head. It was not an answer but a begging to be let alone. On the way to Drane she did not speak a word – no more than did Hansy. I wanted to ask him what had happened, but was as much afraid of his answer as of what Babs might do or say. She sat, and what I could see of her face was white. When I made to touch her she pulled away.

The Merc pulled up outside Carvel. Hansy opened the near-side door and said, 'Good night, Babs.' She went up the front steps without a word.

I slid out and said, 'Listen, thanks for all the trouble.' Him and me always shook hands when we met or went our way; this time he bowed and as near as dammit clicked his heels.

Babs was already upstairs, sitting on the edge of the bed. I said: 'All right, let's have it. Did he chance his arm?'

'*What?*'

'Trot it out. He tried it on with you, is that it?'

She said: 'Are you mad? I wish he had. No; no, I don't, God forbid. All I mean is that at least that would have been natural.' When I stared at her, she shouted at me: 'Are you thick? It was him and that young fellow with the dyed hair. Martin or Maurice or whoever he was. It was the pair of them. At it!'

She began to sob.

'Jesus, at what?'

She let out a hiccup.

Looking back to those days, I think of how narrow-minded we must seem now, but that was the way of it. A man kissing another man was a thing not to be talked about, at least not by nice people like Babs, and with her it was even worse because of her fondness for Hansy. The word she spoke was nearly funny because it was so tame. 'Oh, the . . . the *boldness* of him.'

She cried into her pillow, and I left her to it. Next morning over the breakfast, the first thing she said was: 'Well, I'm not going to the Picture House again.'

'What's the Picture House got to do with it?'

She said, straight out: 'Because he might be there, and I don't want to see him.'

'Ah, now.'

'Ever again.'

She kept her word the following Saturday, but I went on my own to see *The Wagons Roll at Night*. He moved to the seat beside mine.

'Babs is not with you?

'No.'

'It is because of me?'

'What do *you* think?'

He said nothing for a minute while he found the right words. 'And you and I, are we still friends?'

'I don't know.'

'You don't know?'

'What you did – what Babs said you did with him – with –'

'Marius.'

'I don't know about those things. I have to sort myself out. It's –'

'Oh, yes?'

'It's as if you were all of a sudden someone else.'

'I am the same person.'

'No, you aren't,' I said. 'Not to me.'

He said: 'You can tell Babs that I vill not come here again. Not until you and she have – vot is it you say? – sorted yourselfs out. You know vhere my house is.'

I told Babs about our conversation. She said: 'Oh, so His Royalty is letting me go to the pictures, is he?'

'Now that's silly.'

'He's bloomin' noble, isn't he? Well, I won't give him the satisfaction.' She was always not giving someone the satisfaction.

I suppose I was selfish. It was bad enough for a fellow to live in a town the size of Drane without having to give a November of a nod to somebody he was cool with, but I knew I would miss the outings and the bit of gas and the bite of suppers Sean would do for us up at Heimat. We weren't hangers-on but the pair of them were company. They made it easier for us – well, for me, at any rate – to live in Drane.

And a question I actually asked myself was: *Does Sean know about Hansy*? I mean, well, it goes to show.

It was two Saturdays after that Second Sunday when Dermo drove up in the Jensen at half-nine in the morning. I was shaving.

'Wipe that stuff off and get dressed.'

'What's up?'

'I won't tell you. Then you won't have to lie to Babs. Hurry.'

'Where are you going?' she wanted to know.

'Tell you later.'

Dermo drove himself and me to Dun Laoghaire and pulled up outside the open door of the red-brick courthouse in George's Street.

'Hey, today's Saturday,' I said.

'I know. Special sitting.'

I had never been in a court of law before. There were a few expensive-looking men sitting askew on the benches and talking in low voices. My heart jumped when I saw that Hansy was there in the company of a well-dressed man who looked like George Sanders when he was the bully in *Man Hunt*. His head might have been on a swivel; it turned as if a camera behind his eyes was photographing everyone in the courtroom: me, Dermo, the expensive men, the court officials and the two Gardai.

After a time, the judge came in. He was nice enough, but too young for the part. We were told to stand and then be seated, like in the pictures. Somebody said: 'Put up Harold Pringle,' and at this who else but the bold Marius Corby came into the courtroom shaking his goldy locks. I could not believe what came next, because the charge was read out, and it was of gross indecency in a public place. One of the expensive men said, 'Your worship,' and went into a huddle, and all at once it was feeding time in the hen-run. They came clucking around; the judge listened and said that he would hear the case of the defendant Pringle in camera, and that the other defendant, Mueller, would lay claim to diplomatic status. With this, Dermo and me and a few others were turfed out.

Dermo lit up a cigarette. Without waiting for me to ask, he said: 'Would you believe it? The pair of them – Hansy and Goldilocks showing off their credentials in some picture house or other. Not in *my* Picture House, for God's sake, don't think that!'

'Oh, Christ.'

We waited. A Garda was holding the courtroom door open an inch or two. He let go of it and turned to us. 'The blondie young lad has promised to go back to England by this evening's mail boat, and the judge said, "Proper place for you. And –"'

The door was flung open and Marius or whoever he was came out. We heard the judge shout, 'And good riddance,' after him. Maybe a minute later, Hansy came out with the quick walk of a man being followed. He grabbed my hand and Dermo's.

'Sank you, sank you. You are good friends.' He looked over his shoulder towards the courtroom. 'I sink they vill send me back to Germany. You must find Sean for me. Please, find him, find him.'

The courtroom door opened again, and before you could blink Hansy was gone from us, out into the street. The man in the good suit had come out and not only did he look like George Sanders but had the self-same walk, as if he was in a bad way to get to the jacks without breaking into a run. He gave Dermo and me a look. 'Will you know us next time?' Dermo asked. George

Sanders caught Hansy by the arm, but not in a comradely way, and led him to a car that was waiting.

'Him and his "Find Sean",' Dermo said. 'Now how the hell are we to find Sean if we don't even know his last name? Do you know it?'

'Ask me another.'

He said: 'You have shaving soap all over you.'

'Wherever we're going,' I said, 'would you call in at the house? Babs'll be worried.' So we drove to Carvel, and on the way I asked him why Sean was no longer at Heimat. He said: 'Search me. Either the Krauts gave him the boot or he humped off.'

'Why would he want to hump off?'

'Well, what else would you do if your wife got up to a lot of dirty andrewmartins with a young fellow in the Pillar Picture House?'

'Wife? Whose wife?' I was beginning to feel like one of the world's innocents.

'Hansy's shaggin' wife. Name of Sean,' Dermo said, getting into a right wax.

'Sorry?'

'His wife's name, are you thick?'

We stopped outside Carvel and I let myself in while Dermo waited outside in the Jensen. Babs was in the kitchen, all smiles. She was pouring tea for a visitor.

'Sean dropped in,' she said.

I signalled to Dermo from the front door, and mind you, when he came in and saw Sean he recovered in a blink. He smiled and said: 'Well now, the dead arose and appeared to many. The hard man. Where did you –'

Babs was staring, but not at him. He turned to let his look follow hers and saw that the dead were in full attendance, for Hansy, as if he had been hot on Dermo's heels, was two short steps behind him. He faced Babs, gave one of his stiff bows and this time clicked his heels. He said: 'Madame Babs, you will please to forgive me if I intrude.'

Sean said: 'She may, but I damn well won't.' He took three steps across the breakfast room and slapped Hansy's face, hard.

Hansy kept his eyes on Babs, knowing that she did not want him in our house. Whenever she moved between the Primus and the table to make fresh tea, he leaped to attention, and the look she gave him was more scalding than the splash of boiling water in the teapot.

'Vee Chermans are a sensible people,' he said. 'Vee believe that a door iss for people to come through, so vile they are watching the front gate and the front door of Heimat, I come out through the back vindow.' He gave me a little smile that for some reason was between me and him. 'I had a little call to make on my vay, and here I am. *Gut*, eh?'

'Anyone would think you'd been caught robbing an orchard,' Sean said. 'I hope you know you can't go back there.'

'Oh, but I am to be a guest of the German embassy,' Hansy told him. 'And next veek the National Socialist Party is to send me on a . . . vot is it called? A *Kreuzefahrt*, a cruise. It is a ship *mit* a cargo that goes to the vest of Afrika, and in a month I will be at home in Germany. And ven I am there in case I get lost they vill giff me a pink star to vare. That vill tell the peoples vhere I am and vhass I am, and vhere I am going.'

Sean said: 'Would you like another belt?'

'No, sank you, Sean.'

'Then what are you grinning at?'

'Because you are so angry that I know you vill save me.'

I wondered if Sean was going to hit him again. Instead, he said: 'You can't go back to Heimat, and you can't go anywhere else. Whatever is to be done has to be done today, and we get only the one chance. I have an idea and I don't know if it'll work.'

Babs said: 'I can't sit and listen to this.' Hansy stood up. She snapped at him: 'Oh, sit down, you . . . you . . . you . . .' She went out and upstairs.

Sean said: 'On the Isle of Man –'

'On the vot?'

'Just shut up and listen. I hear tell there's an internment camp on the island for enemy aliens. They lock you up, but at least you stay alive. Now if you could get that far in the *Liebling* –'

Hansy clapped his hands with delight and crooned: '*Mein Liebling*. She vill save us. She iss a *gut* girl.'

'Hey, hey,' Dermo said, getting excited, 'this might work. Only thing is, how are you for diesel?'

'We have lashings,' Sean said, 'and the tank is full.' He looked at Hansy: 'He's been siphoning it out of the Merc. A gallon or so every week.'

'*Ptih, ptih,*' Hansy made a face and a spitting noise. 'So that vee can go fishing,' he said, with a great smile on his face and not a care in the world.

'Then that's it,' Dermo said. 'We're elected.'

'It won't work,' Sean said.

'Why won't it?'

'In this bloody country?' He had a face on him like the ace of spades. 'When does anything ever work?'

I said: 'Sean, you're being a misery.'

Hansy was not listening. All of a sudden he was von Runstedt on the Russian front. 'It vill verk, I know it vill. First of all, ve must vait until it is dark –'

'No! That's what we mustn't do.' Sean nodded towards the sea. 'We won't wait. We have to go now, this minute.' He was back in charge of Hansy. 'Broad daylight.'

Dermo opened his mouth and said sweet eff-ahh.

'It's a Saturday, and look at the weather. Not a cloud in the sky, and the bay is black with yachts, so who's going to notice a little matchbox the size of ours?' Sean got to his feet.

Hansy said: 'Sean, you vill come with me?'

'And supposing I don't? Who's going to navigate? But I'm shagged if I'm going to be interned along with you. I'm no enemy alien.' He spoke to Dermo: 'We'll hug the coast as far as

Clogherhead, then head a bit north by east, and it should still be daylight by the time we pick up the Calf of Man. Can we take a loan of the Jensen as far as Dun Laoghaire?'

'Leave it anywhere, I'll find it,' Dermo said.

As Hansy reached for the teapot to pour himself a hottener, Sean said: 'None of that. We go now. Now, this instant. They're looking for you.'

Hansy's eyes filled with tears. He reached for me.

'You've had enough of that,' Sean said. 'Now come on. Bye for now, then.'

Dermo gave him the car keys and went with me into the front room to watch them leave. Sean looked up and down the road, this way and that; then Hansy blew a kiss to someone above our heads. I knew – no, be honest; I hoped – that Babs was waving goodbye to him from the front bedroom.

Later that afternoon, Dermot called. He had found the Jensen parked safely in Dun Laoghaire harbour outside the Royal Irish Yacht Club, and the *Liebling* was gone from her moorings. All that evening and into the next day Babs was not worth her salt with worry. At two in the afternoon I went to Jemima's for a Sunday paper. The good weather was holding. I looked out at the yachts. Some of them were cadging for a wind, and I thought to myself: *There is no war, no Hitler, no Hansy and no Sean.*

When I got to the paper shop, even the placard outside it was as unreal as what was in that day's *Independent*. The words jig-danced in front of me: TWO MEN DIE IN BOATING ACCIDENT.

It was not until the inquest a week later that we learned at least some of the truth of it. The Irish naval vessel, the *Naoibhe Gráinne* had hailed the *Liebling* which had passed Lambay Island and was outside the three-mile limit. Instead of coming alongside as signalled, the two male occupants went into the cabin and appeared to have opened the sea-cocks. By the time a line could be thrown, the *Liebling* was low in the water. The occupants were taken ashore, but were dead on arrival at

Skerries. The inquest was adjourned *sine die* at the request of the coroner.

Captain F. M. Mooney, the commanding officer of the *Gráinne*, said that the deceased were known to him and that he had hailed them as on previous occasions in the belief that they might have accepted a gift of herring.

When I came out of Jemima's I went and sat on the harbour wall and waited for the sea and the yachts to be real again before I went home to Babs. I looked at the rest of the paper, which in those days was only a few pages long, There was an item on one of the inside pages headed, ACT OF SENSELESS VANDALISM AT DRANE.

And here, if this was a film, I would have Hansy speaking in what is called a voice-over, saying what he said when he came into Carvel on that last day, the Saturday: 'I had a little call to make on my vay, and here I am.' I could even hear violins over the end titles. Some person or persons had broken the padlocks on the doors of the four pumping stations on the flagstones leading up the hill behind Drane. Pending repairs, people would be obliged to obtain their domestic water from a pump.

When I got home, I went straight up to Babs's little sewing room, not out of callousness but because I wanted at least to tell her that Hansy had left us a little present. I pulled the wireless in and switched it on. The reception was as bloody hopeless as ever.

Chapter Ten

The Canon's Bewk (1)

Canon Turmoyle died in September, and the town gave him a great turn-out. The body was laid out in the parochial house, all dressed up and tuppence-to-talk-to in its canonicals, and one woman was heard to say that from his appearance he must have suffered like a martyr, while another, more on the cheerful side, declared that he looked very like himself. Maddie Dignam from the hot bread shop had prepared the corpse for the lying in state and now sat by the head of the canon's bed, telling her beads as callers filed past and sprinkled a few drops of holy water on him so that before an hour had passed he looked like a Kerry Blue run over in the rain. She wore the calm look of a widow who was looking forward to a rest.

The canon had no sooner had his stroke than his house-keeper, a small, fat woman by the name of Mag McClure, declared herself unable to lift anything heavy or well-fed, such as the canon. She was only too delighted when Maddie offered, free of charge, to do the nursing part of looking after him and got dug in with great devotion. 'It is an old saying and a true one,' Mrs McClure declared, 'that God never sends a mouth, but He provides meat to put in it.' She was a dab hand with old and true sayings, and, as for Maddie, the only payment she was after was a savings account in heaven. When the end came for the canon, she washed and dressed him after first sending the curate, Father Luke, and even Aloysius Gunn the undertaker from the room for decency's sake.

As it happened, my Babs was one of the women who twice a

week queued in the hot bread shop for Maddie's loaves, which on account of the war became a darker shade of brown with every passing month – it was said that the sales of senna pods at the chemist's fell off as the bread got browner. Maddie told the women that her only concern had been to do what the canon would have wanted.

'It must have been hard for you,' one of the old ones said with a tremble of daring running through her like long grass shivering in a breeze.

'It was the right thing to do, I know that,' Maddie said, and added, simply: 'I kept thinking of my latter end.'

This was all but too much for the old rips, and there was no reply they could give but to sigh as deeply as their stays would permit.

'I did what I could for him,' Maddie told them, 'and I could feel my years in purgatory falling from me like leaves off a calendar in a fillum. That's more than many a one could say.'

She had always been a town joke. The corner-boys would say 'Howyah, Maddie?' as she walked the length of Easter Street, and the red-faced pissers coming out of The Ebb Tide would wink and tell her 'Fine girl y'are!', causing a blue vein to run down her forehead like forked lightning. She was six feet tall – taller, if you included the white paper glengarry that kept the flour out of her hair – and without a hillock of flesh on her from foot to face. If you were to go raving mad and dream of bending her at the middle, she would have snapped.

Babs and me were not mass-goers, but we went to the funeral. In that year of Nineteen Hundred and Forty-Three a person who did not attend church, chapel or meeting was looked upon as no better than a heathen; however, being a writer of plays and books, I was regarded as no more than a queer fellow and exempt from the everyday decencies. Even so, not to draw the window blinds as the funeral of a priest went past would have been beyond the beyond.

The parish church, St Begnet's, was packed, and a Miss

Blánaid McRoarty sang 'Faith of Our Fathers' and, as a particular request of the deceased's, 'I'll See You Again'. The Bishop of Mungret officiated and preached the homily. 'We are saying farewell,' he said, 'to a man who was a saint in the making,' and at this there was a great nodding of heads. I was impressed. Praising the guest of honour to the skies is part and parcel of any funeral – a kind of amicable nail in the coffin – but you can always tell the difference between what is only old palaver and the real Ally Daly. This was a true bill.

The canon's remains were taken by hearse to Westland Row and by train across the country to Ballaghaderreen in County Roscommon where a ga-ga older brother, the last of his surviving relations, lived. That ought to have been the last of him, and it would have been except that at his funeral and before you could shake more holy water over him, the Bishop of Mungret and the curate of Drane, the Reverend Tadgh Luke, discovered a passion in common for the songs of Percy French. It was expected that Father Luke would have stepped into the canon's shoes as the parish priest of Drane; instead, he woke up one morning as the bishop's new secretary. The life of a country priest, and for that matter a bishop, was a lonely one, with only hare-coursing and the occasional altar boy to break the desolation. It was said that from the Bishop's House in Mungret the congenial and melodic sound often came of a duet that began:

> *The harems of Egypt are fine to behold,*
> *The harlots the fairest of fair,*
> *But the fairest of all was owned by a sheik*
> *Named Abdul Abulbul Amir.*

The new parish priest of Drane was a Father Chancey, who brought his own housekeeper with him, and Mrs McClure was given a retirement pension of God's blessing on the one hand and a handshake with the other. As for what happened with

Maddie Dignam, we never learned the full story, but when Babs called into her shop as usual Maddie put a finger to her lips, warning her to bide her hour till the place was empty. She waited, and when they had the shop to themselves Maddie rummaged under the counter and said: 'This is a little something for yourself and himself.'

Babs could not credit what she saw, which was a loaf of bread made with the whitest of white flour. She had not seen the like of it since the Emergency started. Before an ear-wigging customer could come in and interrupt, Maddie made a parcel of the loaf and lobbed it into Babs's shopping bag.

'I'd like a word with himself,' she said in a hoarse whisper.

Babs said: 'Himself?'

'With yours,' Maddie said, meaning me. 'At seven o'clock.' As the doorbell jingle jangled on its spring, she jerked a long thumb towards another door, this one down a step at the back of the shop. 'In there. If it suits him.'

'It'll suit,' Babs said, taking a great deal upon herself.

She hurried home with the smell of the new-baked bread causing people to follow her with their eyes and noses the length of Easter Street. At home, she put the loaf on the kitchen table and did not so much unwrap it as unveil it. She told me what Maddie had said.

'Now what have you got me into?' I said. Then: 'And before you wrap it again, give us a cut.'

She took the bread-knife and sawed two heels off the loaf, one from this end, the other from that, and scraped a mingy dab of rationed butter over both, one for her, one for me. The fresh bread sucked the butter in; it might have been blotting paper, but even so it was lovely. No, it was better than lovely; it was peace-time. And there was more to come, for on the blow of seven I was at the hot bread shop with Maddie showing me into the bakery at the back. She cut two thick doorsteps off another white loaf and put them into her Aga to turn crispy. She took them out and began to slather butter on them – fresh country butter that you would break a window to steal at two in the morning – and then she put the slices back in the oven.

'That's how you make toast,' Maddie said.

She had mugs of strong tea all wetted and ready for the pair of us in her living room at the back of the bakery, and there we had our tea and toast with more holy pictures and statues than you could shake an aspergillum at, all of them looking down at us like they were dying with the hunger. Was there ever a fat saint? Anyway, there were maybe a half-dozen Sacred Hearts, not to mention statuettes of St Anthony and St Francis, one hooshing the Infant Jesus on to his shoulder and the other fondling a spring lamb. There were two Little Flowers, a St Sebastian pin-cushioned by arrows, and a model of St Catherine spinning on her wheel and labelled 'A Souvenir of Knock'. There was a picture of a child who, Maddie told me when I gawked, was Holy Nellie of Little God although I suspected that she got it arse about face and it was more likely Nellie that was Little and God that was Holy. There were photographs, a few of them with rosary beads hanging over the frames like scapulars.

'That's the canon,' Maddie said, pointing to the mantelpiece, and I saw the likeness of a man of sixty with a fine head of dark hair. 'Did you ever lay eyes on him?'

I told her that I had seen him a few times when Babs and me were new in Drane, but not for long enough to make an impression. The truth was that he had come up to me in the street with his hand outstretched and said: 'You're welcome in the town, and God bless you.' He kept his head tilted to one side, and I was told that he had been blown up as a chaplain in the first world war. I could have mentioned this meeting to Maddie Dignam, but by then I had formed an infatuation for fresh air. Her house was dirty.

The holy statues had never seen a duster; the little table where my mug of tea sat was fretting for a dab of polish, and there was not a clean saint in the place. Worst of all, there was a smell in the room, and it was not of new-baked bread but of mouse shite.

Maybe, I thought for a minute, the bakery was spotless at the expense of the sitting room; then I thought again that chance would be a fine and lovely thing. I looked at my watch, but before I could make an excuse to go, Maddie had a drawer open and was lugging out a fat copybook held shut by an elastic band. She put it on my lap and looked at me like an owl that had fed a mouse to its young and was waiting for a hoot of appreciation.

'What is it?' I asked.

'It's his bewk,' she said. 'The canon's bewk.'

I took a squint into it. It was the size of an accounts book, with slanty blue-black writing that was as easy to read as print, with every 't' crossed and every 'i' dotted. It took only the one look to know that what I was looking at was a class of a diary.

'And I'm no robber neither,' Maddie said.

Her voice was so angry that I said: 'I'm sure you're not.'

A few days after the funeral, she had been putting the presbytery in order. 'That Maggie McClure had it like a pig-sty,' she said, and I thought to myself, *You can talk*. She was in the main bedroom when the new priest's house-keeper came upon her and took her for one of the old ones of the town doing a bit of scavenging. Maddie explained herself, but the old rip, although in the wrong, would not climb down. 'There's no need for you here,' she said. 'Take what's yours, if anything is, and be off with you.'

I looked at the book on my lap. 'But what has this to do with me?'

'Bewks, bewks.'

'Excuse me?'

'Do you write them,' she asked, 'or don't you?'

'Well, I used to, now and again, but –'

'There you are, then. And you could make what's there into a proper bewk. Couldn't he?'

She spoke the last two words to the array of saints and blesseds, and it would not have surprised me if they had answered that yes, I could, and she was not codding.

I said: 'Excuse me, but I can't take this book. It isn't mine.'

'It's nobody's,' Maddie said. 'The canon hadn't a soul belonging to him except for that old brother that was a crust short of a fippenny loaf in Ballaghaderreen.'

'Then it must by rights belong to the diocese.'

'That lot!' Maddie said with disgust.

'Well, whoever owns them, it's not mine to take.'

I stood up and what was left of my cut of toast slid on to the floor. As I put it back on the plate, she said with a frown: 'You'll folley a crow for that yet.' Then in a softer and wheedling voice: 'You'll do it. You'll make a bewk of it. Say you will.'

I had been down this road many a time. It was like taking someone to a film and explaining what a director was, and I could spend until tomorrow was a fortnight telling her about publishers and the difference between me and them, and at the end of it she would be none the wiser.

I tapped the ledger. 'Have you read what's written in here?'

'Ah, sure it's like himself was,' she said. 'He was lovely.'

'But have you read it?'

'A prayer bewk,' Maddie said, closing the door on me, 'is enough reading for anyone.' All of a sudden she was on her feet and jovial. 'Now what you do is this. Take it home with you . . .'

'But –'

'Refuse me no refusals. You have a read for yourself of it, and then come back to me. Go on now, off you pop.'

She all but pushed me through the bakery and the shop and out into the street, squeezing my arm in her bony hand till it hurt, then clamping it tight on the book. I took it home with me as I was bid and put it in what we called the sewing room, deciding that there it would stay for a few weeks until I gave it back to her with some old cod of a yarn as to why it would not make what she called a bewk. And that would be the end of it. As for Babs, she was no more interested in Canon Turmoyle's memories than I was; what concerned her was the state of Maddie Dignam's bakery, and from then out she got our bread in Cussen's shop at the far end of Easter Street. It was baked by Johnston Mooney and O'Brien, and every day when their van arrived, pulled by a horse, it was followed by kids chanting:

> *Johnston, Mooney and O'Brien*
> *Bought a horse for one-and-nine.*
> *When the horse began to kick,*
> *Johnston Mooney bought a stick.*

From week to week I put the idea on the long finger of opening the door of the hot bread shop and facing Maddie again. Walking on purpose on the opposite side of Easter Street, I could see her serving her customers and my feet itched to step it out and get clear of her and away. I had a coward's imagination. I could see her coming after me. Then one day that was what she did.

'Mr Perry, I want you, if you please.'

I was cycling to the Robin Hood for a jar and a talk with Dermo Grace about the autumn programme for the film society. I looked and saw Maddie catching up with me on those long legs of hers that could outrun a horse, never mind a bike like mine that needed oiling. The back wheel locked and the tyres skidded. My head whirled with a rag-bag of excuses.

'Miss Dignam –'

'It's the mercy o' God I caught up with you. Have you that bewk I gave you?'

'Yes, I was going to call in and –'

'Set fire to it.'

'Excuse me?'

'Get rid of it before I'm destroyed, and yourself along with me. We're going to get gaol over it.'

She was as white as the bread she had made toast with. She put a hand on my shoulder to steady herself. 'Excuse me.' She stood there, swallowing to get her breath back and licking her lips for a drop of wetness to go with it. She was a woman of sixty and weak with fright.

'What is it? What's happened?'

'Father Chancey, that's what,' she said, 'and Father Luke. You remember Father Luke that was the curate?'

'The bishop took him,' I said.

'He's back,' she said. 'I had the pair of them beyant in the shop. They say that whoever took the canon's bewk out of the presbytery is a robber and will be put in gaol. They were leppin' with rage.'

The people that are dead and gone were afraid of three kinds of caller at the door. The first was a policeman who might disgrace you and yours for stealing sticks of firewood; the second was a doctor telling the world what was none of its business, that there was consumption in the house. The third – the priests, that is – were the worst of all. There was that double smell off them, of carbolic and God, and what was more, it was a God that had it in for you. I got over that kind of old rubbish, same as every other chiselur I grew up with, but once in a while the old fellow with the beard would sneak up on me in his bare feet, same as now. He was there for no more than a second, and I hunted Him, but he was as real as that capital H.

'Maddie, there's nothing in that book,' I said. 'The priests are only chancing their arms. Tell them to shag off.'

'Now you're saying a curse,' she said.

'Listen,' I said. 'I don't want the book, honest to God I don't. If you tell me to, I'll make a bonfire of it out in the yard. Will that do you?'

She had her mouth open to answer. Instead, she looked past me and said: 'Oh, jumpin' Jesus.'

I turned to look. In the Emergency, motor cars were so scarce that if you saw a black one you looked for a hearse in front of it; but one of them had pulled up across the road from Maddie and me. Even from where we were, by the harbour wall, I could make out a pair of Roman collars you could play hoop-la with.

I said, 'Isn't that –?' but Maddie was already half-way across Easter Street. The saying must be true that God never shut one door without opening another, for the door of the hot bread shop had not jangled and slammed before Father Chancey came out of the car with a smile on him that was the wrong size for his face.

He had a voice that carried. 'Mr Perry, isn't it? Can we have a word?'

I have never enjoyed being called out of my name in a public place. What was more, he stopped half-way across the street, obliging me to prop the bicycle against the harbour wall and cross over.

'We haven't met,' he said. 'Tom Chancey.' A scrubbed hand came out of the black sleeve. 'And I know you know Father Luke.'

They were a proper pair, both smiling. One smile was too big for the face it was pasted on, and the other too small, with yours truly trying to work out which was which.

'Will you sit in with us?' Father Chancey said. 'Just for a private word.'

Father Luke gave me a handshake of his own as I slid into the front seat beside him. His smell of soap was the same as Chancey's, only different; it was Lux, maybe, as befitted a bishop's bathroom. I was looking for fight and ready to take on the pair of them. Maybe it was because they had put a scare into Maddie, or it might have been because they were trying to put one into me.

'Not wishing to be rude,' I said, wishing to be rude, 'but I was on my way to an appointment.'

'Grand,' Father Luke said. 'And no more than ourselves. We're having luncheon with his Lordship.'

It was not so long ago, I thought, that the same Father Luke had called lunch 'dinner'. Howsomever, himself and Father Chancey seemed in no mad hurry to get the double-damask off the episcopal table and on to their laps, so they sat in the car for the town to see, teasing at me like dogs worrying a bone. I said nothing, and priests cannot abide a silence, so at last it came out that the new housekeeper, Mrs McCrum, had found Maddie Dignam not only upstairs in the presbytery but in the act of making off with certain property.

'Was it something valuable?' I said, all innocence.

'Oh, not at all!' Tweedledee said.

'Not worth tuppence!' Tweedledum said.

It was more, Tweedledee said, like a memento of the late Canon Turmoyle, R.I.P., but now it was not to be found, and Maddie Dignam was swearing black-was-white that she never clapped eyes on the notebook –

At this, Tweedledum gave Tweedledee a private look that told him to bite his tongue off or the bishop would do it for him.

'I mean,' Tweedledee said, 'it was only old rubbish. Page after page of scribbling and scrawling.'

'Oh, aye?' I said.

'Do you know, Father,' Father Luke said cosily to Father Chancey, 'I wouldn't be surprised if abstracting property from a priest's place of residence or –' and he gave me a hard smile over the rim of his starched collar – 'being in possession of same was not one of the reserved sins.'

'Begod, that's a thought to conjure with,' Father Chancy said to Father Luke.

'You gave me a kind of look just then,' I said.

'A look?'

'Well, I thought you did.'

They could have dropped dead with amazement. '*Us?*'

'I mean,' I said, 'what have I to do with this?'

Tweedledee smiled and said, 'Nothing,' and Tweedledum smiled and said, 'God forbid.'

Father Chancey said: 'Begging your pardon, but we saw you just now, yourself and Maddie. And the pair of you seemed to be very great.'

'Did we?'

'Well, so it seemed. Colloguing, dare one say?'

'Oh, dare away,' I said.

At least that got rid of the smiles.

'Now, now,' Father Luke said. 'Sure all we want is to clear the air.'

'Which let us do by all means,' Father Chancey contributed.

Father Luke took the ball and ran for goal. 'Not to hem and hee-haw about it, and to avoid any note of . . . ah –' And here he said a word that I would not presume to use myself, being only a self-educated man; but I would lay odds that 'acerbity' is not pronounced with a *k*. '– may we assume that the object of the little chat you had with Maddie was not about the property that is missing from the presbytery?'

I could have told the sanctified pair of them to feck off and assume whatever they liked, but at least there it was, out in the open for me to answer. And they were cute, I'll give them that much; they had looked at Maddie and at me, and they had us taped.

I said: 'Well, you see, my wife has a birthday coming up.' Which, if you think about it, is true of every person on God's earth.

'A birthday?' one of the Tweedles said.

'And I'm trying to persuade Maddie to make her a cake.'

'A cake?'

'With icing so thick you could skate on, and white flour.' Then I said to Father Chancey: 'I suppose you wouldn't oblige us with a few candles?'

I started off towards the Robin Hood, nursing the way I would tell the story to Dermo Grace; instead, curiosity took hold of me on the way and I did an about turn and went home to Carvel. 'What brought you back?' Babs said as I went past her, upstairs to the sewing room. I went through the canon's book with eyes that were dying of hunger, and at first it seemed that Fathers Chancey and Luke had been getting their soutanes in a twist for no reason. I told myself to have sense; there was nothing that a simple old priest could have writ down that was worthy of a prod from a bishop's crosier. Most of it was his life story and not in the least pass-remarkable, and then, while flicking through the last half of the book I noticed that that was when the diary began. It ended, I guessed, not long before the canon had his stroke.

Life in Drane was never as full of excitement as one of the folleyer-uppers at the Picture House, and the book was what you would expect: a cure for insomnia that was all pieties and prayers and accounts of local baptisms, weddings and funerals. It was of a sameness, except that on Saturdays the word *Confessions* was written in red ink. I took a quick look and looked again. The hair stood up on the nape of my neck. They say that a snake is not a cold creature like people make out; well, one that was made of ice came hissing up my back, and I felt its tongue.

Under that heading, *Confessions*, the canon had set down initials instead of names and then written details of sins, including how often committed, the penance given and his own comments. I read one of them and was not the better of it. Then I took another dekko at the initials: *R.R.J.C.* What was written kicked off with: 'Today, I was honoured – honoured to begin with, that is – when his Lordship on a visit to this parish to enjoy the sea air asked me to hear his confession. The experience quickly became one of profound sorrow and repugnance.'

I looked again at the initials. The *R.R.* stood for Right Reverend; the *J.C.* was for James Cootehill, and he was the Bishop of Mungret. I turned the page to put the rest of it out of my sight. I thought of hell and myself in it.

My eyes fell on another confession on the following page, and I could not help but see that it had been made by a *D.G.* I slammed the book shut. The snake was even colder and wetter and its hissing was angrier as I went off to keep my appointment with Dermo Grace.

Chapter Eleven

The Canon's Bewk (2)

There is an instrument called the celeste; it gives out the sound of bells, and when you hear it in a Warner Bros film you know that Bette Davis is heading for heaven. At two in the morning I was dreaming I was in a band and playing one of these yokes when Babs nudged me and said, 'There's someone in the house,' and the music turned into a serenade of broken glass, followed by the bang of the hall door and a bullying October wind.

'No, there isn't,' I told her, for I could hear the quick crunch of gravel and the sound of shoe-leather on the front steps. I got out of bed and went to the window. The street was dark and empty. Downstairs, there was a jigsaw of stained glass on the floor of the hall, and someone had reached in and undone the chain. The door was swinging open in the wind. 'Phone the police,' Babs said. 'I'll do my hair.'

Like forked lightning, a squad car arrived half an hour later. Both of the two Gardai were Corkmen. 'Oo're a great woman,' one of them said to Babs. 'Whatever oo did, oo musta put the fear of God into dem.'

'We didn't do a hand's turn,' Babs answered. Her paleness turned pink at the compliment.

The two policemen foostered for a while. One of them, a right Charlie Chan, gave his deducement that it was a ha'sh old night out. The first rummaged in his tunic pocket and found a card for a glazier in Ballybrack. The other one said: 'Most likely all it was was divilment. Young lads on deir way home from a hop.'

'There aren't any hops,' I told them.

'Well, on their way home from some do or other.'

'There aren't any dos.'

'And it a Saturda'? Dis must be a right kip of a town, so.'

They were gone, and Charlie never said: 'And the murderer is . . .' A Saturday, I thought. It had been the day for confessions at St Begnet's. I thought of people jamming the pews outside the confession boxes, bums banging into bums as they shifted on their knees towards absolution and heaven for sure certain; then the slide was pulled back and it was 'Bless me, Father, for I have sinned, it's been three months since my last confession, and I called me sister a bitch and me mother a rip.' I went back to bed shivering. When it comes to being a hero, then even in a bad light no one would mistake me for a Jimmy Cagney or a Humphrey Go-Cart. I was not two-fisted, but one-fisted, and that same fist was clenched now in the middle of my chest.

Babs said: 'I'm not the better of that.'

'I know. Go back to sleep.'

'I mean, what in God's name have we that anyone 'ud steal?'

'Thanks a heap, Babs.'

'You know what I mean.'

I did, and the thought of the canon's diary had strayed into my head and now sat there side by side – Tweedledee and Tweedledum again! – with the notion that someone had tried to throw a fright into the pair of us. Not that I had breathed a word to Babs about the book; she was no holy Mary any more than I was a holy Joe, but the thought of having the sins of the whole town under our roof to be looked at and dribbled over would have given her the habdabs.

Before long there was light in the sky. I heard the clunkety-squeak of oars in the rowlocks of the boats going past and knew that in the city next evening there would be lobsters on the tables at Jammet's and the Red Bank. I was ready for sleep because by then I had decided to make a parcel of the book and send it to Father Chancey from the post office at Bray where no one knew me. I would tip the wink to Maddie Dignam and, if she had the sense to keep that long gob of hers shut, it would be the end of it. Good, fine, splendid, as the fellow says in *Peg o' My Heart*.

The only thing that moved fast in Drane was bad news. I made what I thought was not a bad fist of glueing the broken glass to a piece of cardboard and wedging it into place – Babs, who was forever the hurler on the ditch, watched me and said, 'That won't stay.' Then I walked around to Jemima's for the Sunday papers, and P. Linehan said with one of his leering looks: 'I hear tell yous were robbed.'

'Not at all,' I said. 'It was hooligans.'

'That so? I thought they might have been after the crown jools.'

I said 'Ha-ha,' and promised myself that on the morning of the revolution he would be the first person to be put up against a wall. The consecration bell rang from the chapel; and on my way home the mass was already over, with the congregation out and coming towards me. You would take it for a regatta, with a fleet of the little yachts they called waterwags bobbing around a tall full-rigged ship, which was Maddie Dignam. I was delighted to see her. She came towards me with her prayer book held tight against the ironing board that was her front.

'Maddie . . .'

Her nun's eyes did not look at me. 'Go 'way from me.'

'What?'

'I was at the altar. Don't come near me.'

When a person said that they had been at the altar it meant that they had taken communion. They had knelt with eyes shut and mouth open like a baby bird; which signified in turn that they had been to confess their sins the day before, and in Maddie's case it meant that she had turned informer and dropped me head first into the Number One. Now in a state of grace, she was heading home to the hot bread shop with Jesus in one eye and her breakfast in the other.

I turned and trotted along beside her. 'Maddie, listen to me –'

'The divil's cure to you. Hoosh.'

There were people all around us with their eyes and ears out on stalks. The blue vein did a zig-zag down Maddie's forehead.

'Maddie, just tell me how the –'

'I'll tell you nothing. 'Twas all your fault, and I near damned me soul over you.'

'All I want is –'

'Ask me arse,' the holy communicant said.

Tall ship that she was, she spread a bit of extra sail and all but capsized tacking into Easter Street and out of sight. What puzzled me was me how Father Chancey knew or had guessed what was in the canon's book, and maybe the last person to ask was Maddie. A prayer bewk, she had said herself, was enough reading for anyone.

That afternoon, although all I could find was Christmas wrapping paper with Santas on it, I started to make a parcel of the book. While nosy by nature, I was as good as gold and did not give the pages as much as the flick of a thumb. Then Babs called to me from downstairs. The bits of stained glass had come unstuck from the cardboard and were blinking up at us from the tiled floor.

'I told you it wouldn't stay,' Babs said. 'Now it's bunched.'

I kept my temper, and rang the number the Garda had given me. A voice answered: 'Gerry the glazier, seven years' good luck guaranteed.' I started to explain myself.

The voice cut in on me. 'I'm sorry for your trouble, but do you not know today is a Sunday?'

I said: 'Yes, I do, thanks very much, but you see last night we had a burg–'

'And if you would read your catechism you would see the commandment about keeping holy the Sabbath Day –'

'Excuse me?'

'– and you would know that any sort of what is called unnecessary servile work is not only a sin but may be deemed a mortaller. And –'

I said: 'Look, would you kindly let me get a word in?'

'Oh, certainly.' Gerry the glazier was enjoying himself, and I was down the field and riding a three-legged also-ran. 'And what is the word you want to get in?'

'Go and fuck yourself.'

I slammed the phone down, all but breaking it. Babs stuck her head out of the kitchen. 'Is he coming?'

'No,' I said and put the wrong joke in the wrong place, 'but he's breathing hard.'

I went past her up the stairs, and for once she was speechless. Then I think I must have had a kind of blackout, for when I came to myself I was going through the pages of the canon's book, not reading it, you understand, but in a roaring red temper, the worst ever, cursing burglars and priests and policemen and glaziers. Like I mentioned, I am inquisitive – you could say it was my stock in trade – but I take my affidavit that I was neither looking for secrets nor finding them. I was turning pages, like a man counting a pack of cards. Then something did catch my eye. It was a solitary sentence: *Father Luke persuaded me to go to the pictures this evening.*

Well, there could be no harm in running an eye over *that*. I did, and what the Canon had written was:

The last film I saw was *The Life of the Little Flower*, which was all in the French language, but the words were set down in English at the bottom of the screen. I can vividly recall the bit where the dotey little child, Thérèse, said 'I hope that Papa will die,' and at this her parents were as cross as two sticks and fit to be tied, but then she said, 'Because then Papa will go to Heaven.' And the next thing you saw was her father laid out with the hands crossed on his chest and him stone dead. Well, more power to the child, I thought. I cried.

The picture I went to this evening with Father Luke was called *Thou Shalt Not Kill*, which was an American film, with people talking through their noses. It was all about a priest, and an actor by the name of Charles Bickford took a very good part. He hears the confession of a man who did a murder, but then an innocent man is arrested for it, and because of the Seal of the Confessional the poor priest does not dare to say a word.

By the mercy of God it all comes out right in the end, but the priest is nearly killed, and I must say that the film gave me food for thought. Next day, I could hardly read my Office for worrying. What if he had died and took his secret with him to the grave, as the expression has it?

It is fourteen years now since I came to Drane as the new parish priest and I have to say that at first I thought bad of his then Lordship, the late Bishop Mulhuddart, for sending me to such a parish. God forgive me, I thought him unjust. In my vanity, I believed that I deserved better than to be a – and the wretched creature I was deserves no better word – than to be an inmate of this sad and sorry town. And then God spoke to me.

As usual I had gone to Kattygollaher-and-Lugduff on the yearly pilgrimage to the top of what is a double peak of the same small mountain; even so it is not a patch on Croagh Patrick away off in Mayo, where the pilgrims must make the climb in their bare feet. However, on Katty-gollaher-and-Lugduff they must not only achieve the ascent in the month of February with their shoes and stockings off, but walk every step of the way backwards. It was bitterly cold, and the snow and the east wind were cutting the ears off me on the aptly named Lugduff when I heard God's voice as clear as clear, saying: 'You must carry out my divine will. I command you to tell the world how, even in a place as forlorn as Drane, the devil still holds sway. He works his evil will, and no soul is too common-place to be passed over by his net. I have chosen you, to bear witness for Me in this world, and for My part I promise to punish the evildoers with the fires of Hell in the next one.'

And so I knew what I had to do. For two years now I have been setting down the evidence that Satan is here, thriving amongst us in Drane. In so doing, I have broken no rule of silence, but the proof is here, whenever needed, that the devil walks abroad. I know that it was God who sent me to see *Thou Shalt Not Kill*, for when Father Luke and I left the Picture House the question was in my mind: 'What if you were to meet with an accident here on the street this very night? What if you were called to your mansion in Heaven and someone was to find your book and read it?' Well, God asked the question, and God provided the answer. And so I will do as He directs me. This very night I will write a letter addressed to my reverend successor in Drane and –

That was when Babs called me from downstairs. 'What are you doing? Are you going to be up there all day?'

I answered her with my breath in my fist: 'In a minute, in a minute.'

All I could think of was that the late Canon Turmoyle had had more than just the one slate loose; he was missing a whole roof-full. 'A saint in the making,' the Bishop of Mungret had called him at the funeral, and I thought to myself, *We'll see about that.* I put two blank pages into the typewriter and, out of habit, a sheet of carbon paper between them and copied down what I had read, my fingers hammering away like a whoor on a bank holiday.

Before I had rightly finished, the sewing-room door banged open and Babs was looking at me and at the typewriter. A smile came on her face. 'Don't tell me you're going back to work?' she asked, ready for a 'Yes' answer. Then she saw the canon's book.

'Perry, what are you doing?'

'Nothing.'

'Don't lie to me. You were typing.'

'Well?'

'What's going on I don't know about? Is that Maddie Dignam's book?'

'You wha'?'

In my foolishness, I turned the page as if to hide it from her, and of course there under my eyes was the page after it, with the confession that had the initials *D.G.* I had time to read: *The blackguard defied me and refused to name the woman,* then I slammed the book shut, shut for evermore, and looked stupidly at Babs.

'Perry, answer me.'

I told her all there was to tell and how I had been waylaid by the two priests in the car. The words spilled out of me.

She said: 'Is that why we had a break-in?'

'I dunno. Maybe.'

'And that old divil wrote down everybody's sins?'

'Well, not everybody's, no. The good ones.'

'The what?'

'I mean the bad ones.'

'And you were reading them? You know all about who did what?' She looked at the book. 'Oh, Sacred Heart, what am I married to?'

'I never read a single one of them,' I said. 'Honest.'

'You were copying them down. Don't deny it, I heard you typing.'

I said: 'I was copying this,' and showed her what I had typed. She gave me an uncertain look. I told her: 'It's all right. You can read it.' She dragged a chair over to where there was light. Halfway through, she broke off for long enough to look at me and say, 'Oh, my God.' She read the rest of it and let the page lie in her lap.

'You see?' I told her. 'He wasn't only cracked, he was *Loony Tunes.*'

'Amn't I nicely circumstanced?' she moaned.

'It isn't my fault,' I said. 'Don't pick on me.'

She said: 'What for do you want to go copying it?'

'Because I want to nail the old bugger.' I pointed at the page. 'And there's the proof.'

'Proof me elbow,' she said. 'How can it be proof when it's only typed? Why didn't you just tear the page out?'

'Because –' I took a few seconds to think. 'Do you know, it never occurred to me.'

'Give me patience,' she said.

She got up, fanned herself with the typed page and said, 'You stay here and don't budge.' She went out and shut the room door after her. There was no sound for a minute, then I heard her shouting, which in Babs's case meant that she was on the phone. She screamed goodbye, and when she came back I said: 'Why didn't you just open a window?'

'What's a beetle drive?' she asked.

'A what?'

'Whatever it is, it's on today and Father Chancey is in charge of it.'

'You ought to know by now that the P. P. is always the head buck cat. What were you phoning him for?'

She said: 'Go for a walk.'

'Beg your pardon?'

'It's a gorgeous day out. And be back here at half four. No later, mind.'

'Excuse me, but who put you in charge?'

'Do as you're bid.'

I did as I was bid. That was Babs; she was either a private or a general, and whatever was not a wedding was a wake. I walked to the harbour, sat on an overturned boat and talked to the fisherman who owned it. He was in his Sunday clothes, wearing boots you could see your face in, and a blue suit so shiny that it was ditto. After ten minutes of colloguing, me and him nodded goodbye, and I walked as far as Ravello Point, a place of rocks, crab grass and gorse where I sat with my back up against a slab of granite, and the sea and myself looked at one another.

'So what are we going to do about it? Will you answer me?' It was a woman's voice.

Sitting in a kind of gully where there was not a breath of wind, I must have dozed off. I looked at my watch. Half past three. I should have stood up, excused myself and flaked off across the rocks. Instead, a finger wagged inside of my head and told me that it wasn't small talk I was listening to. I stayed put.

She said: 'You might give a body an answer.'

'I'm thinking,' a man's voice said. 'I'm thinking.'

There was a silence. 'I thought,' she said, 'that we were supposed to have a talk.'

'We're having it,' he said. 'We're having it.'

'The trouble is,' she told him, 'that we're too ordinary. You aren't in anything dangerous like the polis, or the fire brigade, or maybe one of the lifeboat men.'

'What's that got to do with it?'

'Nothing.'

'Maybe,' he said, 'what you mean is that I ought to go and do the decent thing and get myself knackered. Thanks, Christine, thanks very much.'

She said: 'Don't be cross with me, Eddie. I'm only saying.'

Eddie said: 'Did you do what you said you'd do?'

'What was that, then?'

'Did you go to confession?'

'I couldn't,' Christine said with her voice begging him to have pity on her. 'Father Chancey 'ud read me off the altar. And I'd have to promise not to see you again. God, I'd hate to do that.'

At this there was a lot of short sucking sounds.

'Eddie . . .'

'What?'

'There's a fillum that's banned here. *Brief Encounter*, it's called. It's about this couple that's like you an' me are.'

'Do they go all the way?'

'Well, nearly. Same as us.'

'God.' Eddie said the name as if God was a bowl of oxtail soup put down in front of him.

'Only he goes off to the south of Africa. He's a doctor, do you see? And she goes back to her husband, who's an awful stick.'

'I can't go to the south of Africa.' Now Eddie's voice was on the rise. 'I'm not a doctor. I'm in the Gas Company.' To explain it properly, he said: 'People in the Gas Company don't go to the south of Africa.'

'Go on, tell the world, why don't you?'

'Africa, huh. All I can say is, it's well for some people.'

They said nothing for a while, and I wondered if they had gone. Then she said: 'And we can't run away together, the pair of us I mean, never mind about Finbar at home. Think about poor Mammy.'

It occurred to me, forgetting where I was, with my ears out on sticks, that girls in films who are circumstanced like Christine was circumstanced never seem to have mammies worth fretting about. Sometimes they have old fellows who get all obstreperous like the da in *The Barretts of Wimpole Street*, but need you ask, he was an old bags.

Christine said: 'I have to get Finbar's tea ready for him.'

'He does nothing but eat, that fellow,' Eddie said.

'Don't. It's a sin to laugh.'

There was a scrabbling of shoe leather on the rocks and then more sucking noises like a heifer in a bog. When I got up the nerve to look, I saw them. At least, I saw the backs of them. Eddie had white hair, but was young in his walk, while Christine by the build of her might see thirty again, but only on a hall door. He helped her over the rocks and let go of her hand when they got to the road. He waited to follow until she was ahead of him and around the first bend, out of sight.

I got back to Carvel on the blow of half-four, and Father Chancey was there ahead of me, drinking tea in the kitchen with Babs for company. He said, 'Ah, here's the man himself!' then stood up and produced a dead eel from his sleeve for me to throttle. The kitchen was a hothouse, with the Aga stoked up and roaring.

'I was just telling your good lady,' Father Chancey said, 'that you weren't the only persons interfered with last night.'

'That a fact now?'

'It is, then. Your neighbours, the Hoseys, were victims also. And another couple.'

He was telling us, covering his bum in case the subject came up, that whoever our housebreaker was, the parochial house had neither hand nor part in it. Babs excused herself and went out. To break the silence, I asked his reverence how the cockroach drive had gone.

'The beetle drive.'

'Oh, excuse me.'

'Not at all. Ah, God bless them, people are easily amused. They ought to be out of doors enjoying the last of the good weather. St Luke's summer, is that what it's called?'

I said, 'I thought the name for it was an Indian summer.'

'Ah, that would be the pagan appellation,' he said.

He was about to say more when Babs came back holding the canon's book. My heart did a lep. I looked from it to him, and the dead eel all but made a snap at it.

She said: 'Father, maybe you know what this is. A certain person forced it on my husband, and now he'd be glad to be rid of it.'

'I see.' Words were elbowing their way out of him. 'Ah, yes. Glad to be rid of it, yes. To be sure, to be sure.' He kept looking at the book. If you had a dust-pan handy, you could have swept up his eyeballs.

Babs said, as bare-faced as you like, 'We don't know what's in it, and we don't want to know, but when there was the break-in last night, we were wondering if it was to steal the book. Neither my husband nor I were worth our salt. We thought, maybe the book was worth something.'

'What? Not at all.' The sincerity was lapping over his collar like a spring tide.

'You're sure, now?' And Babs was as innocent as an unhatched egg.

'You have my word on it,' Father Chancey said.

'Oh thanks, Father. That's a great relief for us. And now the least said, the soonest mended.'

She picked up the kitchen poker and used it to flick open the window of the Aga. And it was only then I noticed that while I had been on my walk she had ripped off the binding of the canon's book so that all the pages were loose. It made them easier to burn; and I knew too why she had stoked up the stove. Father Chancey stood there and gawked at her as she shoved the book, bit by bit, into the Aga, and I have never seen a man, priest or layman, get such a lemoner. Inside a minute all she had left in her hand was the carbon copy of what I had typed, about what God said to the canon while he was walking backwards up Kattygollaher-and-Lugduff.

As for me, I had begun to think I was the Invisible Man, but Babs gave me a smile that you could spread on a cut off one of Maddie Dignam's loaves. She handed the sheet of paper to Father Chancey and said: 'This is for you, Father. As a souvenir.'

That evening, Dermo Grace was on the steps of the Picture House as usual, and the letters above his head spelled out *J. Cotten & T. Wright – Shadow of a Doubt – Dir. A. Hitchcock*. 'I hear tell it's great,' I said. 'One of his best,' Dermo said.

Try hard as I did, I could not shake the initials *D.G.* out of my head. There was sure to be a Declan Gallagher in the town or a Daniel Gleeson or a Denis Goode, but in my mind I kept seeing Dermo in his Jensen on one of his jaunts into town, and beside him feeling his leg there was a blonde bit of stuff I could not put a face on. 'Stop thinking about him,' I kept telling myself, but it was like saying, 'Don't think of penguins.' Only shut your eyes and they're waddling all over the kip.

As Dermo did his little back-step to the door to take our tickets he said: 'Come for a jar afterwards. At the hotel.'

'Something up?'

'More trouble in our native land,' he said. 'Babs, you'll come.'

Well, *Shadow of a Doubt* was great and gave Babs such a fright that she said she would never hum the *Merry Widow* waltz ever again. Afterwards, we walked to the Robin Hood, where the barman took our orders for drinks and asked us to wait for Dermo. Judge Garrity and his wife were already there at what was their usual table. After a few minutes the man himself came in. He said: 'Sorry for taking so long. I had to lock up my takings.'

As if it was a signal, Babs and Margaret Garrity began gabbing about Joseph Cotten in *Shadow of a Doubt*. 'Oh, when he looked out of the screen at you,' Mrs Garrity said, 'and talked about – what was it? – the "silly wives" –'

'Yes!' Babs said. 'And you knew that these were the poor women he had done away with!'

'Ladies, ladies,' the Judge said, to shut them up. Then, 'My dear Dermot –'

'Dermo.'

'Whatever, whatever. About this film society of yours . . .'

'What fillum society?' Dermo said.

'Oh, please, give me credit for a little intelligence,' the Judge said. 'Not to mention a little tolerance. Do you really think that Margaret or I would run to the authorities, and all because you chose to put on some silly film about the war?'

'I'm afraid you have the advantage of me,' Dermo said, cagey bugger that he was.

'Now look here. The world and his wife have known all about it this long while, and neither my own wife nor I has ever breathed a solitary word, until now. We have kept your secret, and with small thanks.'

Dermo said nothing.

'I'll not put a tooth in it,' the Judge said. 'The word around the town is that there is a brand-new film you intend to show. What now is the name of it? *Mrs Monaghan.*'

'*Mrs Miniver,* pet,' his wife said, shyly.

'And I'm being warned off, is that it?' Dermo asked.

The Judge laughed. 'My dear friend, we want to *see* it.'

'You what?' Dermo was flabbered.

'At least Margaret does. And I have to confess myself rather partial to that Miss Garson. An actress of great dignity, don't you think? Lady-like.'

'What's more, she's Irish,' his wife said.

'So I believe,' the Judge said. 'Northern Irish, however . . . the County Down.'

'There, now,' Mrs Garrity said.

'But surely you know that *Mrs Miniver* is banned here?' Dermo said. 'Because it's a war fillum. It's anti-German.'

'Oh, I daresay that Herr Hitler will survive,' the Judge said. 'We all of us remember how the *Skibbereen Eagle* declared that it was keeping its eye on the Czar of Russia. Well, I'm sure that the Germans will manage without the approval of the people of Drane.' It was his joke for the week, and he took out his handkerchief to wipe his eyes.

'Oh, Dermo, let us see *Mrs Miniver,*' Margaret Garrity said. 'Say you will. Do.'

She put her hand on Dermo's wrist, not on his sleeve but on the bare skin, with enough force to leave, just for a second, the white imprint of her fingers.

'There now,' the Judge said, smiling. 'You are even making my wife forget herself.'

Chapter Twelve

Love Laughs at Andy Hardy (1)

In the heel of the hunt there was no way to keep the Judge and his wife out of the film society. Babs sat with them in the residents' bar of the Robin Hood waiting for *Mrs Miniver* to begin, and I was next door keeping Dermo company while he threaded the 16-mm film – away from the Picture House he was his own projectionist. 'I'm going to get six months in the 'Joy over this bloody fillum,' he said. 'You'll see!'

Not expecting an answer, I asked him how he worked the hookery of getting banned films into the country. He made no bones about it. He said: 'The same way as I get sweepstake tickets *out* of the country.'

He was even chatty on the subject. Tickets for the Irish Hospital Sweepstakes were against the law across in Limeyland, and had to be smuggled from here to there to be sold in pubs and clubs and hucksters' shops. Dermo ran what you might call a clearing house. His contact was the chief purser on the Dun Laoghaire mailboat, and the next man along the line was a detective superintendent at Holyhead, and from him the tickets went to God knew where. The counterfoils came back the same way and ended up inside a drum on a stage in Ballsbridge, where a nurse turned a handle as if the yoke was a barrel-organ; only instead of 'The Good Old Summer Time' what came out was the names of horses.

'It's a nice little sideline,' Dermo said. 'And sneaking the odd fillum past the customs is no more than doing me a favour. And free of charge, would you believe? Mind, I could still be put in the clink for it, fillum society and all.'

'Not if you had Judge Garrity as a member,' I said.

'That's an idea,' Dermo said, sniggering. 'We could frame him.'

Mrs Miniver turned out to be such a winner that it had to be put on twice. When the Nazi airman jeered at Greer Garson and she slapped his face, people raised the roof and someone said, 'Good woman yourself!' At the end, when the little station-master, Mr Ballard, was killed in an air raid, buckets were shed.

When it was over, Dermo went off to lock up his can of film in the hotel safe, and Babs and me sat in the bar with the Garritys and held a kind of inquest. The Judge made a chapel roof out of his fingers and said: 'To my mind the film was without a doubt Allied propaganda, but it had restraint. I was not offended.'

I could hear Louis B. Mayer sighing with relief all the way over in Hollywood.

Mrs Garrity asked: 'And what did you think of it, Mr Perry?'

More for a joke than in earnest, I said, 'I thought it was a load of old codology.'

Babs clucked and said: 'Oh, Perry.' To the others, she said: 'Don't mind him.'

Mrs Garrity said: 'Oh, Mr Perry, surely not.'

'Well, let's say it was *entertaining* old codology,' I said.

'You thought the film inauthentic?' the Judge asked.

'That's a good word,' I said.

I got two looks, one from Babs, and another from the Judge that had six months in it without the option of a fine. 'Well,' I said, 'it was all a fake. I mean, the Minivers' parlourmaid was called Gladys and her boyfriend was Horace.'

'What of it?' his nibs said. His nose twitched, maybe because I was getting up it.

'Well, why in films do upper-class people – toffs, like – always have upper-class names? Greer Garson would never have been called Gladys, now would she, and can you imagine Walter Pidgeon being christened Horace? And the same Gladys wore a baldy old fox fur and said, "Ooo, ta, mum, ever so, I'm shoo-err!" and when Horace was offered a drink he said, "I don't mind if I do, and 'ere's my best respects to you, sir." '

'You have been in England, have you?' the Judge asked.

'Not yet.'

'Ah.'

'Mind, I will one day.'

'When?' Babs said, as if daring me.

'But I've met a few Limeys,' I said, 'and I never seen one of them pulling at his quiff and going, "Begging your pawrdon, mum",' any more than I ever heard an Irishman saying "Begorrah".'

'Do I detect a socialistic note?' the old bags said.

'Well, excuse me, Judge,' I said. 'I don't know what you detect and what you don't, but I'll bet there doesn't exist a village in England the likes of the one the Minivers lived in. At least not on this side of Culver City.'

'Of where, did you say?'

'It's where the MGM film studios are. And of course did you notice the name of the Minivers' cook? She was called Ada. And –'

'Now, Mr Perry.' It was Margaret Garrity digging a hole and putting the hatchet in it. 'Why don't we talk about something else?' And Christ, for a second I thought she was going to prod me on the wrist, the same as she had done with Dermo. Instead, she turned to her husband. 'James, tell them about our house.'

'A house? You found a house?' Babs was thrilled to bits. She gave me a look that said I had disgraced her.

'Well, it very nearly found *us*,' Mrs Garrity said. 'There was an old mansion above The Ramparts at the far side of the Point, and two months ago they pulled it down to make room for a tennis club. Six courts, isn't that so, James?'

Looks were flying. After our little set-to, the Judge was giving me one that stuck like a plaster and, as if he was sorry to see it coming loose, he said: 'I believe so.'

'And we persuaded them to let the old gate lodge stand and sell it to us,' his wife said. 'We bought it for – What is your expression for it, James?'

'For a rather expensive song,' the Judge said.

I looked at his wife and wondered how it felt to be living with W. C. Fields.

'It needs renovation,' she said. 'But Timothy –'

'Our son, you know', he said.

'. . . is getting the boys in his youth club to help him. He's doing a degree in classics, you know. And my goodness, already you would not recognise the place.' Her laugh tinkled at us. 'Leaps and bounds.'

'Bounds and leaps,' the Judge said, getting in another thigh-thumper.

'Your young lad is in a kind of a youth club?' I asked.

His look pitied me. 'Not *in* it, Mr Perry. There are leaders, you know, and there are followers, and Timothy is by nature one of the former. He is the Deputy Leader.'

The young lad's mammy was lit up with pride. I thought of her fingers – nice fingers, come to look at them – pressing Dermo's wrist and wondered again if it had been my imagination. Why had that bloody old canon not minded his interference instead of writing down initials that could have belonged to another D.G. altogether? In my fancy I had pictured Dermo in the Jensen with a blonde beside him – a woman I could see but not put a face on. Now it was different; there was a face, and it was Margaret Garrity's. She was a nice woman, not the sort who would carry on. And she was a lady, not like the kind that lived in Foxrock or Herbert Park: the jumped-up kind that had a smell of herself and was all fur coat and no drawers.

Annoying the Judge was too easy; I got tired of it. 'Would it bother you,' I asked him, 'if myself and Babs were to go out to The Ramparts and take a dekko? My da was a joiner, you know. He would often make a good fist of a job that a man with a degree 'ud turn his nose up at.'

One thing you could depend on about the Judge was that you never knew what way he would jump. Instead of taking offence, he said: 'Now in that, Mr Peregrine Perry, I would agree with you. My own father was a cabinet maker. So one could say they were brothers under the skin, eh? Yes, pay a call to The Ramparts by all means. I'm sure Tim would be delighted.'

It was then that Dermo came in, off duty and ready for his jar. I could not help but watch him and Margaret Garrity like a hawk, but they might hardly have been in the same room. One time, when he asked her about her favourite film, she said: *The Song of Bernadette.*

He said: 'Well, if you'd like to see it again, Mrs G., I might show it at the Picture House. By public demand, you know.'

'That would be lovely,' she said. Then she went red. 'Mind, if I had a choice –' and her voice went down to a whisper '– I'd rather see that new film, *Casablanca*.'

We all laughed, even the Judge.

Next day after school-time, myself and Babs got on our bikes and went to look at the gate lodge at The Ramparts. It was a mile and a half from Drane, and a couple of trees had been felled to give a view of Killiney Bay, with Bray Head, the two Sugar Loafs and the strand at Shanganagh. It was a snug class of a house; right for three but tight for four. A couple of builders were turning two rooms into one and a plumber was working in the bathroom. The Garritys' son, Timothy, was overseeing seven or eight young lads from the national school. They were doing harmless jobs, putting on dabs of paint and slathering Polyfilla into cracks. Timmy's name for them was 'Men' and 'Gang', except for one dark young fellow he called Leo. Leo's eyes were such next-door neighbours that they all but over-lapped; you looked twice in case he had only the one instead of a pair. With the other lads he was the hurler on the ditch, giving orders and doing bugger-all himself. I was put in mind of your man, Tom Sawyer, letting on to the kids that whitewashing a fence was great gas, so that they all paid him to be let have a go.

'Leo is my Number One,' Timmy told me.

I said to the two builders: 'Well, I see you're not short of little helpers.'

The men turned their eyes up.

Next thing, Margaret Garrity appeared out of nowhere, like the Blue Fairy in *Pinocchio*. She had been in the kitchen, making tea for the builders and the plumber on a primus, and there was lemonade for the kids and thick slices of barm brack and gur cake. 'Very nice,' I said and she answered that the workman was worthy of his hire.

'And he's takin' us to the pitchers,' one of the kids said.

'For a treat, next Saturday morning,' Timothy said. 'Mr Grace is putting on a special double feature.'

'What is it, let me guess,' I said. 'I know! A Gene Autry and a Hopalong Cassidy.'

A couple of the kids laughed, and one of them, a right little get, said, 'Eh, wouldja ever go and –'

The one called Leo gave him a hard punch on the arm. The kid said: 'That hurt.' Timmy gave no sign that he had noticed. I looked at this one-and-a-half-eyed Leo; he faced me down, and I faced him back. Not being a da myself, I can take kids or leave them, but a suitable place for little gurriers is in a sack and under water.

'Mr Grace gave me a list of films,' Timmy said, 'and then we did it the democratic way. I mean, I picked the second feature, and the gang here voted for the big picture. Hey, kids, let's hear it for *Love Finds Andy Hardy*.'

The boys came out with the kind of jeering heave you would hear in a picture house whenever Ireland was mentioned.

'And what was the other one?' I asked. 'Break it to me.'

Leo grinned and said: '*Angels with Dirty Faces*.' A different kind of cheer went up.

Well, that was not too bad, I thought. There was a bit of *bang-bang, yer dead* in it right enough, but the bully – Bogart, who else? – got the works in the end, and God came out on top. Good old God.

When the tea things had been cleared away, myself and Babs cycled back to Drane, and Timothy gave his mom, as he called her, a lift home on the crossbar of his bike. She created a to-do about it, saying that people would look at them.

'What about it?' he said. 'You're my best girl.'

She made a pretend slap at him and said, 'Timmy.'

He said: 'Well, aren't you?'

I looked at Babs, but something or someone on the peak of the Sugar Loaf across the bay was getting all her attention. Mrs Garrity sat sideways on the crossbar of her son's bicycle with her arm around Timmy's waist, and they went wobbling down the White Rock Road ahead of us. When the hill got contrary and went up instead of down we got off and walked our bikes.

Timmy said, 'Sir . . .'

It took me a few seconds to cop on that I was being talked to. I said, 'Present.'

'Do you mind if I ask if you have ever seen *Angels with Dirty Faces*?'

Babs laughed. 'Ask him if he sees his face when he's shaving.'

Timmy said: 'You see, it's new to me, and I was wondering if it was suitable for kids. I mean, seeing that in a way I'm responsible.'

'Are there really angels in the film?' Mrs Garrity wanted to know.

'Well, no,' I said, 'I wouldn't go that far.' I told her and Timmy the gist of it. 'James Cagney is this gangster, you see, and –'

'A gangster,' she said, not best delighted.

'And his best friend is Pat O'Brien, who's a priest. And there's a gang of boys – street kids who live in the slums and think that the sun shines out of Cagney. He's their idol. They want to do like he does and be tough guys. And he eggs them on. Only he has this falling out with Humphrey Bogart and he shoots him and gets sentenced to the chair.' At this, Margaret Garrity smiled at me and, thinking she might ask if it was an armchair or just a fireside, I said: 'No, the electric chair.' She said 'Oh' again.

I said: 'But Pat O'Brien visits him in his cell and asks him not to set a bad example to the boys. "Rocky," he says, "when they take you to the hot seat I want you to pretend to be afraid. For the good of their souls I want those boys thinking you died a coward. When the executioner pulls that switch and turns on the juice –"'

'For God's sake,' Babs said, 'do you need to make a breakfast, dinner and tea of it?'

'I'm trying to tell a story,' I said, 'and I'm trying to tell it proper.'

'And what happens?' Timmy wanted to know.

'Well, when the time comes,' I said, 'what does Cagney do but start screaming, "I don't wanna die. Oh, please, Warden, don't kill me. I don't wanna die!"'

'He's off,' Babs said.

'And next day all the papers have what they call banner headlines saying, ROCKY DIES YELLOW.' Then, quick before Mrs Garrity had time to ask if being electrocuted made you change colour, I said: 'But you never know for sure if Cagney was really a coward or was putting on an act to oblige Pat O'Brien and teach the lads that being a gangster is only a mug's game. It's left for you to decide.'

Margaret Garrity gave a shudder and let out an 'Ugh' sound to go with it. Timmy said: 'But, Mom, I call that a very moral ending, don't you?' To me, he said: 'Thank you, sir. I really am obliged.'

By now, the road had levelled out; we were in the town with people around, and Mrs Garrity said in earnest that she would prefer to walk rather than climb back on the crossbar. Out of politeness, Babs and myself kept her company while Timmy went ahead on his bike. He was doing his hop, skip and leg-over when it occurred to him to stop and ask: 'Oh, sir, while I think of it, a few of us were wondering if you would find time to give a talk in aid of the youth club.'

Before my jaw could hit the ground he said: 'Any subject you like.'

I said: 'I never give talks. Sorry.'

'Sir, I should explain –'

'Never have done, never will do.'

'. . . that it would be in the nature of a public lecture, at the Picture House with a charge for admission. Maybe "Fifteen Years of Talking Pictures".'

I shook my head, and Babs said, 'Don't be so disobliging.' Then, to Timmy, as if I was somewhere else: 'The bitter pill again. He's always the same.'

Margaret Garrity put her hand on my wrist, but without a prod from a finger, and said, 'Say you will.'

When Babs and me got home the door was no sooner shut than she said: 'I noticed that you said yes when *she* asked you.'

'I didn't say yes,' I said. 'I gave no answer whatsomever.'

'No answer counts as a yes.'

There was no pleasing some people. She gave me damn all credit for the stage fright I would go through or the lying awake every night for a week thinking of rows of faces looking up at me like mackerel, gutted, cleaned and waiting for the pan. And if I did give the talk, it would not be to oblige Timmy's ma, but the lad himself. God, but he was keen. He was tall and lean and scrubbed and with not a bad tooth in his head, and hair that was – and excuse me for showing my frilly knickers – the colour of the strand at Killiney. There was goodness in him, and another quality as well that kept dancing out of my reach. When you looked at him, and I tell no lie, you as near as dammit said a prayer that the world would never get at him.

Inside of a week he had a photo of me – God knows how come by – on display in half the shops in Drane. There I was, fifteen years younger, wearing a collar with the front stud showing and looking out at the world from the box office of the Picture

House, the reception desk of the Robin Hood and the glass door of Jemima's. Going for the paper in the morning, I saw myself surrounded with snapshots of lost dogs and cats and cards – there were three of them – all advertising double-sized bedsteads for sale, second-hand.

That started me off. It reminded me that in American films it was not allowed to show double beds. Like I had told the Judge the time he was giving out about immoral films, the studios had to abide by what could be seen and what had to be kept out of sight. You could not show stocking-tops or underwear or garters, and it was beyond the beyond to have two people kissing with their mouths open instead of sealed as tight as a court order. And somewhere up high on that list was double beds.

There had been a film called *It Happened One Night*, and when Clark Gable took his shirt off and showed that he had only his skin on under it, the upshot was that the sales of vests took a header. The question slid into my head: in Drane were people doing the same thing, mimicking the pictures by swapping their double beds for singles? I looked at the three 'For sale' ads and asked myself if they might not be part of a fashion. The cards that were sticky-taped to the glass of the door had box numbers instead of names and addresses.

'Are you thinking of buying a doubler?' P. Linehan said. He had come out of the shop folding my paper and was standing in the half-open doorway. He had had another heavy night; it was early yet and his watery blue eyes were taking their first snapshots of the town and its begrudgers.

'Would you be interested,' he said in a drawl, 'in bedsprings with a bit of bounce in them? Mind, I would have thought, that by now you and your good missus might have worked your way up to – what is it they call them? – four-posters.'

'We did that long ago,' I told him, 'but the pair of us kept breaking them.'

I took my paper and walked away. Not to be diddled out of

having the last word, he called after me: 'I'll tell the advertisers that you'll be in touch.'

'Maybe you'll be treated to a nice lunch,' Babs said.

'Yeah, at the Russell, maybe, or Jammet's.'

'God, but you're a right misery.'

'The fellow I'm to meet – Fitz whatever it is – is probably a chancer.'

'Then what for do you want to drag all the way into town?'

'Because, because. I'm beginning to forget what it looks like.'

She asked: 'Will I do you a sandwich? If the day clears you could sit and have it in the Green.'

'No, thanks. I thought I'd go to the Goodwill.'

She made a face. '*That* place?'

'Well, there's a bit of life in it.'

She watched while I put a copy of my banned book, *The Gramophone on the Grass*, into my briefcase. She said: 'I think he's right about it making a great play. I always liked it.'

'I told you. I think he's a –'

'– a chancer. You said. Just like you're never done giving out that you'll do no more writing. Now all of a sudden you can't wait to get mixed up in more of it.'

'That's not true. I –'

'I know. You want to see if the Liffey is still there.'

Putting in her prate where my work was concerned was not Babs's style, and all I could think of to say was: 'I don't want to miss the train.'

Now that she had started, there was more. She said, straight out: 'I'm an awful bloomin' grouch. I know I am. I bite your head off, Perry, and I don't mean to. I blame this place. Moving out of the Widow Gamble's Hill was a mistake. And you were wrong to give up your work and I was wrong to let you.' I looked at her, and she said: 'I'm just saying. Now go for your old train.'

Now it had been dragged into the open. She had no liking for Drane any more than I had, but it was thanks to her that it was out now, ready to be talked about. Later, maybe. No, not maybe; later for sure. I nodded and went for my old train.

The chap I had arranged to meet in town was called Fitzgerald and, whatever else, he was not a chancer. He was young with a chin so sharp it would cut you, and a brain to match. He talked umpteen to the dozen and said that there was a play buried deep in *The Gramophone on the Grass* and I was the one to mine it. When I told him that I had promised myself never again to write a play or a book, he laughed and said that the whites of my eyes were brown. While I was working that one out, he told me that I would write it and he would produce it. In those days there was no such thing as a director of plays; if you wrote one and needed someone to make an utter balls of it, you called him a producer.

Next thing, Fitz and myself were shaking hands on it. We had a pint, not in Neary's because I thought of Paddy Kavanagh, and not at the Shelbourne because it was there that I had met poor old Hansy, but in Davy's; then we had a second handshake and a second pint, and I walked down to the Goodwill restaurant to have my lunch.

It was in College Street, opposite Trinity. There were no tablecloths and the waitresses all but threw the knives and forks down the long tables. They called you 'love' and their 'old segotia' and served you your lunch with 'Get that down you.' What you ate was plain and nourishing, and the Irish stew was the best gristle south of the river. There were benches to sit on instead of chairs and you needed to do the high jump to get over them. I squeezed in and found myself facing Timmy Garrity across the table.

He was not overjoyed to see me, and the reason was sitting next to him. She was fair-haired and might have been a year older than he was. One day she would be a nice piece of stuff. And some girls have a certain look that they wear like a brooch or a badge; it tells you things about them; not everything, maybe, but enough. Not her, though; at least not yet. When I said hello, she looked away from me and at him as if I was something not to be stepped in. He introduced us.

'Mr Peregrine Perry . . . Orla McAdoo.'

I smiled at her and she gave me a look that said I needn't have bothered.

I asked him: 'How did *Angels with Dirty Faces* go?'

He said: 'Great. It was great.'

'Terrific ending, what?'

He gave me a wink and a thumbs-up.

'And hey,' I said, 'what about your man Cagney? And that lingo of his. "Hello, Faddah . . . whaddya hear . . . whaddya say?" Did you know that he picked it up on the streets of New York, when he was a kid?'

Orla asked me: 'Were you ever in Jammet's?'

'Excuse me?'

'Jammet's the restaurant. It's the last word, so I hear. Only a few yards from here.'

'Is that so?'

'Turn right out of here and then left. You ought to go there,' she said.

'Yes, well, I've been a couple of –'

'Like now.'

I started to get up from the table. 'No, no,' Timmy said. 'Stay. It's past Orla's lunch hour.'

She said: 'No it isn't.'

The pair looked at one another, and I stayed where I was, standing crooked with the edge of the bench twisting my legs into a hairpin. Now she was showing that brooch I had looked for, only it was in the voice and not the look. I am a Dub and I talk a Dublinese you could cut with a blunt knife, and never mind that she had the kind of accent that shouted out the Five Lamps, or Irishtown or the Coombe. No, with that one it was not the words she spoke, but the colours that showed through them.

Timmy told her: 'Mr Perry is the gentleman who will be giving the talk at the Picture House.' To me he said: 'Orla will be doing the box office. She's a great help to us.' The look on his face begged her to flake off. 'And you met her brother, Leo. He's my Number One out at The Ramparts. A great worker.'

Jesus, I thought.

'A Trojan,' he said.

Mary and Joseph, I added.

Orla said: 'I'll see you later. At the place.'

She gave him a look that stayed after her. I sat down again.

Timmy said: 'Orla is the best in the world, Mr Perry. One of a kind.'

'Oh, I'm sure,' I said.

'She's a bit rough. Hasn't had the advantages, so she's a bit shy with strangers.' He gave the door a look that begged her not to come back through it. 'I wonder if I might ask you for a favour.'

I was already ahead of him and out of sight. 'Ask.'

He leaned across the table. The waitress said, 'Hey up, lads,' and a plate of oxtail slid between us on its way to a man in a hard hat.

'My dad is a great man. I mean that. A truly great man, sir. A prince.'

'Got you,' I said.

'I can speak to him on any subject. For as long as I can remember – in fact, sir, since I was knee-high to a grasshopper – we have had man-to-man talks.'

I had a picture in my mind of Mickey Rooney – even though Timmy could have given him a good six inches – getting all his problems solved by his da, Lewis Stone as wise old Judge Hardy. In fact, the two judges – Hardy and Garrity – always kept the same tight grip on their lapels. There should have been violins playing, but the only music in the Goodwill was the man in the hard hat working on his oxtail.

'And, sir, if I ever amount to anything, it will be because of what I have learned from Dad. I guess he's just about the wisest man I know. But he and I come from different generations. Nowadays there are things he might not understand.'

I said: 'Such as . . . ?' and nodded my head towards the door of the Goodwill.

Timmy said: 'Such as Orla. Gosh, sir, you're pretty wise yourself.'

'Just a wild guess,' I said. I kept thinking of Orla's brother, the One-eyed Reilly.

Timmy said, very earnestly: 'Not that Dad is a snob, not in a million years; no, sir! But he and Mom . . . they might think that maybe Orla was . . . well, that she wasn't our sort. They've made so many sacrifices for me, you know. And I'll bet they think I'm too young to . . .' he blushed, '. . . to be going steady. So gosh, Mr Perry, be a sport.'

He reached across the table and caught hold of me by the wrist. Like mother, like son.

'Sir, please don't tell them that you saw Orla here with me today. Don't snitch, huh? Don't spill the beans.'

People were looking at the young lad and the middle-aged nancy-boy. I took my wrist back and said: 'It's none of my business.'

He said: 'Jiminy Cricket, thanks. I'll never forget you for this. Nor will Orla. You just wait till you get to know her better. And Leo. He's terrific.'

At The Ramparts, it had occurred to me that Timmy had two qualities, and one of them was his goodness. The other quality had not been so easy to catch hold of, but now I had it. The lad was a fool.

Chapter Thirteen

'Love Laughs at Andy Hardy' (2)

Before I go on with what happened to young Timothy Garrity, I should mention Ben Moone, who, if he was not the only doctor in Drane, was beyond any argufying the drunkenest. He was rarely seen in a state of advanced ossification; if he was ever indisputably in the jigs it was at home and within the decency of four wallpapered walls; but in public a daily drink or two, judiciously spaced, was enough to keep him topped up. He was a widower and a bird-alone. He drove a car that he had crashed four times and written off twice. It was so decrepit that in the town it was known as the Accident.

He rarely missed an evening at the Picture House and had his regular seat on the side-aisle where he could be rooted out in case of an emergency. He sat there hugging his bag of tricks on his lap like a woman breast-feeding an infant and lapped up whatever film was on. Once he was sufficiently oiled he liked nothing so much as a good cry; even Mickey Mouse and Goofy would start him off.

Thomas Mitchell was his favourite actor, and the Doc, as he liked to be called, would unfailingly poke his red nose into the box office to ask the cashier, Miss Lally: 'Does the fillum have Tommy Mitchell in it?'

'I have it worked out,' Dermo told me once. 'It all began with *Stagecoach*. Best cowboy fillum ever made.'

'True for you,' I said.

'And the bold Thomas Mitchell was in it, smacking his lips the way he does and being as real as the man living next door to you.

He was great in *Stagecoach*; they ought to have given him an Academy Award.'

'They did,' I said.

'Did they, so? Well, more power to him. And in it he was taking the part of this doctor that was forever so maggoty drunk that he was being run out of town. So he was on the stagecoach, have you me?'

I wanted to remind Dermo that I knew the film frontwards and backwards, but there was no stopping him; you might say that he had the reins of the stagecoach between his teeth. 'And when this woman passenger was having a baby, Thomas Mitchell, pissed and all as he was, swallowed a gallon of black coffee, did an upchuck, then delivered the kid, and it was a girl. Not only that, but later on there was a sudden *whhhhoosh!* and the little whiskey salesman –'

'Donald Meek,' I said.

'– got an Apache arrow driv through him. So what did the bold Thomas Mitchell do but shoot at the Indians with one hand – *khirr! khirr!* – and pull the arrow out with the other.' (This bit was news to yours truly.) 'And listen, the first time I showed that fillum I heard a snuffling from the soft seats near the back, and I saw Ben Moone taking a wad of cotton wool out of his doctor's bag to dry his eyes with.'

'He thought *Stagecoach* was sad?' I asked. 'Get off.'

'Sad my royal Irish backside. In his mind he thought he was Thomas Mitchell. What's more, he still thinks it.'

'You're raving,' I said.

'Maybe somebody is raving, but don't look at me. Listen. No, don't laugh. I know you well enough now to give you a puck for yourself.'

'Go on, then.'

'So there's two doctors, right? One up on the screen that's called Boone, and another sitting in the tip-up seats by the name of Moone. Boone and Moone, like.'

'Well?'

'And on top of that there's a definite resemblance. Now don't say there isn't.'

'Same build, maybe,' I said.

'For God's sake, man, the Doc is the spit of him. But wait, I didn't tell you the best bit. The evening after *Stagecoach*, I was showing *Only Angels Have Wings*. And the Doc comes up to the box office and – just by the way, you know – asks, "Is there anyone any good in it?" "Cary Grant," I tell him. "And your woman, Jean Arthur, and Thomas Mitchell and –" With that, he gives a buck jump and says "Tommy Mitchell? Oh, begod, we'll have one-and-thruppence worth of that!"'

'Everybody has favourites,' I told him. 'We all do.'

'That's the exact same word I used to him,' Dermo said. '"Thomas Mitchell," says I. "Is he your favourite?" And with that he taps me hard on the chest as if I was a patient of his and one more clean shirt would do me. "There are people in this kip of a town," he says, "that take a man's character because he is partial to a few quiet, harmless jars. 'Pissed again,' they say. Well, Tommy Mitchell showed them what was what. In that fillum, *Stagecoach*, he proved conclusively that in certain cases" – and he tapped his own chest this time and all but knocked himself over – "a drop taken in moderation can elevate competence into what you might call genius. Nay, artistry!" And at that he clapped his hands and was Tommy – I mean Thomas – Mitchell to the life.'

'Well,' I told him, 'God send that I never get sick in this town.'

And I didn't, but Babs did. During that first winter in Drane, she had a fall in the kitchen and cut her head.

'I tripped,' she said.

'No, you didn't,' I told her. 'I was looking, and you fainted.'

There was nothing for it but to call up Doc Moone. He answered at the first ring, and when I heard him say: 'Whash up?' I thought: *Oh, Christ, he's peluthered.*

I had seen him only two evenings before at *Kings Row*, and when the gurriers in the wooden sixpennies jeered at Ronald Reagan when he reached for his missing legs and cried out,

'Where's the rest of me?', the Doc stopped his sobbing for long enough to stand up and shout: 'Shut up, you gang of moronic whelps!'

He was with us inside of half an hour. A smell of whiskey came into the hall and took a right turn up the stairs with himself chasing it, and me in third place. I told him that Babs seemed to have taken a weakness. 'She just —'

He said: 'That was a good fillum the other evening. And didn't whass-his-name, Claude Rains, make a great doctor, what?'

'So I put her to bed in case —'

'Did you cop on to the old chat that came out of him? "I seem to be in a vein," says he, "of epic grammatic sententiousness." Jesus, I couldn't shay that if I wash cold sone stober.'

He all but put his fist through the bedroom door with a knock. Babs was in bed, under the covers and wearing a slip. One of her eyes was half closed; the other was big with fright at the sight of him. The cut was across her right eyebrow and by now the bleeding had stopped. 'Well, no problem there,' the Doc said. 'We'll put a stitch in it.'

All I could think of was that in the state of him he might staple her to the mattress. 'Now what about this weakness of yoursh?'

'Tell him the truth,' I told her.

She said: 'I don't know. One minute I was putting a casserole in the oven, and next thing I was on the floor.'

'Can you get to Austria?' the Doc said.

I thought she would add a second faint to the first. She said, 'Excuse me?'

'For there's only the one doctor who can save you,' he said, 'and he's in Vienna.'

Vienna was another bit out of *Kings Row*. To show that he was joking he gave her a smile and hummed a bar of a Strauss yoke – *Roses from the South*, I think – and then turned to me and pointed a stubby Thomas Mitchell of a finger. 'I want a drop of lukewarm water, if you please. And then stay clear. I have to put this lady through her catechism in private. Never fear, we'll get her to Lordsburg, and the baby with her.'

As I closed the door, he was saying: 'We'll get that bit of hemstitching over and done with, and it won't leave a mark on you. But tell me, did j'ever see *The Bride of Frankenstein*?'

The whiskey fumes apart, he had a great bedside manner. When I next clapped eyes on Babs, she was wearing sticking plaster and cotton wool and was all smiles.

'Your wife,' he said, 'is a cashulty of this bloody war.'

'Excuse me?'

'No protein in her diet, whish is why she's falling out of her shtanding. The woman is starving herself. I've made out a prescription for beef extract and a tonic. And can you get Bovril and Marmite at Cushen's?'

'At Cussen's? He keeps it for special customers.'

'Then fuck him,' the Doc prescribed and turned to Babs with 'Pardon my Irish, ma'am.' He said that he would talk to Mr Cussen, ordered her to stay in bed until he came to take another look at her, and told us that he would see himself out. We heard him fall on the stairs.

It was because of the Doc that Timmy Garrity is still for all I know in the land of the living. Bear with me.

Less than a week after meeting young Timmy and his mott, Orla McAdoo, in the Goodwill, I was at work and as happy as Larry, turning *The Gramophone on the Grass* into a play. It was going well; the more so because Babs and me had sat down to have our talk and it was two-nil for clearing out of Drane and finding a place nearer to town. I found a snug house for sale on Vavasour Square where on a Saturday you could hear the roars of the crowd at Lansdowne Road. We got an order to view, and Babs was mad for it. The stone in the shoe was that we needed to sell Carvel to a muggins who was as thick as we had been when we bought it. It was a lobster pot of a house: getting into it had been a pudden; getting out was like herding mice at a crossroad.

Babs asked: 'Could we not move and take out one of those what-you-may-call-'ems?'

'Do you mean a bridging loan?'

'And sure maybe we could get rid of Carvel in a month or two?'

'A year or two more like,' I said.

That kept her quiet, but she fretted. We advertised the house for sale, but the name of Drane was like a magic wand; you had only to wave it at a buyer and he melted. 'The good news,' I told Babs, acting Job's comforter, 'is that the house on Vavasour still has the *For Sale* sign up.' It was true; what with the war and all, money was only a rumour; you could have bought the whole country for the tosser we hadn't got.

M. J. Mulrooney, the same estate agent who had sold us Carvel, put a *For Sale* sign up in front of the house, and when we went to the pictures that evening, Dermo said, 'I see you've had your fill of us.'

'Excuse me?'

'They say you're on the move.'

'Oh, that. Easier said than done.'

He said, 'Well, I suppose you think you can do better for yourself.'

Maybe there was English blood in me and I was born guilty. Before I could go red he had turned his back to us to talk to another patron. I said: 'Come on, Babs, we'll go home.'

By the time we were at the foot of the Picture House steps, Dermo was after us. 'Hey, what's up?' He gave one of his grins. 'Know something? You take things too personal.' He was not peeved at us, only upset.

Long threatening comes at last, and so starved were the people of Drane for a crumb of diversion that the tickets for my talk were selling as if John McCormack was coming to sing *Panis Angelicus*. The prospect of standing in front of a packed audience had me in such a lather of funk that I went for walks at night-time, speechifying to hedges and sermonising to stone walls. People crossed the road when they met me.

On the evening before the talk there was a new moon that took the curse off the blackness and I sat for a while until the wet grass of the White Rock field told me to feck off home. My road took me past The Ramparts, and I saw the wink of a candle in one of the windows. The first thought I had was that Timmy Garrity and his 'men' were putting in a bit of overtime; the next was the idea of sticking my head around the door, and saying 'God bless the work', like an Old Woman of the Roads in an Abbey play. So I did; at least I went in, saw that the light was coming from under the living-room door, pushed it open and got as far as the 'God bless'.

There were two people lying on the floor; at least she was on the floor and he was lying on her with his backside pumping like a fiddler's elbow. At the sound of my voice, he sat up, and in the light of the candle, faint as it was, I saw that he was the one-and-a-half-eyed Leo. The girl lifted herself on the heels of her hands, and there was hardly a stitch on her. She said, and it was more of a scream: 'Who are you? What do you want? Fuck off.' There is a saying about not recognising your butcher at the opera, so it took me a second to see that she was Orla McAdoo.

I think that what I said was: 'Oh.' Then, 'Sorry.' Then, for the big finale, 'Excuse me.'

I went out, slowly as far as the front door, then fast, down the hill. Before I saw the lights of the Robin Hood between me and the town, I heard footsteps hurrying to catch up with me. Sooner than let Leo come at me from behind, I turned to face him. I said: 'Don't try anything.'

'Try what?'

Dark as it was, I could see that he was grinning. He fell into step alongside me. He said: 'Listen, head. You don't want to go carryin' tales, right? I mean, you don't want to get the girl into trouble, now do you?'

'*Me*?' The nerve – no, the wickedness of him – made me want to scream, and maybe I did. '*Me* get her into trouble?'

He said, 'Hey, hey, turn it down.'

He was small; one good hoosh could have lifted him over the granite wall next to us, with the railway line below, the same as one good clout of his fist south of the border could have burst me. I was faint from the shock of what I had seen at The Ramparts. My teeth were chattering. He said: 'Hey, what ails you?'

I said: 'That kid is your bloody sister.'

'You what?'

'And you're going to end up in gaol, and the divil's cure to you.'

'Me sister . . . who says?'

'Well, isn't she?'

He said: 'How would you like a belt in the snot, your dirty oul' get? Jasus, that's a good one . . . That's a howl. Orla, me sister!' I saw the white of his face come close to mine in the dark. 'She's an effin' nurse child.'

'You what?'

'I'm tellin' ya. Me oul' one and me oul' fella adopted her.'

I said nothing because it had to be the truth.

'Do you not know?' he asked. 'Everyone in the shaggin' town knows.'

'Timmy Garrity doesn't.'

'That's his lookout. Too shaggin' posh to consort with the likes of anywan but hisself.'

'Listen . . .'

'Shaggin' Lord Muck.'

'What age is Orla?'

'Dunno.'

'You do so know. What age?'

'Fifteen.'

This time I got out a proper roar. 'How old?'

'Shurr up. Jasus, do you want to get me hung? I mean, it was only a bit of an oul' coort.'

187

'You little liar,' I said. 'You were poking her.'

At this he laughed. He liked hearing it said. My strength was back, and I caught him by the throat, banging his head off the granite wall. He called me a name and said, 'Let go o' me. I don't want to hurt you.' I caught hold of him by his greasy hair, and he let a yell out of him that came back from the side of the hill above us.

'Little Sir Echo,' I sang to him, 'how do you do? Hello.' I banged his head again and enjoyed it so much I did it a third time. 'Hello.'

'You're fuckin' mad,' he said.

'I am,' I said. 'And now I'll tell you what you're going to do. You're going to mark Timmy Garrity's card for him. You're going to tell him what you've been up to with that kid.'

'Like hell I will.'

'Because if you don't I'll tell Judge Garrity.'

All of a sudden he was afraid. He said, 'Hey, hey, hey.'

'Do it tomorrow,' I said, 'or by tomorrow evening you'll be in Glencree.' In those days Glencree was a reformatory up the mountains.

He jeered at me. 'You will in your hole. I'm too old to be sent to a –'

And there he stopped, for there I had him.

'Are you?' I said. 'In that case it'll be Mountjoy Gaol.'

I pushed him away from me, hard, and walked as quick as I could towards the lights of the Robin Hood. He shouted after me: 'Informer. Fuckin' informer.'

My talk about the films I grew up with had a jaw-breaker of a title: *Mr Laurel and Mr Hardy and other friends*; and Dermo, who was never backward about coming forward, had proposed himself as the MC. And of course once he was in charge nothing would do him but to make a full evening of it by kicking off with a couple of Stan and Ollie two-reelers – *The Music Box* and

Laughing Gravy – as well as the dance in front of the saloon from *Way Out West*.

'I bet he's doing it on purpose,' I said to Babs. 'Fixing it so's I have to follow Laurel and Hardy.'

'I know, I know,' she said. 'Everyone's against you.'

Before I could thank her for the vote of confidence, she kissed two of her fingers, touched them to my forehead and put on a sham Cork accent with: 'Errah boy, sure all oor cygnets are swans!'

All of the front row of the tip-up seats – the clatters, as they were called – was reserved for the Garritys, with Babs and Dermo next to them, and then a sleep of borough councillors. Father Chancey and his curate had been invited and declined – the affair of Canon Turmoyle and his book had not been forgotten, nor would it be – and Doctor Moone had been talked into moving to the front row from his usual seat near the back. 'It's an honour,' Dermo said to him, but the real reason was to put him near the door in case he lost the run of himself. The helpers – the kids from the youth club who checked tickets or were ushers – were put sitting and free of charge in the hard sixpennies at the front. There was no sign of Leo, but I saw Orla in the box office; she was wearing a gash of lipstick and a woolly off-the-shoulder thing that was too old for fifteen.

I sat next to Babs while the Laurel and Hardys were on, and at the interval the audience moved out to the foyer for cups of tea with Marietta biscuits and lady-sized wedges of Margaret Garrity's gur cake. I felt like throwing up and had a mind to get out into the fresh air, but the Judge was standing in my road. He took a grip on his lapels, pulled himself perpendicular and said: 'We are expecting great things from you this evening.' I nearly told him that there was no harm in expecting, but already he had turned away to congratulate his white-headed boy for making the event a success. What with nerves and all, I had not noticed Timmy until then or copped on that he was trying to smile with a face on him like a sick ghost. Then Orla came over, pouring out refills from a ginormous tin teapot. She smiled up at Timmy, as brazen as you like; he turned his back on her, and I knew that he knew. 'Mark his card,' I had said to Leo on the White Rock Road, and either himself or Orla had paid heed to the side their bread was buttered on.

She pointed the spout of the teapot at me. I said, 'No, thanks.' She grinned at me and said in a low voice: 'Hey, Peepin' Tommy, will I pour it on your foot? That might slow you down from carryin' tales.' Out loud, she said for all to hear: 'Go on, have a hottener. Aren't you the star of the evenin'?'

I reminded myself that she was only a kid and there was no harm in her except maybe a bit of divilment. A bad part of my mind said: *After last night, God send that divilment is all that's in her.*

My talk, when the time came, lasted for just short of an hour, and it went like a bomb, although twice I thought that it and me would go up the spout. Dermo did the intro and when I walked up on the stage it was to a gramophone record of the Laurel and Hardy tune that goes 'Dum-de-dum, Dum-de-dum, Dada-de-dum'. 'The Waltz of the Cuckoos' is the name it goes by, and the audience kept time by whistling and clapping their hands. And later, when I described how my ma and me used to go to the pictures in Ringsend after my da died, the Doc began to cry in his seat in the front row of the soft seats, with a 'Sorry' after every second sob.

Afterwards there was a great carry-on. I was hardly off the stage when Dermo came bounding up with his hand out. He said: 'Sound man, I wouldn't doubt you.' Mrs Garrity's eyes were shining; she said it was splendid. And what Babs said was: 'There now, you were grand after all your carrying on and ullagoning.' I told her: 'If I *hadn't* been carrying on and ullagoning I'd have gone down like a lead balloon.' The audience went off home in dribs and drabs, and there was so much goodwill that I said to Babs: 'Still and all, it's not too bad of a town.'

She looked as if I had hit her. 'Perry, you said –'

'I know, and I meant it. We're on the move, don't worry. Once we get rid of the house.'

'When?' she said.

'Soon, soon.'

We were nearly home when Timmy Garrity's voice called my name. He was standing inside the entrance to a private avenue. 'Mr Perry, sir, could I have a word? Will you excuse me, ma'am?'

I told him: 'I'll just see Mrs Perry home safe.'

The three of us walked the rest of the way, saying nothing. When we got to Carvel Babs asked Timmy if he wanted to come in.

And I couldn't credit it; what he said was: 'I take that right kindly, ma'am' – years later I thought of him when I saw Sergeant Tyree – who during the War Between the States had been *Captain* Tyree of the Confederate army – taking off his cavalryman's hat in *She Wore a Yellow Ribbon* and holding it to his chest – 'but I won't impose.'

Babs went into the house and me and Timmy went over to the harbour wall. He said: 'Sir, I have demanded satisfaction from a certain person.'

'Excuse me?'

'In Quintillon's Park at eight tomorrow evening. I thought you might do me the honour.'

I said: 'Timmy, what the hell are you talking about?'

'The honour of seeing fair play. I guess you would call it of being referee.'

'Oh Jesus, no.'

He said: 'That person and that girl –'

'You're never going to fight Leo McAdoo?'

'They lied to me.'

'Is it a fist fight?'

He said: 'Sir, I'm asking you because you know about her and me, and I've got a hunch that you may also be aware of more than you let on.'

'He'll slaughter you.'

191

'My dad told me, if a man doesn't stick up for his honour, then he is less than a man.'

In my mind I cursed the Judge and his man-to-man talks. I said: 'Timmy, that fellow is a guttie, a gurrier, a slag. I grew up with him and his like. He knows every dirty trick there is, and I'm telling you that he'll step out in front of almighty God and take your sacred life.'

Timmy looked me full in the face, and I swear to you that what he said was: 'A fellow's got to do what a fellow's got to do.'

Chapter Fourteen

'Lordsburg'

The fight, when it happened, lasted all of a minute and a half, maybe less.

Quintillon's Park was ten acres caught between the end of Kish Road and the sea. The late Canon Turmoyle had had a great leg of someone on the borough council and in consequence there was a street lamp, not on the street itself but inside the park gate, where its light could dim the ardour – I suppose this is what you might call a paradox   of any couples putting the grass to immoral purposes.

I was there at ten minutes to eight and was looking at the double beam from the Kish lightship when Timmy appeared. He had two young fellows from Trinity with him; he introduced them as Gavin and Michael and said that they were his seconds. One of them was carrying a canvas bag. It struck me as peculiar that anyone would need one second, never mind a pair of them, just to have the lard beaten out of him.

Babs had put me through the wringer. The previous evening, once Timmy had asked to have a word with me on the q.t., nothing would do her but to ferret the story out of me. The first thing she said was: 'Didn't I tell you not to go next or near the Goodwill Restaurant?' the answer to which, if I had a mind to waste my breath, was, 'No, you did no such thing.'

Next, it was, 'What call had you going into that Ramparts house?'

'I saw a light and thought young Timmy was in there.'

'Huh.' Which was shorthand for *Now pull the other one.*

'Do you want the truth or don't you? How was I to know I was going to trip over the One-eyed Reilly?'

'Who?'

'I mean the pair of them. Him and her. At it.'

'There's no need to be common.'

'Going all the way.'

'I said that'll do.' She was quiet for a minute; then her curiosity nailed her decorum to the mat. 'And you're sure they were . . .?' She was leaving it to me to say what she wouldn't.

'Hammer and tongs, and knickers off,' I said.

She scalded me with a look. She said: 'Well, you'll have to tell Judge Garrity.'

'What about?'

'About Timmy and that little sleeveen.' A sleeveen was a mountainy man with a mountainy kind of mind. 'So as he can put a stop to their carry-on.'

'I think,' says I, being as wise as Lewis Stone, 'the lad should fight his own battles.'

'Yes,' she said, 'and I'm sure he'll win them.'

That was the end of it, except that next evening when I left the house she lassoed me with my red scarf and tied it fit to throttle me. 'You mind yourself,' she said. 'You hear me?' And sign's on it, there I was in Quintillon's Park, waiting with Timmy Garrity and his two comrades.

It was the end of October and bitter cold. Eight o'clock came and went. At twenty past I was telling Timmy that he might as well throw his hat at it when we heard voices. It was the Prince Charming – Leo – and his band of seven little helpers – Doc, Sleepy, Sneezy, Grumpy, Bashful, Happy and Dopey. And Snow White – Orla, that is – was with them. The talking stopped when they saw us. Timmy took off his overcoat and the jacket under it, so that he was in his shirt sleeves and shivering. One of his two friends opened the canvas bag and my eyes went out on stilts when I saw two pairs of boxing gloves. If that was the kind of a fight it was going to be, I thought that Timmy might as well open one of his veins and an artery along with it for good luck, then lie down on the grass and die decently.

Leo said nothing. He stood with the others at his back and kept pounding one fist into the palm of the other hand. I muttered to Timmy: 'Watch him, he's a leftie.' The young lad named Gavin put a pair of gloves on Timmy and started to lace them up. Michael offered the other pair to Leo, who said, 'What the fuck is this?' He took the gloves, looked at them again and said in a toff's voice for his pals to hear: 'Ooh, orn't we orfly grawnd,' then threw them away from him as hard as he could. You could say it was the rock he perished on.

He made a crouching move towards Timmy. I put myself between them and said: 'Not yet. The man isn't ready.'

Leo said: 'Well, tell the man to *get* fuckin' ready.'

I said to Timmy: 'Listen, are you going to wear those yokes?'

He told me, calm and matter-of-fact, like: 'Oh, yes.'

'Honest?'

He said: 'I always wear gloves.'

I turned to Leo and started to say that there was to be no gouging or acting the animal, but before I could get two words out he said that he was effing freezing and that he was putting up with no more of this effing ballsology. He made a run at Timmy like a dog that was off its chain, knocking me out of his way so hard that I went down on one knee. When I looked up, Timmy was high-stepping it away from Leo. Fred Astaire wasn't in it. Next, he came back with three or four straight lefts to the face, and you could almost hear Leo's brains or what there was of them rattling like marbles in a kettle. The dwarfs were shouting, 'Come on, Leo,' and 'Finish the fucker off,' although he had yet to lay a fist on Timmy, and Snow White was screaming, 'Kill him.'

Leo had not much temper to lose, but he did his bestest. He made another rush and this time Timmy hit him a tat-tat-tat of hard jabs in the short ribs. Whoever taught him had done it well. Leo stood still, gasping for breath and Timmy gave him an almighty belt in the face and then another one that sent out a fine spray of red. Leo was panting. He said, 'Fuck you,' and at this Timmy stopped boxing and began fighting. He opened Leo's eye and turned his nose into a memory.

The gang stopped their cheering. Leo sat down on the wet grass. 'Get up,' Timmy said and stirred him with his foot. 'He's kickin' him,' one of the gang shouted. Leo stretched out and turned on his side as if he could not care less. The grass was changing colour, and it was over, as quick as that.

Timmy let Gavin pull his gloves off, then shook hands with me and said: 'Thank you, sir. Much obliged.' Michael took a lemonade bottle from the bag and offered it to Leo. 'What is it?' Orla asked. 'Just water,' Michael said. Gavin went to hunt for the gloves Leo had thrown away.

I said to Timmy: 'You and your butties, call in at Carvel. Cup of tea, or a bottle of stout if you take a jar.' I kept my voice down; there was no sense in being overheard and getting a brick through our front window.

Timmy shook his head and said: 'By right he wins. I shouldn't have touched him with my foot.'

'I think we should go now and rather quickly,' Gavin said. It was the first proper sentence out of him, and he spoke in a Protestant accent. When we left the park, the dwarfs were standing around Leo, saying nothing and waiting for him to sit up.

By the time I got back from the off-licence with a dozen stottles, Gavin and Michael were in our kitchen, watching Timmy, who was putting on one of my clean shirts. Babs was holding up his own shirt that had spots of Leo's blood on it.

'I'll wash this for you,' she said. 'You'd be a nice sight, going home to your mammy with a Russian flag wrapped round you.'

He thanked her. When I put the corkscrew to work on the bottles of stout – we had no crown tops in them days – she looked down her nose. 'And you, Perry Perry. You ought to have more sense than to go pouring drink for . . . for children.'

'Hardly out of their cradles yet!' I said and winked at the three lads. One of the bottles was foaming, and as she went to bring tumblers I asked Timmy where he had learned to be a second Joe Louis.

He said: 'My father said that a fellow my age should know how to defend himself, so he sent me to Sergeant Hannigan who trained the Gardai boxing team. He's a highly remarkable man.'

'This sergeant?'

'Oh, yes, him too. No, I meant Dad. I model myself on him.'

I said: 'No better man.'

He said: 'I couldn't agree more, sir.'

Two days later was Hallowe'en, and to mark the occasion Dermo showed *White Zombie* and *The Bride of Frankenstein*. Kids went traipsing through the town banging on doors and bawling 'Any apples or nuts?' and the young lads wore their sisters' dresses and masks of papier-mâché that took less than an hour to go soft and mushy around the mouth. Babs remembered how she and other young ones would dress up every Hallowe'en along where the Dodder meets the Liffey in Ringsend and had a basin of fruit and sweets in readiness as well as ten bob's worth of thruppenny bits – one for every caller.

At school, it was explained to us with a leather strap that Guy Fawkes was a Catholic, and it was consequently a sin to let off fireworks on November the 5th, the day he dirtied his bib. Not to be denied their bit of diversion, the RCs, as the Proddie-Dogs called us, did their bit of divilment on Hallowe'en. Then the war happened and fireworks were banned altogether no matter what foot you dug with; but on either evening, the 31st or the 5th, you would see the odd rocket climbing and bursting over the sea, or a Roman candle or Catherine-wheel out on the headland. So when we heard the bell of a fire brigade going past Carvel late on Hallowe'en we came to the conclusion that some gobhawk was after making a hames of letting off a rocket. Twenty minutes or so later the telephone went and it was Dermo.

'The Ramparts is on fire,' he said.

I told Babs, who let out a wail and said 'Oh, no,' and started taking her curlers out. 'It's a fire,' I told her, 'not a dress dance.'

We took the bicycles, pedalling like mad, and by the time we were passing the Robin Hood there was a lick of flames from the direction of the White Rock Road. 'That's not the dawn,' I said. 'That's Manderley.'

'What?'

'Nothing.'

'You and your fillums.'

We passed people running, anxious not to miss the excitement. By the time we got to The Ramparts it was not so much a place for living in as a bonfire. The house was tinder, and for all the repairs and tarting up, the old plasterwork had still been there between the ceilings and the roof. There were two units of the fire brigade, and the east wind sent the spray from the hoses like rain over the gawpers.

Straight off, I saw the Judge, sitting on a spur of granite with his wife and Dermo close by. Babs went straight to Margaret Garrity and put an arm around her. I looked for Timmy and saw him coming through the crowd with a silver flask he had fetched from home. He gave it to his da, who offered it to Mrs G. She shook her head. One of the firemen told the Judge he ought to move a bit further away from the fire.

The Judge said: 'A countryman of yours and mine was Richard Brinsley Sheridan whose theatre in Drury Lane caught fire. Somebody brought a chair, and he sat watching the flames as he partook of a libation. When he was spoken to as you have spoken to me just now, he said –' The fireman moved away and the Judge told the end of his story to the night air. '. . . Sheridan said: "May a man not enjoy a glass of sherry wine by his own fireside?"'

Dermo said: 'Those bloody fireworks ought to be banned.'

The Judge said: 'Surely they *are* banned.'

The head buck cat of the firemen heard him. He said: 'Mister, like holy hell this was fireworks. Not unless a rocket came down in three or four places at the same time.'

No one said anything for a while, and I knew better than to look at Timmy. The only sound was of water from the pump and the hoses, then a fireman led the Judge to a safe place. A moan went up from the crowd as part of the roof fell in. There was a roar and a crackling as the fire found more to feed on.

Timmy said: 'I have to talk to my father. Come on, Dad . . . Mom. We're going home.'

'Home,' Margaret Garrity said and started to cry.

I saw Dermo squeeze her hand. She looked him in the face for a second, and it was long enough for me to know for certain and at last what was between them. They had hidden it well, mind.

Timmy took charge and led his parents away. As they started down the hill, a man and a woman came towards them at a half run. The woman was panting. She said: 'Ah, don't say we missed it.'

A few days later, I got a note, short and sweet, from the Judge.

Dear Mr Perry, Timmy has told me his story. I want you to know that in my opinion both you and he have behaved as I would expect of gentlemen. Yours truly, James J. Garrity.

Then a week went by and Leo McAdoo was arrested.

The charge was arson or a dozen long words to that effect, and the town could talk of little else. Leo was let out on bail, and he walked – paraded, more like – along Easter Street either with Orla holding a death-grip on his arm or the seven dwarfs trotting behind him, feeding like pigeons off the crumbs of his being famous. One evening, him and the gang tried to get into the Picture House, but Dermo was having none of it. 'The management reserves the right,' he said, 'to refuse admission.'

The case came to court in January and Leo pleaded not guilty. There was evidence that the fire had been started on purpose;

Leo had bought paraffin from Drane Hardware, and two empty tins had been found at The Ramparts with his fingerprints on them. That was enough to settle his hash, never mind that Timmy was called to give an account of the fight in Quintillon's Park. When he was asked the reason for it he said it was a personal matter.

It was like seeing an iceberg popping out of the water. The fight itself had come into view for all to see, and the out-of-sight bit was Orla, aged fifteen and getting poked by Leo while letting on to be his sister. I held my breath, waiting for this to be brought out, but maybe the judge was an old buttie of Judge Garrity's, for he got all twinkly and said: 'An affair of the heart, was it, boy?'

Timmy went red and said: 'Yes, sir.'

The judge looked over his glasses at one of the lawyers in wigs and said: 'Do you wish to pursue this, Mr Kinch?' The wigger, who was on Leo's side, must have been tempted to make Timmy look as thick as a double ditch, which of course he was, but Leo would come out of it the worse by a long chalk. He gave a disgusted shrug, folded his arms and said: 'Unimportant, my lord.'

The judge shrugged back at him and said, 'You may think so, Mr Kinch.'

The jury stayed an hour and a bit in the jury room for the sake of decency, and for all anyone knew they were playing blow-football. Leo got two years hard. A moan went up, and Orla shouted a name at Timmy. The wigger asked for leave to appeal. 'Appeal all you like,' the judge said, 'and much good may it do you. Bail is continued.'

Whatever andrewmartins Dermo was up to with Mrs Garrity – and, to tell the truth, in a horny corner of my mind I envied him – he turned out to be a friend in need. The Judge and herself and Timmy had long since moved out of the Robin Hood to endure the come-down of a pebble-dashed house in St Oona's Villas on the edge of the town. Now that The Ramparts was only four walls and no roof, they had resigned themselves to staying put, but Dermo bullyragged them into coming back to their old hotel suite. He took no refusals, and if you were so bad-minded as to drop a hint that maybe he wanted to have Margaret where he could conveniently carry on with her, then in my modest opinion the devil's cure to you.

'Was The Ramparts not insured?' I asked Dermo.

He shook his head. 'The Judge said it would be time enough when there was furniture in it.'

So the Garritys moved back into the Robin Hood, and they went like lambs, for there was little fight left in them. That could and should have been the end of it, except that young Timmy was never one to let ill enough alone.

March came, and the *For Sale* sign in front of Carvel was blown crooked by the wind. Babs took to moaning, 'We'll be here for ever,' and Leo, waiting for his appeal to come to court, was still strutting around the town. He did more than strut; he boasted that a few months in Mountjoy would not take a feather out of him. Late one night, our phone went.

'Bad news,' I said, getting up.

In the dark, Babs's curlers made her look like a sheep in a bush. 'How do you know?'

'And I'll lay you ten to one it's Dermo.'

I went downstairs, picked up the phone and said into it: 'What, now?'

'You're so bloody smart,' he said. 'Listen, this is serious. Get your clothes on.'

'Break it to me.'

'Tell you in the car.'

'*Again?*'

I was downstairs pulling my coat on when the lights of the Jensen made daytime of the front hall. Dermot finished his U-turn and pushed the near-side door open.

I said: 'Where are we off to this time?'

'Easy on the jokes. Loughlinstown.'

'Do you mean the hospital?'

He nodded. 'Young Timmy Garrity. And it's bad.'

'Oh, God. What happened?'

'I dunno. The police came to tell his parents, only whatever the news is it gave the Judge a bad turn. A collapse, like. So he's in bloody Loughlinstown, too.'

'Christ on rubber crutches.'

'Margaret went with him in the ambulance. I think it was just a weakness. I hope so.' For a minute Dermot drove and was quiet. He said: 'Of course I couldn't go with her.'

I looked at him. He was squinting at the road, harder than he needed to.

'It wouldn't be proper. I mean just her and me and no one else. You know the way tongues wag. And as a matter of fact –' he cleared his throat – 'the Judge has had a letter.'

'Oh?'

'About myself and Margaret.'

'You're coddin'.'

'Insinuating this and that, like. All filthy lies, of course.'

'Sure.'

'And whatever else about the Judge, he has sense enough not to believe blackguardism in whatever shape or form. I mean, Magser and me, would you credit it?'

I was trying hard not to say, 'Yes, I flaming well would,' when he said: 'That's why I took the liberty. I mean, of dragging you out at this hour. Sorry, mate. Last thing I want is for people to see herself and me together, just the pair of us. So you're the beard, like.'

The word was new to me. 'Come again?'

'No sense in giving the scandalmongers a field day, what? And oh God, do you see what I see?'

We had turned through the hospital gates, and there to greet us was the sight of Doc Moone. He was half-seas over and speechifying to a nurse and two ambulance men. He gave us a wave without stopping to draw breath.

He was saying: '. . . So one of the Plummer brothers picks up a shotgun – Tom Tyler, the actor that took the part, was a foreigner, name of Vincent Markowski, I never had time for him. And him and his two brothers, Hank and Ike, make to go out after the Ringo Kid and gun him down in the streets of Lordsburg. Except that Doc Boone – the bold Tommy Mitchell, that is – stands in his way. "I'll take that shotgun, Luke," says the Doc. "You'll take it in the belly if you don't get out of my way," says Plummer.' At this, Doc Moone gave a great Thomas Mitchell smack of his lips. 'And says the bold Tommy – and sound man himself – "I'll have you indicted for murder if you step outside with that shotgun." '

Doc Moone swung an arm to include Dermo and me in his fan club. He said: 'Only this evening on the pier over there in Drane there was no shotgun, just hobnail boots, a couple of bicycle chains and the shaft off a box-cart. And instead of the three Plummer brothers there was seven little gurriers, and they were –'

Dermo hustled me away from the Doc and his story and through the door marked *Casualty*. Margaret Garrity was inside talking to a doctor, with a Garda doing referee. Of course Dermo was a familiar face there, the same as everywhere else.

'Good man yourself,' the doctor said on seeing him come in. 'Try and talk sense into this lady. The boy isn't conscious, and if she sees him now she'll only be upset.'

Margaret wrapped her arms around Dermo's neck, held him tight and began to sob. There was passion in it; she was Timmy's ma and Dermo's woman, the two in one. We were told that the Judge had been given medicine and was asleep one floor up. Most likely he had a grip on the lapels of his py-jams; at any rate, he could bide his hour.

'The boy will be grand,' the sawbones said. 'Once we've done the x-rays and know what's what, then the swelling will go down and he'll be the image of himself.'

'Please God,' Mrs Garrity said, kissing Dermo.

As for me I might as well have been the Invisible Man.

It was a week before I was allowed to see Timmy, and I would have given odds that his young good looks were a thing of the past. His face might have been one of them barrage balloons, but inside of a month or two it mended itself. The real damage was to his brain, and by the time the surgeons were done with him there was a fear that his walking days were over. He went from a wheelchair to two sticks and then to just the one, and it was a full year before he was back in Trinity. He was his good-looking self again, but he looked used, like a book that has been read.

It was a while, too, before we found out what had happened to Timmy that was bad enough to rob him of a year of his life. And there, if you like, was a wonder; not only did the memory of it come back to him; he could not be stopped from talking about it. His story was that he had seen Leo going into Max Finnerty's betting shop in Easter Lane. He waited for him outside and walked up to him without as much as a how-are-you.

He said: 'How would you like a travel permit to Holyhead?'

Leo looked at him as if he was cracked, and Timmy went one better. 'And with fifteen pounds in your pocket. You needn't ask for more because that's all I've got.'

I can see Leo now, outside the bookie's with his last tanner lost on a nag that came in so far down the field as to need a road map, and nothing in store for him except two years in the 'Joy, not counting the usual time off – too much of it – for good behaviour. He looked up and down the lane for a sniper and under his feet for a land mine, then gave Timmy a long look with his eye and a half.

He said: 'Where's the catch?'

'Come for a walk.'

They went down the pier of Drane's little silted-up harbour, and stood at the wall that gave on to the sea.

Timmy said: 'I know a fellow that can get a travel permit in your name. He can have it for me by tomorrow.'

'I assed you, where's the catch?'

'Those seven friends of yours, they think the sun shines out of you. Wherever you go, they follow you. They don't go to the youth club any more. We've lost them. I want you to help me get them back.'

'Me?'

'Well, that's what you might call the catch. Fifteen pounds in your hand, and you won't go to gaol. And gee willikers, Leo, I'm breaking the law, I hope you know that. Still, I guess it's for a good reason.'

'So what am I supposed to do?'

'Well, you could write a note. Or you could talk to them. Gee, I dunno, you could say that you're jumping bail because you're afraid to go to prison. Something like not being as tough as you thought you were.'

'You want them to think bad of me?'

'I guess you could say that.'

Leo grinned. A front tooth was missing from where Timmy's glove had hit him in the mouth.

'What's so funny?' Timmy asked.

' "Rocky Dies Yellow",' Leo said.

'Pardon me?'

'Nothing.' Leo looked out at the sea as if he could already see Holyhead sixty miles away. He said: 'Okay, you're on.'

The arrangement they came to was that him and Timmy would meet the following evening at seven on the self-same pier. That would give Leo time enough to get to Dun Laoghaire and catch the twenty-to-nine mail boat. As soon as he had the fifteen quid and the travel permit in his mitt, he would give Timmy a goodbye note he could show the dwarfs. 'Mind,' he said, 'I don't make a great fist of writin' letters.'

I said to Timmy. 'And you believed him, you sap? Along with the banshee and leprechauns.'

He looked at me through eyes that were still half shut. It hurt him to smile. He said something about there being so much bad in the best of us and so much good in the worst of us. I very badly wanted to hit him a good dig.

Next evening, Leo was on the pier waiting for him. Timmy had three English five-pound notes in one hand and the travel permit in the other. Leo reached out for them. Timmy said: 'Hold on. You were to give me a note for the fellows.'

'Bejasus, you're getting more than a note,' Leo said. He raised his voice and called out: 'Hey, lads. Here's the fella that wants me to act the yella-belly.'

All seven of them came into sight, over the wall on the bay side of the pier. If Timmy had not been such a gawm he would have copped on what he was in for. They came at him together. In the couple of seconds he delayed, one of the dwarfs dropped on his hands and knees behind him and another pushed Timmy so that he fell backwards. Someone else – Grumpy, maybe – hit him hard on the side of the head with a piece of wood that had a nail driv through it. The last thing he remembered was the sight of Orla sitting on the wall with one leg on either side.

He had no recollection of being kicked in the head and chest or of Orla shouting to the gang to shag him in the harbour where, with the tide out, the fall would have killed him; neither did he hear Doc Moone's old Ford scuttering along past the pier-head.

The Doc was on his rounds and fluthered as usual. He thought at first that a crowd of young lads were stamping on a conger eel to kill it. Then he looked again, stopped the car and got out waving the starting handle. He came staggering down the pier twirling it with a shout of 'Baaast-aaards' that would have woken up even the more misfortunate of his patients. Thomas Mitchell would have been proud of him.

'Get away, you whoors' ghosts, or I'll swing for yiz,' he roared.

They scattered, and he made one of them a hospital case with a belt of the starting handle in the small of the back. 'Self-starters?' he said afterwards. 'I have no feckin' faith in them.' As for Timmy Garrity, the Doc's considered opinion was that one more kick in the head would have done for him.

'Ama-chewers,' he said. 'They don't know how to maim a man without killing him.'

Four of the dwarfs were had up in court and would have gone to a reformatory but for Father Chancey, who gave them a character reference on account of their parents were regular mass-goers. As for Leo McAdoo, his appeal was never heard. The joke was that he did jump bail, but the sly little bugger let the mail boat sail without him. He went to Belfast, crossed over from Larne and kept going till Wolverhampton. Either there was a dire manpower shortage on account of the war or else he was suited by nature for a certain line of work, for he joined the police and word came back that he was a credit to the force.

As Timmy Garrity said, there is so much good in the worst of us.

Chapter 15

'A Free French Garrison over at

Brazzaville'

The door of Doc Moone's house, St Luke's, was locked, with a sign scrawled in pencil: *Gone out – Feed colds, starve fevers.* I went hunting and found him and the bar counter of the Robin Hood shoring one another up.

'Can I talk to you?'

He put me into focus; he might have been forcing an old horse over a low fence.

I said: 'I think my wife is suffering from depression.'

'Tell her a joke.'

I gave him a stare and kept it going until he sighed and took a notepad from his waistcoat pocket. He said: 'Tomorrow, three o'clock. Your place.'

I asked him: 'What's wrong with your surgery?'

He shook his head. 'Not for depressives.'

'Sorry?'

'The wallpaper.' It was Abbott and Costello.

On my way out I noticed Judge Garrity. He was on his own and signed to me to sit down. I asked: 'How is Timothy?'

'He goes from day to day. We have hopes that he will be home within the month. And then he will require what they call good nursing.'

The day after the Judge's bad turn, he had been discharged from Loughlinstown, but there was a greyness in his face. He made what I thought was a queer remark. 'It's a task for which

Margaret is more suited than I am. There may after all be an advantage in having a younger wife.'

Before I could do more than look wise, like Lionel Barrymore telling young Dr Kildare how to cure a case of Gogo on the Magogo, what the Judge then said put my life standing on its head. It was: 'Would you be interested in selling Carvel back to us?'

It was a bit early for Christmas, but I could hear 'Jingle Bells'. He said: 'I notice that your *For Sale* sign is still up. As regards The Ramparts, I am told the borough council will be disposed to look favourably on the question of malicious damage.'

Like the town thick, I thought: *Duhhh.*

'Compensation, you understand?'

I was a man on a cliff face who sees a ledge. The Judge beckoned to the barman and said in a voice you could hear in the Four Courts: 'If you would favour us, my man . . . ?' While he was ordering a jar for us both, all I could think was *Oh, Auntie Em, there's no place like home!* I could all but see the snug house in Vavasour Square, and on the front gate there was a new name-plate with one word on it: Kansas.

'But that won't be payable,' the Judge said, 'until the next financial year.' Now I was off the cliff and on a switchback railway; first he told me the good news and then the bad. 'And the people who sold us The Ramparts have abandoned their notion of using it for tennis courts. All of a sudden the zoning laws are as chaff before the wind.'

'Beg your pardon?'

'More corruption. They want the property for a block of flats and are offering to purchase The Ramparts, or what is left of it' – the switchback was on the rise, then down it went again – 'but only for a pittance.'

There was a confetti of ifs and buts, but the Judge wanted to buy Carvel as bad as we wanted to be quit of it and had enough money in his fist to pay a deposit. I cannot and never could come at things sideways and, as common as cabbage, I asked how much. 'The same price as you paid for it. Fair, would you say?'

I said: 'Why don't we shake on it?'

As we did, Dermo came into the bar, and the Judge said: 'Now where have you been?'

Doc Moone was still at the bar a few feet away. Putting in his prate, he said: 'He won't tell you, but I will. He's been upstairs playing with his train set.'

I laughed. The mood I was in, I would have split my sides at a Bette Davis. It did not occur to me until I was on the way home carrying my great news to Babs, that at the mention of train sets Dermo's face had turned the grey-white of an Emergency loaf.

After I had told Babs my news, nothing would do her except to send for a taxi to take us to Dun Laoghaire station. We caught a train to Lansdowne Road and walked from there to Bath Avenue and around the corner into Vavasour Square. The *For Sale* sign was still up.

'It was meant for us, I know it was,' she said. 'Knock on the door.'

'It's empty. They've moved out.'

'I want them to know we're going to buy it.'

'Tomorrow. Come on home, we'll get a taxi.'

'Oh, sure we will,' she said, 'and there's a blue moon out.'

The sky was full of blue moons that evening, for Glinda, the Good Witch of the North, waved her wand and a hackney cab came into the square. It was one of the rare times when we could not move without kicking an open door. And our luck held; next morning, I saw the house agent and the bank manager, and put our lives in pawn with a ginormous bridging loan. In the meantime the Judge wrote a cheque as a down payment on Carvel. That same afternoon himself and Margaret called on us with a bottle of *fino* sherry. 'I took the liberty,' he said. 'I thought we might mark the occasion.' He was so happy that he all but smiled.

The doorbell went. We had forgotten that Doc Moone was due to look in on Babs; he always made his house calls during what was known as the Holy Hour, the time when the pubs were shut. He was sober, a condition which was quickly rectified.

So we were as happy as Larry, except that something caught in my mind like a stickyback. I said: 'Doc, yesterday you mentioned that Dermo had a train set. That was just a makey-up, I suppose?'

'Indeed and it was no such thing,' the Doc said, reaching for the bottle. 'I heard it with me own ears.'

'Ah, you're saying it is merely a canard,' the Judge asked.

'A duck?' the Doc said. Underneath it all, he was an educated man.

'Unless it went *quack*,' I said, doing my Edward Everett Horton smirk, 'he means it was a train he heard.'

The Doc all but snapped at me. 'Well, I could hardly see it, could I, considering it was under the floorboards?' He went: 'Zum-zum, *bweep* . . . zum-zum, *bweep*.'

Babs and Margaret pawed one another, and the Doc said, 'Oh, laugh away.' The Judge said with the straight face that was his version of convulsions: 'The train was under the floorboards?'

'Amn't I saying?' The Doc was very patient with us. 'Listen to me. One Saturday a year ago there was a wedding in the Robin Hood, and never mind about the jakes being occupied, there was even a queue to use the flowerbeds. So I trotted upstairs for a slash – excuse me, ladies – and I went into his nibs's private apartment by mistake. And there he was, kneeling down, with his ear against the carpet.'

'Who – Dermo?' I said.

'No, the cat's old fella! "Are you took bad?" says I to him. "Doc, you don't belong in here," says he, very narky like. "Excuse me," says I, about to go elsewhere and find a vase. Or is it a vawse?'

'Confine yourself to the point,' the Judge said.

'Except that then I heard it, and it went "Zum-zum, *bweep* . . . zum-zum, *bweep*"' And he gets all flustered because he's been caught playing with trains. "What the hell is that?" says I, giving a buck jump in the air, because the shaggin' thing was rattling along under my feet.

'"It's a Chube train," says Dermo. "A what?" says I. "Same as in London," says he. "But it's under the feckin' floorboards," says I. "Well, where else would you expect a Chube train to be?" says he.' The Doc looked at Judge Garrity. 'Laughter in court, what?'

The Judge said: 'But how do you account for –'

'You're there ahead of me,' the Doc said. 'Whoever heard of a Chube train that had a whistle on it? Am I right?'

'Well, no. What I –'

'So I asked him. "What's the idea," says I, "of the shaggin' bweep-bweep?" Do yous know what he told me? Do yous? "Poetic licence," says he.'

When the laughing stopped, the Doc treated himself to a wheeze, then looked at his watch and at Babs.

'You, my lady,' he said. 'Upstairs.'

'I'm grand now,' Babs said.

'You're not grand. You're on the twitch.'

'She's fine,' I told him. 'We've had a bit of good news.'

'Upstairs,' the Doc said.

She went, and he followed her, and ten minutes later he left without coming into the living room to finish his *fino*. It was not unsociability, but opening time. A few minutes later, Babs came down.

She said, trying to laugh: 'He wants me to go to a specialist.'

Margaret put an arm around her. 'Pay no attention, dear. He's a little bit tipsy.'

'He's maggoty-eyed drunk,' I said.

'Well,' Margaret said, 'whatever. And I know what would cheer us all up.' She gave Babs a little squeeze and looked at me and the Judge. 'Dermot' – not Dermo, mind you, but Dermot – 'is going to put on *Casablanca*.'

'Go to God,' I said. I had been gumming to see it.

'He says it's a little present, just for me.' She blushed, and I all but had to cross my legs, the most provoking sight in the world being a respectable woman. 'Well, he's so silly, just like with his train set.'

The Judge raised his head, the better to look down his nose. 'I assume we are talking of more illegality.'

'Well,' I said, 'I hear tell that Ingrid Bergman goes off with the wrong man in the end.'

'The wrong man?' the Judge said.

'Her husband,' I told him.

He was the original duck's back. 'Miss Bergman always takes a good part,' he said. 'Very wholesome.'

The sort Babs was, by now she had pushed talk of specialists into her purse and snapped it shut. She made a face at me. 'Now you've gone and told us the ending.'

The Doc came back the next day and gave Babs a note with a date, a time and a name—Dr Hubert O'Grady Whitlow—with an alphabet of letters after it and an address in Fitzwilliam Square. Knowing that if she was left to herself she would promise and then renege, he said, 'I'll give you a lift. I have business in town that day.' The liar.

She went with the Doc in the Accident and found herself being talked to by a morning suit. 'Dr Moone tells me you're moving house,' the suit said.

'Oh, yes.'

I wasn't there, but I could see her as clear as clear, thinking of Vavasour and lighting up like a gas mantle.

'And when would that be?'

'Um . . .'

'Um what?'

'Maybe a few months.'

'Um indeed,' he said.

She came home to me in a state of shock. 'He wants me to go into a nursing home.'

'Jesus.'

'For a little rest, he says.' Her voice shook, and I could feel my own eyes filling up. She said: 'Don't you start.'

I said: 'You'll have to go.'

'I'll put it on the long finger,' she said, and, once that was decided, she was all smiles and her own switchback was on the up. 'And don't forget,' she said. '*Casablanca* is on tomorrow evening.'

Casablanca was banned here; but not only did Dermot put it on, he did so in the Picture House instead of just to members of the film society. 'I'll take a chance,' he said; 'otherwise the ones that don't get in will wreck the place. But I'm making them pay through the nose. A bob for the woodeners and half-a-crown for the softies.' He got all sly. 'Hey, how would you like a what's-it-they-call-it . . . a sneaky preview?' So he found the projectionist and slipped him a quid, then had a couple of pints brought in from the Ebb Tide next door, and we watched the film, just the pair of us.

I could see why it was banned. Conrad Veidt was in it, and as usual he could sneer for Germany. And Humphrey Bogart was the chap, which naturally meant that whoever he was against were the bullies. Not far into the film Conrad Veidt asked Humphrey Bogart, 'What is your nationality?' and Bogart answered, 'I'm a drunkard.' I said to Dermo: 'That's good. Doc Moone will give that a vote of confidence.'

When it was over, Dermo sat back and sighed. 'That was great. Would you not agree?'

'I would and I do.'

'And haven't we the divil's own luck?' The song he sang was an old one. 'I mean, you and me, to be born not too soon and not too late. Did you ever pause to consider that if a fellow's life is miserable and a dead loss he can always go and see a fillum and have another one.'

'A jar?'

'I mean a life. I mean, think of all the adventures we can have without getting our feet wet. And if we get married and she turns into a right old rip, haven't we got Ingrid Bergman?'

'And Mary Astor,' I said.

'Jasus, you're going back a bit. And that new one, Rita Hayworth. And Gene Tierney and Ann Sheridan and Deanna Durbin singing and Ann Miller dancing. And good old Marleen and the boys in the back room. And not a woman among them would ever look crossways at you or give out to you. Do you know what I'm going to tell you? I'm a happy man.'

'Watch it,' I said.

'Watch what?'

'My da used to say that if you want to make God break his arse laughing, just tell him that you're happy.'

'Not at all,' Dermo said.

'Dermo . . .'

'What?'

'Were you ever married?'

'Nope. Mind, I don't go short.'

'I know.'

He sat up and took his feet off the seat in front. 'How do you know? And while we're at it, I suppose you know who with?'

'What?'

'Do you know her name?'

'I think so.'

He gave me a long, cool look. He could have asked who I thought his bit of stuff was, or how I had found out, or did Babs know. Maybe he was afraid of the answers, which was why he did no more than nod and say: 'Fair enough-ski.' He looked at our pint tumblers which had been empty since Bogart said: 'You played it for her, you can play it for me.' He said, 'Will we send out for another?'

'Don't mind.'

He called to the projectionist. 'Vincent, good man, same again.' He looked at me and said: 'I think the hubby knows.'

'He might.'

'Tell us. How do you think he looks?'

'Who, the Judge?'

I had named a name. He said: 'You bastard.'

'Not great,' I said.

Right from the start *Casablanca* was the biggest draw Dermo had ever had. There were chairs put down under the screen, and benches along the aisle, and I'll lay a pound to a penny that it never before or since had an audience like that evening in Drane. The only note of begrudgery came from Judge Garrity. First, there was talk in the story of the film about two letters of transit which could not be gone back on, even by the Germans, because they were signed by General de Gaulle. At this, the Judge said, nearly shouting: 'This is consumptive' – or maybe it was 'consummate' – 'rubbish. Charles de Gaulle is not on the German side in this war, so why should his signature carry any weight with his enemies?' Everyone shushed him, and he said: 'Why should we tolerate this?'

Dermo said: 'Because.'

'Because of what?'

'Because it's a *fillum*.'

And later on, when Bogart said that he had come to Casablanca for the waters, and Claude Rains answered him with, 'What waters? We're in the desert,' there was another interruption. The Judge said: 'More balderdash. Casablanca is a hundred miles from the desert!'

From then on he just grunted or here and there let out a short laugh of mockery. Apart from which, the only sounds were the cheering when Conrad Veidt got a bullet through him and the sound of the Doc crying when Ingrid Bergman went off to Lisbon.

At the end, when Bogart said to Claude Rains the bit about this being the beginning of a beautiful friendship, the lights came up and there was more clapping. It got louder, same as rain starting to bucket down, and then dribbled away to nothing when a man in a blue uniform climbed up on the narrow stage in front of the curtain. It was a Garda superintendent. There were three or four bangs as the street doors were slammed by ordinary guards who had been in the projection booth and now ran down the aisle.

'Will everybody stay where they are,' the Super said. 'This has been an illegal representation.'

He tried to be heard over a noise like thunder as everyone jumped up and the tip-ups clattered, all in one almighty crash. It was as if someone had shouted 'Fire!' Maybe they had seen too many pictures with night clubs being raided; at any rate, people fought to get out. The Super said: 'There is no call for panic. All we want is to take names.' He read from a piece of paper, spouting jaw-breakers about the Censorship Acts of 1923 and 1930. Another word he came out with was 'Neutrality'. And I heard Dermo, a few seats from us, saying: 'At least they had the decency to wait until the end of the fillum.'

The Super pointed a finger at him and said, 'Mr Grace, I want you, if you please.'

Babs began to ullagone like a banshee and said: 'I want to go home.'

The Doc heard her and shouted: 'I am a doctor and I have a patient here.'

The Judge called out 'Superintendent!' three or four times until he was heard above bawls of 'Oh, mammy, mammy' and 'Jesus, let me out.' The Super recognised him and made a sign to us, pointing at the nearest door. What with everyone blocking the aisle, pushing the police while the police pushed them back, we might as well have tried to walk through a stone wall.

'Please, please,' the Super shouted. 'A bit of calm.'

Then a woman started to scream. It was Babs, and it froze my blood. It was so piercing that for a few seconds the crowd stopped their shouting and then started up again.

'Let that lady out of here,' the Super said. One of the guards opened a side door and it was like a cork coming out of a beer bottle that had been given a shake. The crowd carried us with them out of the Picture House and into the night air, with Babs still screaming.

'Hush, now,' the Doc said. 'Into my car. Good girl, come on.'

Once she was inside the Accident and we were on our way, she was quiet. After a while she said, 'This isn't the way home.'

'We're going somewhere else,' the Doc said. 'You'll be grand in no time.'

I expected the screaming to start again, but all she said was, 'I don't have my nightdress. Perry, you'll have to bring me my things.'

'I will,' I said. 'I promise, first thing.'

She said, 'I suppose you're taking me to Grangegorman.' She meant a hospital on the North Side that people made jokes about as the Home for the Bewildered, meaning loonies and boozers.

'Not at all,' the Doc said. He caught sight of a telephone box and stopped the car. He asked me for tuppence, and while he was phoning, I held Babs's hand. She was shivering.

She said: 'Don't hold me. I'm not going to run away.'

'I know that.'

The Doc came back and we were off again. I recognised the main Bray road and next thing we turned into the grounds of a house called St John Chrysostom's a mile before Donnybrook. Two nurses were on the front steps, waiting. I said. 'Doc, where are we?'

'Where she'll be looked after,' he said. 'And you're not going in with her. Say goodbye now. She'll be right as rain.'

One of the nurses said, as jolly as you like: 'Bed, bed, bed.'

The Doc told Babs that I would see her tomorrow. She said goodbye in a whisper and let herself be led into the house. As we drove out on to the Bray road, I asked: 'Doc, what's up with her?'

'The woman,' he said, 'is in need of a rest.'

There was not another word between us until we were back in Drane and had pulled up in front of the Robin Hood. Two guards were standing on the front steps. 'Residents only,' one of them said.

I asked if I could see Mr Dermot Grace, and he said: 'Not unless you have a file.'

'Aye, and a hacksaw,' his comrade said. They were a howl.

Then I noticed that there were three police cars tucked away at the side of the hotel. 'What's going on?' the Doc asked.

The guards were young fellows and it was their first excitement. One said out of the corner of his mouth: 'Search warrant.'

'Searching for what?' I asked.

'Banned fillums,' the Doc said. 'What do you think?'

The Doc was right and the Doc was wrong. Which is to say that the guards may have been looking for one thing, but they found another.

Howsomever, and not to trip over my own feet, early next morning there was a phone call from St John's, and a nurse reeled off a list of things that Babs wanted. I put them in a suitcase, humped my bike down the front steps of Carvel and clipped the case on the carrier. It was a lovely spring morning; the sun was well up, and some of the trees had started to bud. What made it different from any other morning was a sound I had never heard before, at least not in Drane.

It was music coming from wireless sets, clear as you like and no interference.

*

It was too early in the year for windows to be open, but they were today, all the way along Kish Road. I wheeled the bike instead of riding it, and from every house it was as if one wireless was saying 'Good morning' to the next. There was talk – the eight o'clock news, maybe – from a few of them, but music from the majority. The whole town was showing off.

I wanted to find out why, and also where Dermo was, but first things first, so I cycled to St Johnwhatsit's. It took me just over a half-hour: no hardship. Babs had a room to herself and was sitting up in bed reading the paper and wearing a pair of headphones. She had had her breakfast; and never mind the rationing, there was egg on her chin. 'Dr O'Grady-Whitlow is coming in to see me,' she told me. There was not a feather out of her.

'And you won't believe it,' she said, 'but I can listen to the wireless.'

'And *you* won't believe it,' I said, 'but so can I.'

On my way out I saw a morning suit getting out of a Bentley. I introduced myself and we shook hands. Dr O'Grady-Whitlow told me he admired my work and asked if I was writing a new play. I told him: 'Well, sort of.'

'Oh, I hope you do,' he said.

For a few seconds we stood there, with him looking at my bike and wondering where his wife's next fur coat was coming from, and me pricing his Bentley and seeing his bill – the worst kind, that had 'With compliments' at the top of it. When I asked about Babs, he called me his good fellow and said it was early days. 'I've seen her only once, you know.'

He took me by the elbow and we walked together, with me wheeling the Raleigh – a lovely sight. He said: 'Your lady wife tells me that you and she are moving house.'

'She can't wait. No more nor I can.'

'Oh, good. Because I've had a chat with our friend, Doctor Moone, and we agree that she shouldn't go back to your present abode. Or even to that town you live in. Drain, is it?'

'Drane.'

When my bike bumped against the front step of the house, he stopped and tapped a buffed fingernail against his front teeth. He said: 'Not at all good for her. About the new house: do you think you might close the purchase while she's here?'

I said: 'She'll never be laid up *that* long?'

The fingernail went tappety-tap. He should have taken up the xylophone.

All the way home, I did my sums. It was a daisy chain. If the people who wanted to buy The Ramparts from the Judge would only part with a few readies, then the Garritys could afford to pay for Carvel, and that meant that myself and Babs could walk into the house I called Kansas. It would take a small miracle, with a bigger one to follow, which would be to light a fire under the solicitors that were feeding off us.

Carvel without Babs in it was as desolate as a house after a funeral, but no sooner had I put a key in the door than the phone went. It was Dermo. 'How is Babs?'

'Grand. She's in a nursing home called St John . . . ah . . .'

'Chrysostom's? Then she'd be a patient of O'Grady-Whitlow.' I said: 'How do you know that?'

'He owns the place. Listen, come on over. You're needed.'

'What happened to you?'

He told me he was out on five hundred quid bail, which was money in the 1940s. He began to laugh, and it was real laughing, not an act.

'What's so funny?'

'It just occurred to me that you can hear all about it on the wireless.'

The Robin Hood was open, but as empty as an Orange lodge on Paddy's Day. No, it was more than empty; it was full of a nothingness that told you to feck off out of it. There was no receptionist at the front desk, no tables set in the dining room, no waitresses, no barman. The only sign of life, if you could call it that, was Judge Garrity sitting like a rheumatic ramrod while Dermo brought him a double Hennessy.

'I insist on paying for this,' the Judge said.

'Do whatever you like,' Dermo said with a stone face on him.

'And my wife and I are moving out of here. If we had to sleep by the roadside –'

'And you can sleep wherever you like, too.'

The pair were not in danger of being taken for Mutt and Jeff. The Judge turned to me. 'My dear fellow, what's your news?'

I told him what I knew. 'And so she's in this place, St John –'

As black out with one another as himself and Dermo were, they did a little duet and said 'Chrysostom' together. I thought: *What a bloody country it is where even the saints have double-barrelled names.*

I said: 'So the doctor doesn't want her to go back to Carvel, or to Drane either. Not till the solicitors get their ruby slippers on and the house at Vavasour is bought and paid for.'

The Judge said: 'I might be of some help.'

'*You* might?'

'Or rather I have several one-time colleagues who could very well make life easier. Wheels might be oiled. We might circumvent the –' he paused for a second, a sign that a sure thigh-thumper was on the way – 'the law's delays, the insolence of office.'

'You ought to put that in one of your plays,' Dermo said to me, winking over the Judge's head.

'In that case,' I said, 'all I'd need is money.'

'Money is nothing,' Dermo said.

'Well, it won't save *you*,' the Judge said to him, with poison in his voice.

'Thanks.'

'You will go to prison, and it will be for at least a year.'

'Oh, come on,' I said. 'Just for showing *Casablanca*?'

'I forgot,' Dermot said. 'You weren't here for the big picture. You remember the bold Hansy, poor old Hansy? Well, need you ask, there's another Kraut doing his job and living up at Heimat. And it was him that put the police on to yours truly. Only his embassy doesn't want to prosecute . . . I suppose it's bad for the image. So I'm to be given a smack-bott and told not to do it again.'

'That's great,' I said.

The Judge drowned his own opinion in his large Hennessy.

'Hold on,' I said. 'If you've been let off for showing the film, how come you had to get bail?'

'I'll tell you how come,' Dermo said. 'Because the Nazis are a bunch of softies compared with the Irish Department of Post and Telegraphs. They're doing me for jamming wireless reception these past six years.'

It was a joke. It had to be. I waited for him to laugh and say 'Gotcha'. Then I saw the Judge's face.

'For Christ's sake,' Dermo said, 'how do you think I got the Picture House filled in the first place? Because there was no effin' wireless reception, that's how.'

It was like a Charlie Chan film, where the murderer is always the last one you suspect.

'And now he's looking at a well-deserved year in prison,' the Judge said.

'Maybe,' Dermo said. 'Maybe not.'

'And what does that mean?'

Dermo grinned at us. 'There's a Free French garrison over at Brazzaville.'

The Judge looked at me, then at Dermo. '*Where?*'

Dermot was Claude Rains to the life. 'It might be a good idea for me to disappear from Casablanca for a while.'

The Judge said: 'You're talking about not answering to bail. I am no informer, but I decline to sit and listen to this.'

He stood up and walked towards the door, then turned and came back for what was left of his Hennessy.

Chapter Sixteen

'A Good Cast is Worth Repeating'

'It's a pudden,' Dermo said.

We were walking, just me and him, on the grass of his front lawn, and he might have been telling me proudly how he had constructed a model Nelson's Pillar out of matchsticks.

'All you do is get hold of a receiver and a transmitter. Now, say you pick up the BBC signal. You put a microphone in front of the set, and you use the transmitter to send it out again on the same wavelength as Radio Eireann. What happens then is that everyone for miles around is getting two stations at once. Give you a laugh. I put a Hornby train set under the floorboards, and that really buggered it up. I even rigged up a whistle on it. Doc Moone saw it, or at least he heard it. The old eejit never copped on.

'That was what they found last night. They were looking for all the pictures I'd smuggled in – propaganda fillums and such – and of course there weren't any. I never kept them; I got them on loan like I told you and sent them back double quick. When the polis found the wireless sets, they thought at first I was a spy – God knows what side I was supposed to be on. Anyway, in the middle of the night out comes the Special Branch. Well, they're not the boys to go trick-acting with, so I owned up. And you know, they didn't see the joke.'

'Get away.'

'No, honest. One of them said, "And I got out of a warm bed and a warmer woman for this!"'

I said: 'You wouldn't really do a flit?'

'Skip bail, do you mean? Well, everyone else does it. They

teach it at school. You know what our national exports are: Aran Island sweaters, black pudden and criminals. Let's go inside and have a jar.'

I said: 'It's too early.'

'It's too bloody late.' He looked up at what I guessed was the window of the suite where the Garritys lived. 'They're moving out, you know.'

'Hard cheese.'

'I'm mad about her. Whatever she wants, I'll do it. I'll answer bail or I'll skip it. Whatever. And yet supposing I did a bunk and went across the water? She'd never go with me, not with young Timmy in the state he's in, maybe crippled for life. But I'll do what she says. Mind you, there's nothing for me here, not any more. Because I made fools of them all, didn't I? And that'll be held against me till Tibb's Eve. No, I'll have to put the shutters up on the Robin Hood and the Picture House, both of them.'

He hustled me through the hotel foyer and into the bar. On the way, he said: 'Would a grand be any use to you?'

'A what?'

'A loan, like. That same Picture House was a little gold mine. Look.' He lugged at his pocket and out came a chequebook. 'Money is easy.'

I thought of Babs and said: 'I don't know what to say.'

'I want it back, mind.'

'Oh, sure, but –'

'Go on, take it, and close the sale.' He leaned on the bar counter and started writing a cheque. 'But you could do me a little favour. And no, it's not a condition. No strings attached.' He tore the cheque from the book and fanned it dry. I looked at it, hypnotised.

He said: 'Magser won't talk to me. I'd die for that woman, honest I would. I have to talk to her. Go upstairs, will you? Have a word with her. Get me five minutes. That's not so much, now is it? Five. Five lousy minutes.'

He shoved the cheque at me. It was for a thousand quid. I kept my hands clear of it. His face reminded me of a painting in the church; it was of St Sebastian with arrows through him, eyes turned up and the face all agonised.

I said: 'Look, can I ask you something?'

'Shoot.'

'It's none of my business. No, forget I asked.'

He was impatient for me to go and talk to Margaret. 'Oh, get it out and have done with it.'

'Yourself and her. How serious was it?'

'*What?*'

I thought: in for a penny, in for a pound, and I could always plead the extenuation of a dirty mind. 'Was it only a bit of a coort, like, or was it what you might call the full thingy? Going all the way, like?'

'Are you mad?'

'I'm sorry. I ought to mind my own interference.'

'All the way? For God's sake, man, you've been going to fillums ever since you were a chiselur, and you're as innocent now as you were then. Do you not remember last night? You were at *Casa*bloody*blanca*, that's where you were, and still you know sweet feck all.' He all but shouted into my face. 'The bloody woman is married!'

'I know, I know.' I backed away from him.

'Did I go all the way with her? Eh? Eh? No, I bloody well didn't. What do you take me for?'

'Sorry.'

He said: 'That sort of thing is not on. There's rules, you know. A man could get killed, or else she could, or maybe the pair of yous. What kind of a world do you think you're living in? And, if you don't believe me, you can find out with the aid of a one-and-thruppenny ticket to the pictures. Have you me?'

'I have you.'

'Grand.' He put a hand on my shoulder. 'Now go and do me that little favour. All I want is for Magser to know that the problems of two little people don't add up to a head of cabbage

226

in this loony world. And wherever she is and wherever I am, we'll always have Drane.'

He pushed me towards the stairs. 'Go on, now; be a pal. I'll never forget it to you.' He waved the cheque at me again. 'Like I say, no strings.'

I went to the Friar Tuck Suite and the Judge answered my knock. I could see past him, and there was an open suitcase with clothes in it on the floor of the sitting room.

'Excuse me. Could I please have a word with Mrs Garrity?'

'Of course. Will you come in?'

'Thanks, I won't.' He spoke Margaret's name into the room. I asked him if him and her had a place to live.

He said: 'Thank you for your concern. We're to stay with friends who live out by the Bride's Glen. That's around from the hospital, you know, so we'll be close to Timmy. And it won't be for long.' His face cracked into a smile. 'My guess is that we'll be drumming you out of Carvel within the month. You'll have vacant possession, what?'

Margaret came to the door. The Judge gave me a goodbye nod and went back into the apartment. She asked after Babs. I told her she was in good hands, which got the palaver over with. I said: 'Dermo wants five minutes. That's all, just five.'

She gave me a long look, without answering.

I had an idea. 'Why don't you just walk a lap of the hotel with him? Front door around to front door, what?'

She thought again and said: 'If I do, will you come as well?'

'Me? God no. The grounds are empty, honest. There's no one who'll see.'

'It's not that. I want someone with us. Otherwise, no.'

'Yes, but –'

'I'll tell James.'

While she was talking to the Judge I went down to pass the word to Dermo. I said: 'Once around the hotel, and she wants me to make it a threesome. Best I could do, sorry.'

227

He said: 'You're a jewel.'

Margaret met him on the front steps and did a slow walk around the building while I hung back trying to keep out of hearing. Dermo did most of the talking, in a low voice, and all I caught from her was when she said: 'Dermot, it's no use. I'm really not that sort of person. I simply am not.'

He tried to touch her arm, and she pulled away from him. The three of us, with me as the biggest gooseberry in the garden, passed the kitchen windows; then we walked past the bar and came around again to the front steps. She gave him no chance for a goodbye; without a word of warning she turned and went into the building.

I caught up with Dermo and said: 'Sorry, mate.'

He said: 'What the hell did you want to come with us for?' He was hopping mad, face red and icicles for eyes.

I said: 'She made me. I told you.'

'You effing Judas.'

'Excuse me?'

'Rubbing up against us, tongue hanging out and your ears on stalks. How could the girl say what she wanted to say?'

'I wasn't listening, honest. I was –'

'And asking if we went all the way.' He pulled what I could see was the cheque out of his breast pocket. 'You see this? Well, here. Take it.' He tore it across, then across a second time and scattered it. The pieces skipped across the lawn.

I said: 'Dermo, listen. You asked me –'

He said: 'Don't talk to me, you back-stabber. Fuck you, and for all time.'

He walked into the Robin Hood, and his back was the last I ever saw of him.

*

He answered to his bail and pleaded guilty. Like Judge Garrity foretold, he got twelve months, but the Irish being bad at sums, he served four. Nobody came out of it well; even though, to put Dermo in a good light, his lawyer made a show of the thicks in

Post and Telegraphs. Over the years there had been complaints from Drane about the wireless reception, but the engineers ignored the town, same as everyone else did. Before ever myself and Babs had moved into the place, Dermo had shown a film called *Lost Horizon* and put out a cod of a yarn to his patrons that Drane was like Shangri-La, a sort of heaven on earth locked in by the Himalaya mountains, which made a hames of the wireless reception. You would think that no one in his senses would swallow the idea of Drane living up to anyone's idea of a paradise or of the hill behind the town being a kind of a Himalaya, but then Dermo always had a neck as hard as a jockey's bollix.

When he had served his four months he took the Holyhead mail boat to the offshore island, as it is known. The last I heard of him, he was a buyer of films for the BBC and was married to a girl who had once upon a time been a starlet in what they called the Rank Charm School. Trust Dermo. The Judge moved into Carvel with Margaret and Timmy. I haven't heard about them except for Christmas cards, and I don't ask.

As for Doc Moone, while avoiding a driver who through a freak of nature was drunker than he was, he ran the Accident into the harbour at half-tide. The crash was so bad that people who ran to the scene had already begun to say nice things about him, whereupon he waded out and told the other driver that he would meet him in Lordsburg at sundown.

All that is left to tell is that after Babs had been in the nursing home for two weeks I got a solicitor's letter saying that the purchase of the house on Vavasour could be closed if I would kindly send him a cheque for the balance due. If worries were money, I would have been Diamond Jim Brady; and in fact when it came to nervous breakdowns Babs could be asked to move over in the bed. Howsomever, they say that God tempers the wind to the shorn lamb, which might be why later on that same day I saw a black Bentley pulling up outside Carvel.

Dr Hubert O'Grady-Whitlow stood back from the doorstep and looked at the house. 'So this is the cause of all my worries!'

I said: 'Don't say she's worse.'

'She's doing very well. I have a courtesy call to make on my friend, Ben Moone, and I thought you and I might exchange the time of day.' He moved past me into the hall.

'Matter of fact,' I said, 'I was going to write to you.'

'Now you can save the price of a stamp.'

I offered him a cup of tea, and he said it was bad for the nerves and that mineral water would be agreeable. I had none in the house, but I showed him into the living room, then skipped out and poured a glass of water from the kitchen tap. When I came back, he was at the window looking out at the sea.

He said without looking at me: 'All going as it should, I imagine that Mrs Perry will be home two weeks from now.'

I said, 'Grand,' and tried to smile.

'The question now arises: "Where is home likely to be?" Because you know it can't be *here*.' He took the water glass. 'Most kind.'

Seeing that I failed to do a jazz dance for joy, he asked: 'Is there a problem?' I gave no answer, and he said, 'Tell Uncle Hubert.' This gave me such a shock that the whole story came pouring out: all about us moving out of Widow Gamble's Hill, buying Carvel, meeting the Garritys and Dermo, The Ramparts and the house on Vavasour Square. 'It's all a bloody mess,' I said.

'Buying a house usually is.' There was a shrug in his voice. 'You said you were writing to me.'

'Because I imagine your bill for Babs will be to say the least hefty. I wanted to tell you that it might take us a while to pay it.'

'Do you know,' Uncle Hubert said, 'most of my patients wait until I send them a bill, and then they ignore it. I have to say I'm impressed.' He played another concerto on his front teeth. 'Do you happen to have a chequebook?'

'But I told you, I can't –'

'Write me out a cheque for the amount you need – plus, shall we say, a hundred pounds. And post-date it for . . . well, shall we say three months? And in return I shall give you a cheque for the

230

same amount less a hundred pounds, and bearing today's date.'

He was lending me the money I needed. 'Why?'

'My dear nephew, a suicidal patient is no earthly good to me. I'm going to speak severely to Ben Moone about this. It reflects on my practice.'

I could hardly trust myself to talk. Under the morning suit he was a nice man and the heart of the rowl. There were still a few of them left. I felt all dewy. 'I'll pay you interest.'

He said: 'No need. That's what the hundred pounds is for.'

No house was ever sold quicker than Carvel, and no house was ever bought quicker than Kansas. Two weeks later, to a day, I called to the nursing home and told Babs to get dressed. 'And hurry up. I'm taking you on an outing.'

She was half excited, half suspicious. 'Where? Are they letting me out? Do you mean home?'

'Yes, home. Now put your clothes on.'

I had a taxi waiting. On the Bray road, she looked out of the window and said, same as on the evening Doc Moone had driven us from the Picture House to St John's, 'This isn't the way.'

'Shush, now.'

We pulled up at the beginning of Vasavour.

She said: 'It's our house, Perry. Can we go in? Will they mind?'

I took a shiny new key from my pocket and held it up. She clapped her hands and took it. 'Is it ours? No, it can't be. When? When will it be honest to God ours, really ours? Tell me.'

I had not said a word to her because of fear of what might still go wrong, but on the yesterday the removals men had come and emptied one house and filled the other. On the other side of the front door it was a woeful, desperate mess with everything outside in and the wrong way up. Babs would go demented when she walked in.

As we came near the front gate she said: 'My God, there's curtains up.' Then she saw the name-plate beside the front door.

She said: '*Kansas*? Is that what you called it? But that's a terrible name for a house. I mean, it's silly.'

'Do you think so?'

'Honest, Perry, have sense.' As she put the key in the lock she frowned remembering. 'It was something you said, wasn't it? What the girl in the fillum . . . Doreen . . .'

'Dorothy.'

'What she said to the little dog? "We're not in Kansas any more."'

She opened the front door, and I said, 'Toto, I've got news for you.'